ONCE A HERO

BOOKS BY JAN THOMPSON

Protector Sweethearts (6 Books)
JanThompson.com/protector

Defender Sweethearts (6 Books)
JanThompson.com/defender

Binary Hackers (4 Books)
JanThompson.com/binary

Seaside Chapel (6 Books)
JanThompson.com/seaside

Savannah Sweethearts (11 Books)
JanThompson.com/savannah

Vacation Sweethearts (8 Books)
JanThompson.com/vacation

Keep up with Jan Thompson's book news:
JanThompson.com/newsletter

ONCE A HERO

PROTECTOR SWEETHEARTS BOOK 2

JAN THOMPSON

GEORGIA
PRESS

Once a Hero (Protector Sweethearts Book 2)

To my Lord and Savior, Jesus Christ, who died on the cross to save me from my sins and rose again from the grave to give me eternal life in heaven.

For God so loved the world that He gave His only begotten Son, that whoever believes in Him should not perish but have everlasting life.
—John 3:16

ABOUT ONCE A HERO
PROTECTOR SWEETHEARTS BOOK 2

A former FBI agent and a treasure hunter must join forces to defeat a mutual enemy in a race to find treasures from the lost Amber Room.

Emerging from a deep undercover operation gone wrong, FBI Special Agent Jake Kessler finds himself suspended without pay and left out of the remaining hunt for the most notorious terrorist in the world. The only person who might be able to help him is a random stranger he meets in San Francisco, who wants something in return even when there is a price on her own head.

A relentless hunter...

They say that FBI Special Agent Jake Kessler doesn't follow orders, and that he deserves to be tortured and left to die on that sinking ship. Whatever. Jake is simply thankful he makes it out alive and in one piece, even though his cover is now blown.

The workaholic that he is, Jake doesn't know the meaning of suspension. On his own time, he goes to San Francisco to follow a tenuous lead. All he has to do is meet an informant who has news for him about the international criminal at large, Molyneux. Something goes wrong, and now Jake is fired from the bureau.

A reticent stranger...

Treasure hunter Beatrice Glynn is also at the restaurant to meet the same person, who would recognize Beatrice if not for her disguise. Beatrice's goal is to find the Amber Room before Molyneux does, thus fulfilling her deceased father's lifelong quest. Beatrice thinks she is very close. If she can only get a few more clues to the whereabouts of the Amber Room...

Beatrice does not want Jake to know who she is, but in the chaos at the restaurant, they meet face to face. Their goals intersect, and their hunting parties join forces.

A ruthless enemy...

Getting civilian into mortal danger when he doesn't have his badge isn't Jake's intention, but dying is the least of their worries when his archenemy finds them no matter where they go.

They can run, but they cannot hide from her. Why? How?

Their best bet to survive is to get ahead of their mutual enemy, who will remove everyone in the way toward finding the remainder of the lost original Amber Room. But how can Jake and Beatrice find something that no longer exists?

Once a Hero is book 2 in *USA Today* bestselling author Jan Thompson's Protector Sweethearts Christian Romantic Suspense series. *Once a Hero* follows the story of FBI Special Agent Jake Kessler, who first appears undercover in *Reach for Me* (Vacation Sweethearts Book 2), where the hunt for an international terrorist forms the undercurrent of that novel.

Once a Hero (Protector Sweethearts Book 2)
JanThompson.com/hero

Protector Sweethearts
JanThompson.com/protector

For Book News from Jan Thompson:
JanThompson.com/newsletter

ONCE A HERO

ONCE A HERO

PROLOGUE

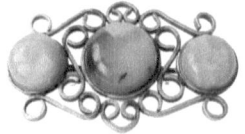

The sounds of his own bones cracking threw FBI Special Agent Jake Kessler into another blinding mental vortex so dark and deep that he couldn't hear his own screams, muffled under the oily, bloody rag they had stuffed into his mouth and tied around the back of his head.

A boot on his chest pressed down on his rib cage and the internal organs inside.

Can't breathe!

Strong hands held his head in an odd position, and if they had pulled him any farther back as he lay prone on the floor, still tied to that chair, Jake was sure his neck would snap—

But then it wouldn't matter anymore, would it, if he died?

God, let me die...

"I told you it wasn't me!" Molyneux screamed into his ear again as she drew the blade of her dagger into his thigh, twisting and shredding his muscles.

The pain was so unbearable that Jake was going to pass out.

Help me, God!

Still, nothing happened.

It was ridiculous to consider how much pain he could tolerate, but here was his test.

Slowly, Molyneux withdrew her dagger.

Whoa. I'm still alive.

God must have something for me to do, yes?

How much could Jake do in his condition, in this place? He opened his one non-swollen eye to look around him in the dimly lit hole in the ground.

Ah, he had been on the other side of this equation once, interrogating suspects, albeit in a more civilized manner becoming of the twenty-first century. He would have extended more mercy to Molyneux's goons. Goons who were now pistol-whipping him again.

Thwack! Thwack!

Funny how it sounded at close range.

God, let me die...

How many times had Molyneux confessed to him, her prisoner? Yeah, she had repeated ad infinitum that she had not been guilty of the Vienna bombings.

Or Tel Aviv.

Or Rome.

Or Barcelona, for that matter.

Oh, and Paris.

The list had gone on and on.

Denials, all.

Tasting his own blood from his busted lips, Jake couldn't process everything the French-born woman had been saying, let alone believe that she was to be absolved of all those terrorist acts that had her thumbprints all over them.

Those had all been signature Molyneux moves.

Operating under the radar through highly secure virtual private networks that even the NSA had envied, Molyneux moved in the darkness of evil.

The first time Jake had met her, he was shocked to find her looking like an ordinary woman who might live down the street from his mother's house.

Big brown eyes, braided brown hair—like she was from small-town America somewhere.

It was hard for Jake to believe that this plain

woman was behind the worst terrorist attacks in the western hemisphere of the world.

And it was even harder for him to believe that she was pushing fifty.

Maybe it's plastic—

A crackle of thunder rocked the room.

Rocked?

Are we on a boat?

Jake couldn't speak, but he could still hear, see, think.

He blinked, trying to recall how he had gotten here. All he could remember was that he had been sitting in a coffee shop in Cannes, waiting for an informant, when something pricked his neck—

The next thing he knew, he had blacked out and woken up in this place.

He hadn't eaten since then.

He felt thirsty, but the oily rag in his mouth only made him gag.

Several peals of thunder rocked the room again.

A heavy door flung open. A tall, well-armed man entered and whispered in Molyneux's ear.

Without another word, she left with him.

And so did her goons.

The room listed. Jake's chair tilted over and slid all the way to a wall.

Now Jake was sure they were on a boat.

In a storm at sea.

In the Bay of Cannes, perhaps?

As if on cue, the sound of thunder boomed through the vessel.

The entire cabin rolled until Jake was looking up at the locked door.

He heard all sorts of metallic and oceanic noises, but what he saw scared him.

Water seeped in all around the supposedly heavy, sealed door...

CHAPTER ONE

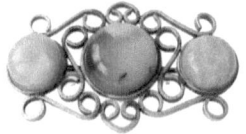

Six months later, Jake Kessler had no idea why Molyneux had chosen to confront him personally, out on a fishing boat in the Bay of Cannes in a thunderstorm, no less.

All he knew was that if his private investigator friend, Helen Hu, hadn't come to his rescue, he would have drowned at the bottom of the sea, leaving the hunt for Molyneux unfinished and someone else's problem.

However, he had lived to tell the tale—albeit through multiple surgeries later—and so, yeah, Molyneux was still his problem, although he had to regroup without a team.

Jake couldn't comprehend the sudden suspension without pay. For what, exactly? For almost dying in the hands of Molyneux?

The Bureau wasn't sympathetic to his life-and-death situation. All they cared about was that their multi-million-dollar operation had ground to a screeching halt because Jake had blown his cover.

Unintentionally, he might add.

But nobody would listen.

The suspension stood.

Helen Hu had offered to pay him a stipend if he wanted to continue the operation against Molyneux.

Who wouldn't?

But first, Jake had to recover from his wounds. Staying in the Paris apartment rent-free with Helen Hu and Reuben Costa while they were on their delayed honeymoon was weird, to say the least, but he mostly kept to himself in his space while they occupied the rest of the luxurious apartment.

In all his life, Jake had never met another couple working through their honeymoon.

Yet they had no choice. Molyneux had bombed Cannes one day after Jake was rescued. All that went into the report that caused Jake to get suspended.

If Jake hadn't gone off script and agreed to meet

an informant in Cannes, perhaps the row of historic hotels could have been saved from the blaze.

In any case, Jake didn't get his meeting in Cannes either. Molyneux's people got to him first.

He thought the informant was dead until she contacted him two days ago.

Which was why Jake was in a transatlantic private jet now, heading for San Francisco.

This time, the informant had better show up.

Stretched out on the reclining leather seat, Jake rolled his head to one side to look out of the window. It was all dark.

He glanced at his watch. He'd arrive in San Francisco in two hours, drive half an hour to the twenty-four-hour restaurant—traffic should be light at two in the morning—and pray that the informant would show up.

At some point in time, the wild-goose chase had to end.

"That all we got on Molyneux?" A voice broke his muse.

Private investigator Earl Young tossed the folder back on the table between them. The way the seats were configured in Helen's jet, Jake couldn't reach for the folder from his reclining position.

Jake glanced over his feet at the end of the

recliner. On the other side of the table, Earl was sitting up, swiping his iPad.

"There has to be something more. She didn't become Molyneux the Doll overnight." Earl didn't look up. "What about family? Parents? Siblings? Spouses?"

"What you see is all we get." Jake pointed to the table. "Four years of work right there."

"And still no fingerprints, no DNA, no first names. For all we know, she might not exist."

"Few people know her real name." Jake crossed his feet. He wiggled his toes in his hiking socks.

The temperature in the cabin was warm, but once they get on the ground, he needed to dress warmly for the low fifties in the middle of the night. Days in San Francisco were mild, but the informant wanted to meet under the cover of night.

"She had to have been born somewhere." Earl tapped his iPad. "Do we know if she has always been a French citizen?"

"You read my report from the Bay of Cannes incident," Jake said. "I looked into her eyes and I talked to her, and if I didn't know any better, I'd say she looked like a neighbor next door or down the street who probably owns a pair of gardening gloves. If she walked in the streets of Cannes or

Paris or maybe even San Francisco, I might not be able to peg her as the world's top terrorist."

Earl nodded. "That's how she has hidden from the law for the last ten years."

"Or more."

"I'll dig into her past and see what I can unearth. How long are you going to be in the States?"

Jake shrugged. "I don't know. Frankly, just between you and me, I want to be done with this operation."

"Well, the Bureau thinks you already are." Earl leaned back and closed his eyes.

Jake had nothing to say about that. He was pulled into the operation when his FBI partner died in Vienna in the explosion. The man was celebrating his twentieth wedding anniversary with his beloved wife. The blast left his wife maimed.

After that tragedy, an opportunity came up for him to go deep undercover in Molyneux's organization. Being single and unattached, Jake took up the multi-year operation.

His sole contact inside the FBI, Stella Evans, had been his only lifeline to the outside world as he navigated the sewers of Molyneux's operation for three years.

And yet, in all that time, Jake never could get

up close and personal with Molyneux until that day in the boat.

Even before he had recovered from his wounds, Jake received the news about his suspension based on entirely frivolous reasons, including turning renegade and arranging a meeting with an informant without proper backups.

Jake supposed that made it all better and hid the fact that Molyneux's people could stab his neck with a needle under the noses of all the FBI agents in the coffee shop that day.

Someday he'd have enough evidence to get his paycheck back.

Meanwhile, he had to keep working on taking down Molyneux, even if the entire Bureau had given up on her. Jake was thankful that when the FBI door slammed in his face, God opened another door for him.

Helen said that Earl and Hugo were her most trusted investigators at Hu Knows, Inc. Hugo was still in Brussels and on another case. Earl had gone to Athens, Greece, for a company meeting with Helen Hu, who hadn't left Europe since her marriage to Reuben Costa.

Since Earl was taking their corporate jet back to Savannah, Helen had suggested that Jake fly home with him. Halfway over the Atlantic, Earl asked to be on the project. The airplane refueled in Atlanta, and off the duo went across the country.

Jake welcomed Earl's help. He needed all the assistance he could get without involving any of his friends still in the Bureau.

Yes, he knew about the FBI mole. However, he didn't think it was going to affect this situation.

Would it?

CHAPTER TWO

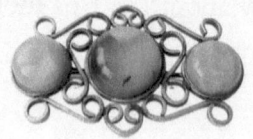

B eatrice Glynn blamed jet lag for keeping her awake at three in the morning on the West Coast—six in the morning in Charleston, where she would have been just waking up to the first cup of coffee that her brother made for her every morning whenever she went to see him.

Instead here she was, waiting for the Ghost of Christmas Past to appear at the next table in the uncrowded brand-new twenty-four-hour café overlooking San Francisco Bay.

Beatrice wondered how her brother was doing these couple of days she had been away, flying back and forth between Europe and North America. He had told her never to call whenever she was out and about, hunting for treasures connected to the Amber Room.

Her brother was even more paranoid than she.

Yeah, Benjamin was just as paranoid as Dad when he had been alive. Dad would still be alive had Molyneux not killed him a few years after Dad obtained asylum in the United States and ended up in the witness protection program as a single father of two kids.

Beatrice was eight years old when Dad died without a body to bury.

She found out later that Dad hadn't been a hero she had thought he was. While nurturing a career as a treasure hunter, in reality Dad was a thief and a partner in crime of Molyneux. Of course, it was all hearsay.

Truth be told, Beatrice hardly remembered the lost years. She was only five years old when she was whisked to the USA and told they would have new names. No longer the Wright family, they would henceforth be the Glynn family. Benjamin was ten, and his story about the event grew more intense and sinister over the years.

I can't blame him.

Beatrice suspected that if she had been ten years old watching her own father be executed, she could be traumatized the rest of her life too. In spite of their loving foster parents, the emotional trauma would remain.

No wonder Benjamin was a recluse now and hadn't left the house for as long as Beatrice could remember. He worked from home, had groceries delivered to him, and stayed away from the public.

As for Beatrice, she had taken the opposite direction. Whether she favored her father or a mother she never knew was beside the matter. The point was that she realized she couldn't be hiding away in a mansion, however nice it was, forever.

Someone had to bring the fight back to Molyneux.

Both she and her brother lived with the fact that any day now, Molyneux would come after them to finish the job she started thirty years prior.

And when she came, Beatrice would be waiting for her.

In fact, rather than let Molyneux find her way to the Glynn siblings, Beatrice was determined to set a trap for the queen rat.

And it had everything to do with the Amber Room.

Ever since she graduated with a doctorate degree in history, with concentration in World War II, Beatrice had set her mind on a race to find the remaining panels of the lost Amber Room before

Molyneux did. Then she could dangle the artifact in front of the terrorist and somehow deliver him to the authorities.

How exactly would she do that last part?

Well, she hadn't figured it out entirely yet, although she'd get there soon.

First, she had to put the remaining puzzle together.

Her contact had notified her that the quarry had left France for San Francisco by way of Mexico. This was the same woman who had tried to meet the FBI Special Agent in Cannes some six months prior.

As if taunting death, Philomena Caddock seemed to be attempting to contact the agent again. Had she found the key to the music box that was supposed to be hidden in a forest somewhere?

And how did Philomena come upon such a crucial piece of information?

Had she gotten it from Dad back when she worked as a nanny and found her way into Dad's bedroom in England? They had carried on for several years before Mom found out about the affair, ending their already fractured marriage.

Being forever branded as the homewrecker wasn't enough for Philomena? Now she revealed herself to be a thief as well, stealing things from

Dad that probably hadn't rightfully belonged to him.

No wonder Molyneux wanted her dead.

Everyone wanted Philomena dead.

Foot traffic was light at this hour of the night compared to six hours before when Beatrice and her team had eaten dinner in the back of a van going up and down Fisherman's Wharf. Raynelle Dryden and Kenichi were simply happy they weren't the ones showing their faces to citywide public security cameras placed all over San Francisco.

Sitting in the van monitoring the situation was a boring task. Yet Beatrice wouldn't have been a successful treasure hunter if not for those two. She kept giving them a raise every year, with bonuses at Christmas.

It had been Kenichi who told Beatrice about the Crete discovery. One single panel from the Amber Room had been buried in a woman's crypt. When the panel was returned to the Russian curators of the Catherine Palace, Beatrice and Kenichi did some research that led them to an FBI mole who revealed that an agent named Jake Kessler had been deep undercover in Molyneux's organization.

The agent was hard to track. He was like a shadow in the night.

However, the wedding of his friend, private investigator Helen Hu, wasn't as secret. It was all over the news because Helen's mother had been convicted of an old crime, also related to the Amber Room.

One thing led to another, and Beatrice and her team had followed Helen Hu and her new husband, Reuben Costa, as they made their way to Paris, where they met up with FBI Special Agent Jake Kessler.

Kenichi and Raynelle tracked Helen and Reuben online, while Beatrice followed Kessler to Cannes. So did Molyneux.

Beatrice prayed that Molyneux had not followed Philomena to San Francisco.

Still gathering her weapons, Beatrice was not ready to fight Molyneux right now.

However, the meeting was tonight, like it or not.

Dressed as a server, Raynelle had done the work of sneaking into the busy café during its peak hours, and assigning Beatrice to the table next to Jake Kessler and Philomena, who made a reservation under the name of Chisolm Wright—which threw Beatrice off for a moment.

Chisolm Wright had been Dad's real name when the family was still living in England. When they approved his asylum application, he came over to the States as Thomas Peterson. His son, Eugene, became Benjamin, and his daughter, Amber, became Amberlyn and then later, Beatrice—after Dad died when they were adopted by a wealthy family in Charleston.

While Dad was still alive, he forbade them to speak of their adoptive mother. Beatrice often wondered what had happened to Imogen Wright, a woman of French descent studying in England who met her treasure hunter husband at Oxford.

To this day, no one knew where she had vanished to.

And now, after twenty-five years, someone had called on Dad's old name.

Why did Philomena ask the FBI agent to reserve a table for two under Chisolm Wright? The meeting had to be about Dad's dealings with Molyneux. How much did Philomena know?

Beatrice was there to find out.

Perhaps she might even discover what happened to Mom. Had she died? Had Molyneux or Philomena killed her?

A wig and a face mask were all it took for Beatrice to subvert the facial recognition cameras outside and inside the café. In fact, it was a requirement all over the city to wear a mask—or face covering—to restaurants and public places, a new normal borne out of a recent virus pandemic.

Ironically, it was going to make it hard for Beatrice to recognize Philomena.

Except for the scar across her left eyebrow—a gift from Molyneux in Cannes. Beatrice remembered watching Philomena escape. They lost track of her after that.

However, she was back on a beautiful night in San Francisco.

A server came to refill Beatrice's glass of water.

She had been sitting alone for a while, playing with her phone. Clearly Philomena and the FBI agent were late.

How did Philomena elude the authorities for twenty-five years?

Well, how did Molyneux?

Why hadn't the two met and dealt with each other in all those years? More unsolved puzzles there.

Beatrice felt no pity for those two women. For one thing, Molyneux had killed so many people that she would never leave prison—if she made it into prison. Numerous government agencies in North America and Europe were after her.

The server returned. "Would you like something else, ma'am?"

"May I have the dessert menu?" Beatrice felt like she had to blend in. Most of the people in the café were eating something.

"Certainly, ma'am. I'll be right back."

At 3:28 a.m., there was still no sign of anyone.

Beatrice's shoulders began to hurt a little. Sore muscles here and there. She had slept poorly in the Gulfstream, besotted with worries about the project to take down Molyneux.

Once in San Francisco, she and her team had booked a hotel room and rented a work van. Then they ate meals in town, got takeout, and went to the gas station.

She had left an enormous trail for FBI Special Agent Jake Kessler.

To wit, if anything happened to her—should Molyneux decide to come after her—she had left enough footprints for Kessler to exonerate her or at least bring closure to her case in the event that it turned into a homicide.

She wouldn't put it past Molyneux to do whatever she could to be the first person to get to the rest of the Amber Room.

The server returned and Beatrice kept it simple with a slice of chocolate cake with ice cream on top. When it arrived, she nearly forgot what she was there to do.

"That looks delicious."

The voice was calm, friendly, and distinctly male.

Beatrice looked up, her fork in midair.

"Such a tiny slice." It was all she could think of to say.

Jake Kessler smiled.

A nice voice that went with a disarming smile.

They finally met, but Kessler would never know that she knew who he was long before today.

He had gotten a haircut since Cannes, though that had been six months prior. Those scars on his forehead and left cheek were healing nicely.

Beatrice wanted to ask about his ribs, which Molyneux's men had broken, but that would give her away to both the FBI and to Molyneux.

She wasn't sure which one was worse.

Regardless, she was glad that he was still alive.

Her anonymous tip to Helen Hu's personal cell phone had been a knee-jerk reaction. Beatrice could not let a fellow human being die in the ocean when she knew where Molyneux had taken him. The sudden storm was something else. She was surprised that Molyneux had escaped in a helicopter before the fishing boat capsized.

Thank God Helen and her team had reached him in time.

Even though Kessler didn't know Beatrice, she had made him her insurance.

The man sat down without another word.

Just as well. Beatrice did not want to say anything that would give away who she was.

Quietly, she scanned the room. By a dark window, Raynelle was eating salad and reading a book. Presumably she had finished her work as a server in an earlier shift. A former CIA operative, Raynelle Dryden was a coup for Beatrice.

Officially, Raynelle was her bodyguard due to some previous death threats. Unofficially, Raynelle's job was to assist Beatrice in finding the rest of the lost Amber Room. That was Kenichi's job too.

Around them, several other tables were occupied, but the people generally looked like customers.

The stage was set.

All they needed now was the woman of the hour to make a grand entrance.

CHAPTER THREE

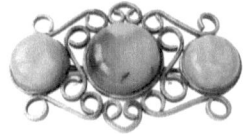

J ake Kessler hadn't meant to make small talk with the woman at the next table, but when he saw that chocolate cake, he almost asked for a bite.

Ridiculous, I know.

There was something familiar about that woman, and he thought she looked almost like someone he had been hunting for the last several years.

Then again, he must have been exhausted to think that a random stranger in the middle of the night could somehow be related to Molyneux.

Everyone looked like her after a while.

He couldn't shake her face from his mind. The big brown eyes, the braids, the dagger in her grip, slicing his muscles from his thigh, the moment he wished God would let him die...

His hands began to shake as he quickly sat down at his table, his back against the wall. That way, he could see the entire dining room.

He opened the menu in front of him to distract himself from the past, which kept resurfacing in his mind.

Six months old now.

Maybe the bureau was right to put him on suspension. There was no way his mind was in the right place right now to do this undercover work.

Yet the informant had called him out of the blue to apologize for Cannes. And she wanted to meet again. This time in San Francisco. Why, though?

Jake hadn't been authorized to conduct this meeting. He was suspended, remember? But he decided not to tell the informant.

Flying under the radar meant that he had no backups, no protection. And yes, as soon as he started recording the conversation at this table, he could kiss his FBI badge and career goodbye forever.

So long. It's been nice.

He could go to work for Helen Hu. She had been asking him when he was going to quit the

Bureau. However, he wasn't sure if he wanted to work for a fiery, feisty person for more than just a few months—although Helen was the only one who had come to his rescue when he was trapped in the overturned fishing boat off the coast of France.

Who had been the anonymous caller with the timely tip of his whereabouts? Why had she called Helen instead of the Cannes police?

A woman of mystery.

Jake wondered if she was the informant herself.

Jake drew deep breaths to calm his nerves, but all he smelled was fresh bread passing by him on a tray. His mind wandered to buttering a piece of toast, putting a dollop of strawberry jam on it, and eating it slowly while watching the sun set across a lake.

He closed his eyes.

"Hello." A woman's voice interrupted his imagined calm.

She sat down across from him at the small table.

Philomena Wright, also known as Philomena Caddock, was in her sixties with short black hair combed neatly and tucked behind her ears. Simple earrings made of gold—or something golden—caught Jake's eyes because they were like two dangling keys.

She did not glance to the left or right.

Customers started to leave around them. The woman at the next table kept eating her chocolate cake. When she asked for a glass of milk from the server, Jake almost leaned toward her and said, "I would too."

But he stopped his wandering mind. Why would a stranger draw his focus away from the matter at hand?

Thank God that Earl was somewhere in the room. Jake slowly looked over Philomena's shoulder and spotted him at a far table, earbuds at the ready to listen to their conversation.

"Take two, huh?" Philomena said.

Jake supposed she was referring to Cannes. He nodded.

"This is all I have for you." She opened her palm, showing him an amber brooch. "From my late husband."

"And?" Jake suddenly felt it was a mistake to meet this crazy woman.

"There's a story behind this brooch," the woman said. "Find the story, find the room."

Suddenly Philomena turned toward the woman at the next table, her eyes widening.

Jake glanced at the woman, now staring at her phone, seemingly oblivious to Philomena's stares.

What is going on?

A new server came to refill their water. "Would you like some coffee?"

"Yes. Two creams," Philomena said.

"Black for me," Jake added.

The stranger at the next table put away her phone and got up. She walked toward her server and pressed a couple of bills in his palm. The server was thanking her profusely when another server bumped into them, spilling liquid all over her blouse. Soda, it looked like.

Jake shook his head. He turned toward Philomena. "I need more than this brooch."

He opened a clean paper napkin and wrapped the brooch in it without touching it with his hand.

"I have nothing more to tell you, except that I regret everything I ever did in my life." Her arms were crossed, as if belying her own words. "If Chisolm were here today, he'd vouch for me. Unfortunately, he's gone, and I have nothing left of him but that brooch."

"What you wanted to talk about was so far in the past that I'm not sure it's relevant for today," Jake said quietly.

Philomena waited for the server to pour her a hot cup of coffee. After the server left, she still didn't speak. Slowly, she sipped the cup of coffee.

Jake wanted to drink his own coffee black, but

decided to ask for cream. He stirred in a small drop into his coffee, which was the color of night and dark days ahead.

At this point, Jake's eyes were on the stranger again, coming out of the ladies' restroom, half her blouse and part of her jeans wet. It was then that Jake realized who she reminded him of—

Across his table, Philomena gagged and choked. Her hands were on her chest. She was gasping for air and trying to say something.

"Whoa!" Jake rushed to her, knocking over his own glass of water on the table. "Someone call 911!"

Across the room, Earl came flying. So did the stranger.

"What's going on?" Earl asked, tapping his phone.

Was it the coffee?

Philomena fell off the chair before Jake could catch her. The maître d' and several servers came over, but Philomena was not breathing.

She was gone.

When Jake remembered the brooch that Philomena had put on the table, it was too late.

The brooch was also gone.

CHAPTER FOUR

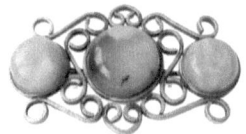

T he night masked their getaway in a van that Kenichi drove. Before Beatrice could calm down, they arrived at their safe house in South San Francisco.

The garage door closed, and the van doors opened. Raynelle led the way to the kitchen door, since she had the key to the rental townhouse.

Kenichi was out of it, having sat in the van and waited the entire time Beatrice and Raynelle were in the café. He went upstairs to get some sleep.

Raynelle put the kettle on to make tea. That woman didn't sleep.

Beatrice closed the kitchen door behind her and locked it for good measure. She washed her hands and looked for something to drink in the refrigerator. It was bare. She found some glasses but they were covered with a soapy film of some sort. She grabbed a paper cup and walked to the kitchen sink. Tap water would have to do.

In the living room, where Kenichi had set up shop—laptops everywhere and all interconnected—Beatrice plopped down on a sagging sofa and kicked off her boots. She lifted the wig off her head and removed the mesh net wig cap.

Her prosthetic nose was still stuck to her face. She'd deal with that later.

The sticky soda on her blouse was drying. The blouse was probably ruined. Or not. She'd find out after doing laundry.

She closed her eyes and thanked God for keeping her safe.

Jake Kessler would be coming after her soon. He might not know about Kenichi and Raynelle, but he had seen Beatrice's face under the wig.

I don't care.

She fished the brooch out of her jeans pocket. On the drive here, Raynelle had explained how she swiped it off the café table when everyone was freaking out over Philomena dying in front of them.

There were three polished amber cabochons inlaid in thick gold.

Pretty, but not what she was after.

On the underside, there was an inscription of some sort. She pressed her thumb right in the middle of the brooch.

Nothing happened.

Her mind was in a fog—jet lag and a lack of sleep—and she tried to remember the notes she had read in Dad's study back in Charleston.

Wait.

If there were two cabochons, then press the bottom.

If there were three...

Beatrice speed-dialed her brother on a secure line Kenichi had set up via a virtual private network. "Good morning, Ben."

At the other end of the line, her older brother, Benjamin, sounded groggy. "What time is it?"

"I think eight where you are."

"Call me back at noon." *Click.*

Beatrice tried again.

"What?"

"Don't hang up. We found the three-amber brooch." She did not explain that Raynelle had stolen it on Jake's watch.

"Where?" Benjamin sounded alert now.

"Our ex-nanny kept it." Beatrice stretched out on the sofa.

"That thief. She stole it from Dad."

"Well, we got it back." Beatrice didn't want to get into details.

"You know it's not enough."

Beatrice sighed. "We don't have the other two brooches."

"We'll have to track down the buyers."

"We? Benjamin, are you planning on doing something? Will you come out here and help me?" Beatrice almost got her hopes up.

There was a moment of silence on the other end of the phone. A long silence.

"Dad has been dead for twenty-five years," Benjamin said. "I've let it go. You should too."

"No. We've been having this conversation for a long time. His murderer needs to go to jail."

"I love you and all, but I really don't agree with you about this. You've spent an enormous amount of your inheritance on finding the Amber Room, and all you have to show for is one-third of a brooch set."

That about summed up the story of Beatrice's career. "I am putting my history degree to good use."

"Right."

"I think we're very close."

"Uh-huh."

"Dad would keep going." Beatrice didn't know for sure, but she thought he might.

"Yeah, he probably would. He's stubborn like that. I don't know who I take after, considering we don't know much about our mother, but I know I don't take after Dad." He paused. "Oh, wait. I forget I was adopted."

Beatrice didn't want to go there. "I'll call you when I find the lost Amber Room."

"Okay. I'll go back to sleep." And he hung up.

The Amber Room was Beatrice's thing, not Benjamin's, but he would help her if he could. He'd been busy looking for sunken treasures instead.

Even when Beatrice had been in college, she was fascinated by the research done on the special room in Catherine the Great's Winter Palace. When Germany raided Russia in World War II, the Amber Room vanished.

That was, until a year ago, when a few panels were unearthed in Agneta Sanna's crypt on the island of Crete. Helen Hu was there, as far as Beatrice knew. She had read the rest of the information from newspapers that four small panels were found altogether.

There had to be more.

"Bee, there is a reason it's called the *lost* Amber Room." Benjamin laughed.

"Whatever." Beatrice was determined to find it. If Molyneux thought it existed, then she would too.

The world didn't care. St. Petersburg had been displaying a reproduction Amber Room to tourists for years.

Those who wanted to preserve history cared about original things, artifacts, documents. Memories of days that had vanished into the vortex of time.

"Okay then. Just don't get dead on the way there."

Benjamin might be a paranoid recluse, but he sure hadn't lost his sense of humor. Beatrice rarely laughed at his jokes, but he was still her brother. She wouldn't want to lose him.

So yes, he could stay in their hideaway in Charleston for the rest of his life if he wanted to. As long as he was alive and well.

How on earth are we going to find two more brooches?

If Philomena was dead, then much information would have died with her.

"Ken, could you check the local PD to see if Philomena made it?" Beatrice texted him. He would see it after he woke up from his nap.

CHAPTER FIVE

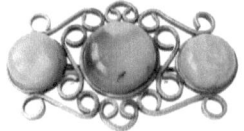

The investigation wasn't moving as fast as Jake would like, and he liked it even less when he received a call saying he had been fired from the FBI.

Forget suspension.

Ten years of service flushed down the drain.

On this rainy afternoon, twelve hours after Philomena had keeled over, everything that could go wrong had gone wrong.

With his only contact dead, Jake had hit a brick wall.

And so at four o'clock, Jake found himself sitting across from Earl in the latter's hotel room suite. Between them, a laptop whirred, and Helen Hu's sunburned face smiled into her camera.

"Autopsy takes time," Earl said. "A few days if we rush it, but without the FBI cooperation—how on earth did you get yourself fired?—it could take weeks."

He was chewing gum and it annoyed Jake. He got it that Earl was trying to quit smoking, but could he do it quietly? "Stop popping new wads of gum into your mouth, will you?"

"Does this bother you?" Earl added another wad and chewed loudly. "As I was saying, autopsy takes time. I bet you she was poisoned. Coffee was all she had."

Jake drew a deep breath. The pain in his thigh persisted. He remembered the rod inside his leg, holding his bones together, and he groaned at the thought of lost muscle and tissue.

Let me be the one to kill her.

This was not the time for Jake to wonder if God would approve. In fact, his entire career at the FBI was probably not approved by God. After all, he had to go undercover for very long spells at a time—sometimes years—and he had to live a lie the entire time. Sometimes he had to do things that his own mother would not approve. Certainly not things he could talk to his pastor about.

Pastor? What pastor? He had moved from place

to place so much in the last ten years that he had no particular church home.

What would it feel like to settle down and stay put in one place for once?

"My offer still stands. Come work with us." Before Helen could continue, her phone pinged. "Okay. We have something here. Streaming it now."

"I should've put the brooch in my pocket," Jake said as Earl opened another window on his laptop to see what Helen was sending them.

On the screen was the restaurant dining room from every angle. Helen zoomed in to the two tables.

The stranger at the next table was eating chocolate cake while looking at her phone when Philomena walked in.

They watched the replay until the part when Philomena fell over, clutching her chest.

What could possibly kill in minutes?

"Slow down," Jake said as the video continued.

He recalled a server spilling liquid on the stranger's blouse. After she came out of the ladies' room, she flicked the edge of her hair.

That was when Jake saw her hairline. "She's wearing a wig."

"Okay, we're getting somewhere." Earl tossed out his squishy wads of gum.

"Thank you, man."

Earl shrugged.

The woman looked startled when Philomena fell onto the floor. She rushed forward, her eyes all wide.

"Stop," Jake said. "Can you please zoom in on her face, snapshot it, and see who she matches?"

Helen saved the image. "Who are we comparing her to? If it's to everyone in the whole world, it would take forever."

"Let's start with Molyneux," Jake suggested. "Remember the sketch we had made?"

There was no photograph of Molyneux anywhere. She must have done numerous plastic surgeries to be that elusive in police state Europe where cameras were everywhere in public and private places.

"Why are we starting with her?" Earl asked.

"The last five years of my life have been about catching Molyneux. That woman looked like a younger version of Molyneux."

"A doppelgänger." Helen chuckled.

"Or her daughter." Jake reminded them about the bits of information that Philomena had already told him. "When Philomena worked for Chisolm, he was still married to Imogen—before she became Molyneux the Doll. Philomena was a nanny to his two kids."

"Where are the kids now?"

"That's the billion-dollar question, right?" Jake waited for Helen to process it. "If Chisolm were still alive today, I'd have many questions for him."

"It's not a match," Helen said. "Truly, we need a real photo of Molyneux, not a sketch."

"I thought her eyes looked familiar." Jake leaned back against the couch. "I've done this too long. Failure after failure. Maybe I should just quit and move back home. Dad could use some help with his farm."

Earl laughed. "You wouldn't last a day. You're cut out for this, Jake. Whether you do it in the bureau or as a private citizen, it matters not. What matters is that you're doing the right thing, putting away evil people for life."

"Evil people?" Jake opened an eye.

"Aren't they all?"

Jake stood up. Turned to Earl. "Do you have a list of the employees at the café?"

"Sure do."

"Let's go talk to the server who spilled soda on the stranger."

"I'll drive." Earl reached for the laptop. "We'll talk to you later, Helen."

Helen nodded onscreen. "Meanwhile, I'll call in some favors at the NSA to see if they can help us identify the woman."

"Don't work too hard," Jake said. "Make sure you have some hubby time."

"Is that the advice of a bachelor to a married woman?" Helen grinned.

"I'm just saying that you and Reuben spent your honeymoon fishing me out of the ocean and saving my life. Get some rest."

"If I hadn't received that anonymous call, you'd be dead by now," Helen said. "Thank God for that person, whoever she is."

"Still no idea who, huh?" Jake would like to thank her in person if possible.

"Nope. Burner phone. Short message."

"She didn't text."

"No. She was a bit freaked out on the phone."

"Surprised at her own information?"

"Shocked was more like it." Helen sighed. "But the voice was filtered. It's not her real voice."

Earl stretched and slapped his thighs as he stood up and put on his vest. "I think it's Philomena, overcome by guilt."

Jake wasn't as sure.

CHAPTER SIX

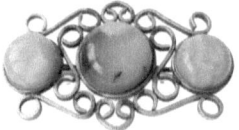

When Beatrice and Raynelle returned to the Fisherman's Wharf at ten o'clock at night, they found the café off limits with yellow police tape across the front door. The rest of the restaurants up and down the bay were still open. Tourists enjoyed themselves, laughing loudly, chatting to one another, taking night selfies.

Beatrice and Raynelle blended into the crowd.

"Whose bright idea was this?" Beatrice quietly said into her Bluetooth headphone. She knew Kenichi could hear her.

He was at the back of the van several blocks away, looking at the world through the cameras on

Beatrice's shirt button and Raynelle's beanie cap button.

"Why are we here again?" Beatrice did not expect an answer. She hadn't slept all day, and she was getting cranky.

In fact, she hadn't wanted to come here a second time in twenty-four hours. However, Kenichi had obtained the security video from the same café and noticed that before Philomena had sat down with the FBI agent, she went to the ladies' room.

The before-and-after photos showed that she went in with an amber-colored brooch on her lapel and came out without it. Had she dropped it some-where on the restroom floor?

"Ladies' room, people," Kenichi said. "I'm not going in there."

"Does it matter? The café is closed. Someone just died there." That was Beatrice's verdict.

Raynelle didn't care if they went or not. She would still be paid whether she sat in their town-house or in the van or accompanied Beatrice into the café.

"You better go with her," Kenichi told Raynelle. "Two pairs of eyes are better than one."

"I guess we could bring a metal detector." Beat-rice was still reluctant. "What if we're caught?"

"Don't worry. I'll disable all the sensors before you go in."

Six hours later, after a dinner of salmon on greens—yeah, Kenichi cooked too—the trio had headed out to the Fisherman's Wharf, and here they were.

Beatrice paid Kenichi and Raynelle very high salaries for their expertise. However, on a crowded street with security cameras all around them, how would they break into a locked café?

Beatrice did not want to hear that her employees hadn't thought through their mission. In fact, if anything, she was to blame. She should have said—

"Walking off your chocolate cake?" A voice said to her.

Beatrice froze. It was the same voice from the café last night. Surely it could not be Jake Kessler.

"I recognize you even though you're wearing a different nose tonight," he added.

Beatrice turned.

"And different colored hair."

It was indeed FBI Special Agent Jake Kessler. Again. However, he wasn't supposed to know that she knew who he was. "And you are?"

"Jake." He was wearing a plaid shirt of many dubious colors—the street lamp distorted the colors in the night. "There. I gave you my real name. What's yours?"

"You must have mistaken me for another person." Beatrice noticed Raynelle distancing herself from them.

She was going toward the café.

"I don't think so," Jake said. "You wore a prosthetic nose this morning."

"I'm sorry?"

"I'm not sorry to see you again. In fact, I want to find you if you're looking for this?" Jake showed her a photo on his phone.

Beatrice tried not to react when she saw the one-amber brooch.

The amber was huge. It was set in...silver?

The resolution on the phone was so-so, but the rest of the brooch wasn't gold. What happened to the gold? Had anyone tampered with it?

"You do recognize this," Jake said. "Let's talk."

"I was just thinking it looks pretty and old. Why are you showing me a photo? Are you trying to sell?"

"Not at all." Jake put the phone back into his pocket. "In fact, I think it will lead me to Molyneux. What do you think?"

"Who?" Beatrice felt helpless. She wasn't sure she could play this game for much longer.

Anytime someone mentioned Molyneux, it was triggering.

She killed Dad.

And maybe even Mom.

Beatrice turned toward the bay and placed her elbows on top of the railing. She did not want Jake to see her reaction.

"Maybe we can work together," Jake said.

"Maybe not. I don't even know you. You're a stranger out of nowhere."

"If you tell me your name, we will not be strangers anymore."

Ping!

Jake flinched and touched his ear.

Beatrice noticed blood under the street light. "Whoa. What's going on?"

She glanced around.

Raynelle was nowhere to be found.

The crowd seemed oblivious to what had just happened.

Jake stared at his wet fingers and touched his ear again. "Did someone just shoot at me?"

Ping!

"Get down!" Beatrice pulled him to the ground. The sidewalk was rough cement, and she was sure she had grazed her elbows through her long-sleeved cotton blouse. "Ken, call 911!"

The crowd was chaotic again. People running, screaming.

Beatrice spotted Raynelle in the middle of the crowd, running across the street and pointing to the second floor of a parking deck. She stopped, pulled out her Glock, aimed at the gunman, and fired.

One shot.

In an instant, Raynelle was surrounded by the local police.

CHAPTER SEVEN

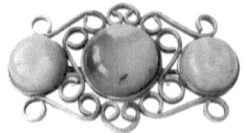

"A treasure hunter, huh?" Earl's voice seemed to say he didn't believe anything Beatrice Glynn had said back at the San Francisco Police Department Central Station.

He pulled the SUV out of the parking spot and eased into traffic outside the police station. Jake buckled on his passenger side safety belt.

"You believe a thing she said?" Earl asked.

Jake didn't know what to think. It turned out that Beatrice had gone at night with her real face. No prosthetic nose. Her face also matched her identification and passport. Jake felt that she had been herself at the police station.

Jake figured that if they sent her data to the FBI, he might call his FBI agent friend Stella Evans to check on Beatrice's real identity, considering he himself now had zero access to any FBI resources.

Alternatively, they could ask Helen to look into it. She had connections at the NSA.

Then again, since Beatrice was an American citizen, the NSA spying on her could be a powder keg of a whole host of constitutional problems.

Jake did not tell the SFPD that he suspected Beatrice to be the same person in the café the night before, and that she had swiped the three-amber brooch.

To his credit, Earl also didn't say a word.

"Who is she, really?" Earl asked again. "I don't buy all that talk about death threats."

"She has proof. Police reports." Jake wasn't trying to defend her. "That ex-CIA she hired as her bodyguard seemed to be doing her job."

"The sniper must be useless if he missed her and got your ear." Earl laughed.

Jake reached to touch his bandaged ear. It still stung a bit, but it would heal. Two stitches at urgent care and he was good to go. "I didn't get a chance to thank her for saving my life."

"You meant when she pulled you to the ground *after* you had already been shot?" Earl didn't seem to agree with him.

"I should try to thank her in person, but we were interviewed separately."

"I'm sure she will show up again. What is she looking for anyway?"

"She didn't say, but the brooches led to one place." Jake looked out the window. "Just like those twelve Petros eggs that Helen and Mama Hu uncovered. They all lead to one place."

"The Amber Room."

"Yep. How could anyone find something that no longer existed in its original form?"

"Beats me. I'm not a treasure hunter. Not my thing."

"Not mine either. I don't even care about the Amber Room. I just want to see Molyneux behind bars. I'm tired of chasing her."

The clock on the dashboard said it was past one o'clock in the morning.

Jake was wide awake on Paris time.

Earl was yawning. And driving.

"Let's go back to the hotel and get some sleep. Maybe tomorrow we'll think better," Jake said.

"It's already tomorrow." Earl laughed.

"We have so many questions. Maybe we're asking the wrong questions."

"And so many wrong answers."

Jake leaned his head on the headrest of the passenger seat, sorting through that day's finds.

He had lost his informant, now in the morgue awaiting autopsy.

He lost the three-amber brooch. Someone had taken it back at the café. Was it Beatrice Glynn? Was it her bodyguard?

Why did Beatrice need a bodyguard? Was she rich or in danger or both?

Speaking of Beatrice, why had she been in disguise at the café but not the next evening outdoors?

If she had taken the brooch, why did she do it?

Why would a sniper try to kill her—them?

It was unclear who the dead sniper was. What was clear was that Raynelle would probably not be charged for the killing. There were hundreds of witnesses who saw the sniper shoot at the crowd. Besides, she had a multi-state license to carry a concealed weapon.

The SFPD wasn't forthcoming to civilians—which Jake now was—about criminal investigations. They didn't answer to him.

How quickly he had fallen from being under-cover to being suspended and now fired.

"What are all the wrong questions?" Earl

parked the vehicle at their hotel. "Ah, like you said, we'll sort it out in the morning."

Jake nodded as he began to suspect that San Francisco had taken him further and further away from his target: Molyneux.

She was probably plotting another terrorist attack in Europe.

And there was nothing Jake could do right now to stop her.

Unless he could find her first.

He was confident there was a connection between the treasure hunter and Molyneux. From all his years of working undercover as part of Molyneux's organization, he knew that she was looking for the Amber Room. Not for history's sake, but to sell the panels to the highest bidder so that she could fund more atrocities.

If Beatrice and her bodyguard were also looking for the Amber Room, they might run into Molyneux.

Perhaps he should join forces with Beatrice.

Hmmm.

He'd have to think about that.

She might not be a friend at all. What if she was hired by Molyneux to look for the Amber Room? Many mercenaries and treasure hunters worked for her that way.

Still, why wouldn't they keep what they found for themselves?

Which side was Beatrice Glynn on?

"Hey, Earl?" Jake thought of something else.

"Yeah?"

"Hugo still in Brussels?"

"Uh-huh. Living the life."

"Can he check on Javier and his pals in jail? Maybe they could shed some light on what Molyneux might be up to regarding the Amber Room. You know how she's been raising funds through the sale of stolen artwork and jewelry."

Earl nodded. "Good idea. Maybe between Hugo and Helen, they could get us more information."

"And see if the name Beatrice Glynn shows up anywhere near Molyneux."

"You worked for her for three years. Never heard of this woman?"

"Nope." Jake shook his head. "I don't know how many people work for Molyneux or who they all are."

"You think Glynn works for her?" Earl made a face to show disgust.

"We don't know, do we? We know that Molyneux cannot leave France—not legally. She has to send people to do her dirty work for her.

Someone who has an American passport would be allowed into the USA."

"Where the three brooches are supposed to be."

"And we lost the one we could have had." Jake wondered who else was working for Beatrice the treasure hunter, and how big her organization was.

And the missing three-amber brooch bothered him. Was he losing his agent acuity? "We're back to square one."

"Yes, we are."

CHAPTER EIGHT

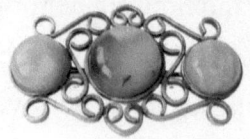

"He's bluffing. He doesn't have the one-amber brooch, but that makes me think he knows where it is." Kenichi seemed confident of his finding, but it scared Beatrice.

It was a rainy morning in San Francisco, and they had finished breakfast without Raynelle, who had gone off somewhere to decompress alone.

Beatrice paced the floor in their hideaway townhouse. "Where did you get that information?"

"Gimme a pay raise and I'll tell you." Kenichi chuckled. "Otherwise, it's best if you don't know because then you won't be liable in court."

"I don't know if that's a failsafe way to protect me." Beatrice rolled her eyes. "I think I know what you did but I don't like it. I don't want you breaking any law to get us to where we need to go."

"What do you think I did?"

"When I was talking to Jake at the wharf, you hacked into his phone via mine because we were mere inches apart."

Kenichi wiggled his eyebrows. "So it's Jake now, huh? Not Agent Kessler or anything formal?"

"He told me his name is Jake." For whatever reason. Maybe to gain her trust. "Okay. So you scanned his phone."

"He's not very techno savvy, but enough to use a burner phone. There was nothing in it. He made a few calls but they were all untraceable. No text messages."

"But he has a photo of the one-amber brooch."

"I wouldn't put it past the FBI to entrap anyone."

"Well, he's not FBI anymore." Beatrice told him what happened at the police station.

"That, I didn't know." Kenichi looked a bit stunned. "Maybe I should keep a better eye on him."

"At the police station, there a man with him," Beatrice said. "I heard the name Earl but I didn't catch the last name. Sounds like someone who works for Helen Hu?"

"Might be. I'll keep one eye on Jake and one eye on Earl then."

Beatrice prayed for Raynelle, hoping that she was okay, and that she would return to them in one piece. Pressure had been the reason Raynelle had left the CIA in the first place.

Treasure hunting was supposed to be a piece of cake compared to what the CIA did every day.

Then again, maybe they should just pack up and go home to Charleston.

"I think I know what you're thinking." Kenichi didn't look up. "You're asking yourself if this is worth the trouble."

"How did you guess?"

Kenichi chuckled. "How many times in the last five years have you asked yourself that very question?"

"Too many times. I may not be cut out for this." Beatrice sighed. "It's getting dangerous. Like tonight."

Beatrice had told the SFPD exactly what she presumed had happened. That Raynelle thought the sniper was going after her. After all, she had hired Raynelle to protect her, having received several death threats in the last year. The proof that the sniper was going for Beatrice again was that

Jake's ears were shot inches away from Beatrice's face.

It meant she was either getting closer to finding the Amber Room, or she was about to cross paths with Molyneux and somebody wanted her out of the way.

"But you end up always saying the same thing," Kenichi reminded her.

Beatrice nodded. "We have to press on."

"The sooner Molyneux is gone, the better the world will be."

"Thank God we don't have to get to her ourselves. We just need to lead the authorities to her. Then again, that's easier said than done. How many times have they failed to follow up?"

"Maybe this time *your* Jake might succeed."

Beatrice ignored his jest. "Did you say you think he knows where the one-amber brooch is?"

"I suspect so."

"Because?"

"Philomena knew where all three brooches were. That's why we tracked her, remember? So she showed up at the café with two brooches—one on her lapel and one in her hand."

"She gave the three-amber brooch to Jake, and Raynelle picked it up for us somehow." Beatrice wished they could have entered the café to find the one-amber brooch, though that was a shot in the dark. "We suspect that the one-amber brooch was either still in the restaurant or maybe Philomena took it off her lapel and put it in her purse."

"All of which would be at the SFPD evidence locker."

"Or the morgue."

"If they suspect foul play, her belongings wouldn't be in the morgue," Kenichi corrected her.

Beatrice sat down. "I have spent too much time and money on this to quit now."

A knock on the door startled them both.

A Sig Sauer appeared out of nowhere in Kenichi's hand. He motioned for Beatrice to get to the back room. Beatrice did so without a word.

Soon, she heard Kenichi call her name. "It's Ray."

When Beatrice came out of the room, Kenichi was saying, "Where did you go?"

"To clear my head." Raynelle washed her hands in the kitchen sink and then found something to drink. "What's been happening while I was away?"

"Did you get any sleep?" Beatrice asked.

"No."

"Why don't you get some sleep and we'll talk later?" Beatrice suspected that poor bodyguard of hers had gone through enough for the night. "I think we'll have more information this afternoon or evening."

"A whole lot more information, I hope." Kenichi got busy on his laptop. "I'm still collecting data on Philomena. Someone killed her, obviously."

"Or she committed suicide. Drank poison or something?"

Kenichi gave Beatrice a look. "You're so old school."

"What? It's possible."

"The more likely scenario is for someone to murder her because she had at least two of the brooches we need to find a map that would lead us to the whereabouts of the Amber Room."

"If we find the rest of the panels, it would be the first time they see light since 1943," Raynelle said.

"But first, we need to complete this brooch set." Beatrice pulled the three-amber brooch from the pocket of her cargo pants and displayed it on her palm. Raynelle had given it to her in the van. "One thing we have to remember, people, is that I don't sanction breaking the law to get ahead of Molyneux."

"We can't get there by the book," Kenichi protested. "That's why your brother...uh..."

"My brother what?" Beatrice was surprised Kenichi brought up Benjamin. What was that about?

Beatrice remembered the time her brother had sent Kenichi to work for her. Benjamin had run extensive background checks on the mononymous Kenichi—although Beatrice had discovered that his last name was Kobayashi—and he was in the clear. No criminal records. Long history at the NSA and CIA and Special Ops. He was at least forty now, but his skillset was perfect for the job of assisting Beatrice on this long quest to find the lost Amber Room.

In fact, it had been Kenichi who had recommended Raynelle, a fellow CIA officer, to work for Beatrice as well. That worked out for all of them because the one condition of Kenichi's employment was that he would never show his face in public.

Unfortunately, the introduction of Raynelle into Beatrice's team made her brother rather upset. Somehow Benjamin detested government agencies, calling them wasteful. Beatrice knew his opinion was probably borne out of the fact that the CIA did not help their father. Once they had no use for Thomas Peterson, they discarded him. He had to make a living somehow, and Beatrice suspected that Dad went back to his old ways—

which caused him to run into his ex-wife, who then killed him.

To this day, Benjamin refused to talk to Raynelle on his own volition. He would only say a few words if Beatrice made him communicate with Raynelle for one reason or another.

Kenichi, on the other hand, had earned Benjamin's respect. Always working in the dark shadows, Kenichi would supply Beatrice with everything she needed. He had fished her out of water so many times she had lost count.

It had been Kenichi, upon her orders, who had discovered the coordinates of the fishing vessel holding Jake Kessler hostage. She had made the call to Helen using an altered voice, but if Kenichi hadn't gotten her the longitude and latitude, Jake would have died.

Jake.

He was only a few inches taller than she was as they stood at Fisherman's Wharf, though she was wearing chunky boots.

He had a pleasant disposition. If she hadn't known who he was, she would never have guessed that he was an FBI agent. That might be how he had been successful in deep undercover for three years in Molyneux's gang.

Who ratted him out?

"Ken?" Beatrice sat down next to him on the couch. "When you have a minute..."

"When do I ever have a minute?"

"Maybe like this week?"

"Yes, ma'am. What can I do for you?"

"Can you somehow find out who told Molyneux that Jake was undercover?" Beatrice asked. "By legal means."

"What for?"

"The more we have on Jake—perhaps the more we can offer him—the more leverage we have." Beatrice and Jake both had a mutual enemy: Molyneux. The old adage might be true. Maybe the enemy of Beatrice's enemy might turn out to be a friend.

Besides, he had a calming voice. If Beatrice were to die, that was the last voice she wanted to hear, ushering her into eternity. Then she would see Dad again.

But who would watch over her brother?

So no. I can't die just yet. There's so much work to be done.

Her fear was that in encroaching on Molyneux territory, death could come before her time.

CHAPTER NINE

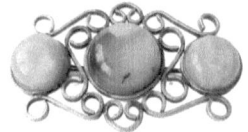

Philomena Caddock owned a pricey log cabin in the woods somewhere outside the coastal town of Eureka in Northern California.

Unbelievable.

"I thought she was on welfare," Jake said, adjusting his seat belt. He leaned back in the passenger seat, trying to get some sleep. It was past midnight, and they had left San Francisco more than five hours before.

He wanted to drive, but Earl had insisted.

It rained most of the time on Highway 101, with the windshield wipers on full speed thwacking away the heavy droplets of rain until they stopped at Eureka to get gas and midnight snacks—even though it wasn't midnight at that time.

They went east, into the forest in the thick of night, with rain all around them and very low visibility.

"She's faring well is all I can say." Earl drank his cappuccino.

"The cabin's worth half a million dollars. Who do you think paid for it?"

"Paid in full, no less."

"Maybe Helen can tell us more secrets in the morning." Jake checked his phone. Out of juice again. He charged it in the USB socket in the car. "Must be nice to have this. My old stick-shift has nothing but AC."

"Cassette player too?"

Jake nodded. "It's broken though."

The rain eased up as they drove on a winding road heading east through the forest. The GPS on both of their phones was intermittent. All they could see around them were tree trunks. The tops of trees were three hundred feet into the dark night of California.

If the headlights on their rental SUV stopped working, they'd have to wait until daybreak before they could find their way off of the long road.

"I want to know why this can't wait until morning," Earl asked.

"We're several steps behind Molyneux already. Don't we want to get ahead sometime?" Jake wasn't sure they would ever get ahead of the terrorist, who seemed to know their every move. How?

Helen Hu's contacts had informed them that the dead sniper at Fisherman's Wharf was undocumented and they had no idea who he was. However, his weapons were military-grade, meaning that he was probably not there to just shoot at the crowd.

He probably had someone in mind.

Which led Jake to wonder if Molyneux had sent him.

"Am I a target again?" Jake mumbled.

Apparently, Earl heard him. "Don't think so highly of yourself. For all we know, Molyneux might be going after Beatrice Glynn and her team as well."

"No schadenfreude for me. I don't want her killed. We know that Molyneux can—"

Crunch! Pop!

The SUV stopped dead in its tracks.

Nothing Earl did moved the vehicle forward.

"Something on the ground?" Jake asked.

"I'll go check." Earl unbuckled, palmed his Sig Sauer, and went outside.

Except for the SUV headlights, the entire forest was dark around them.

Earl came to Jake's side of the vehicle. He rolled down his window.

"Someone put a spike strip on the ground," Earl reported. "The two front tires are blown out. I think we only have one spare tire."

"A prank?"

"Whose bright idea was it to take this short-cut?" Earl asked.

"There's no shortcut. There's only one road. You saw the map. Check your GPS." Jake opened the glove compartment and retrieved more ammunition. He put it in his backpack pocket—

And heard a twig snap.

Earl went around the back of the SUV, turned off the lights, removed the vehicle key, and then retrieved his messenger bag from the back seat.

Jake was outside the SUV now, weapon in hand. When nothing happened, he second-guessed himself.

It was probably an animal in the forest stepping on a twig.

While Earl locked the SUV, Jake listened to

more rustling sounds among the giant redwood trees.

Hurry up. We have insurance. No need to lock it.

They heard a vehicle coming up the road.

"Help is on the way."

Jake stopped him. He pointed to the trees on the side of the road. "Let's make sure."

Quickly, they ran to the side of the road and hid behind the giant trees.

Silently they waited.

The vehicle came by and stopped behind their SUV. Two men came out.

Armed.

This is not good. Jake held his breath.

And Earl's phone rang.

Shots fired in their direction as Jake and Earl ran blindly in the forest. There was no time to check their GPS for suggested walking trails.

There was no time to even breathe!

Or pray!

The forest was dark—pitch black—and Jake pointed his dim cell phone light on the trail in front of him to see the way without alerting their pursuers to where they were.

The bad news was that he had been trying to charge up his phone back in the SUV, but it hadn't charged up much. He couldn't remember if he had another charger in his backpack. If they didn't find help soon, he'd run out of battery before the night was over.

Earl was breathing heavily behind Jake. "I need to lose weight."

Jake couldn't speak a word.

Gunshots!

Jake ducked, as if it helped. If their pursuers had night vision goggles, it was only a matter of time before they caught up with the duo.

Then what? Call 911?

More gunshots!

They were closer now.

Earl stumbled and fell. He let out a short scream.

Jake spun around. Earl's ankle was in a hole by the side of the trail, where a root showed.

"What are you doing?" Jake snarled.

"I was trying to take a break." He gritted his teeth.

Jake helped him get his foot out of the hole. "Is it a sprain?"

Even before Earl could answer, Jake knew. His foot was sideways. He had probably broken it.

Jake helped Earl to hop on one foot so they could hide behind a tree.

Jake tried to call 911.

No signal.

"Give me your phone," Jake said.

Earl looked everywhere for it. "I had it a minute ago."

"Well, if my phone doesn't have signal, yours might not either." It was all he could say.

Jake checked his phone again. His battery power was at ten percent. He texted Helen Hu, who had told them to call her twenty-four seven. Maybe texting would work if voice didn't.

SOS. Send help.

He entered their GPS coordinates.

And prayed.

CHAPTER TEN

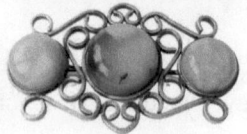

"**D**o you think they've found the cabin?" It was Raynelle's turn to drive, and she was making chitchat to stay awake.

Or at least that was Beatrice's assumption.

Raynelle's job was to follow the signal on Jake's burner phone. Wherever they were going seemed to be in the direction of Philomena's cabin in the woods.

The problem was that Jake's phone had no directions. It had been obvious that Earl's phone was the one with the address of the cabin. For some reason, Kenichi was unable to hack into Earl's phone. It was NSA-grade.

Beatrice was in the back of the cargo van with Kenichi, going over data that he had collected about Jake's time at Molyneux's organization. Nothing so far. When Jake had been undercover there, he was a low-level employee—dispensable—whom Molyneux had deployed to the Great Smoky Mountains several years before to capture a British Special Forces soldier who had been hiding at a top-secret retreat center.

"To answer your question, Ray, I don't know." Beatrice didn't look up from the laptop she had been staring at for hours.

There was nothing there. No leverage.

Beatrice sighed. "So all we have is the three-amber brooch. Assuming Jake has the one-amber brooch, we still can't get the location of the Amber Room."

"Correction, Bee," Kenichi said. "The location of *some* of the panels of the Amber Room. And we still don't know if the brooches are what your dad said they are."

"Hey guys," Raynelle said. "Something wrong here?"

Beatrice tried to stretch but the van didn't have a ceiling tall enough for her to stand up. At five nine, she wasn't that tall, but her thick lug-sole boots didn't help.

Beatrice went to the front to sit down on the passenger seat. She buckled up. "What?"

"His phone is stationary—in the forest."

Beatrice leaned toward the display on the dashboard. They were ten minutes from the location of the phone. "So they added another a few minutes to their drive?"

"Like they've stopped," Raynelle said, eyes on the dark road ahead.

"Maybe they went to the bathroom," Kenichi shouted from the back of the van. He laughed all by himself.

Beatrice wondered... Nah.

On the other hand, yes. "Molyneux might've found them."

"And thereby us, since we're coming up to them," Raynelle said.

"Ken, please check on Jake's phone." Beatrice unbuckled her safety belt and went to their stash of firearms. "What's happening out there?"

"You know what your brother says about you and shotguns." Kenichi laughed.

"That's not my thing." Beatrice slipped two handguns into her vest pockets. It would be hard to get them out if she needed them in an instant.

Kenichi whistled. "Houston, we have a problem."

"What?"

"Jake is in the forest."

"What I said." Raynelle shook her head.

In front of them, two vehicles were parked right in the middle of the road.

There seemed to be someone still inside one of the vehicles.

Before Beatrice could say anything, Raynelle had parked their van, left the headlights on, and was walking toward the driver, who seemed to be looking her way through the rearview mirror.

Beatrice couldn't hear what Raynelle said to the man, but she suddenly yanked open the door, and pulled the man out on the road. What looked like a rifle fell to the road. Raynelle kicked it away.

Why would that person have an assault rifle right in the middle of the redwood forest?

Raynelle stepped on the man.

It looked like she was interrogating him.

Beatrice found some cable ties. She pulled up her bandana mask over her mouth and nose, and was about to exit the van when Kenichi grabbed the cable ties from her.

"Your brother would kill me if I let you walk out there."

"Stop coddling me," Beatrice snapped. "I pay your salary."

"I would still not let you go out there even if you don't pay me anything." Kenichi put on a ski mask. "You're like a sister to me, and I want to see you safe."

And out he went.

Beatrice sat down at his laptop. Onscreen, she could see Jake's phone. It was at five percent battery.

Her eyes widened when she saw the message.

"He texted over ten minutes ago. Where are they?" Beatrice decided to reply, even though it would look weird to Jake. On his phone, if he could see it, it would be as though he was talking to himself.

> Beatrice: Are you okay?
>
> Jake: Who is this?
>
> Beatrice: A friend. Are you injured?
>
> Jake: No. My associate is.
>
> Beatrice: How?
>
> Jake: Broken ankle.
>
> Beatrice: Stay where you are. We're
> coming.
>
> Jake: Who are you?

He had asked a second time. He would find out eventually, but there was no reason to tell him now while they were entering the forest.

> Beatrice: You know who I am. Keep
> your phone on.
> Jake: I'm running out of battery.
> Beatrice: Conserve.
> Jake: One more thing. What's the
> local police number?
> Beatrice: Don't worry. I'm calling 911
> for you.

Beatrice was relieved that Jake was okay. She called 911, but she wasn't sure how long it would take them to come. She made sure to tell them that someone was injured in the forest.

She burst out of the van and ran toward the man on the ground. He was bleeding from the mouth. What did Raynelle and Kenichi do to him?

"He's not talking," Raynelle said.

Gunshots echoed through the forest.

Oh no. They might have found Jake!

Beatrice pressed a weapon on his chest. "Who are you after?"

The man spat blood on her boots—as if he knew she wouldn't shoot.

Sigh.

"Don't mess with me. Tell me now what they want from my friends they're chasing."

He said nothing.

"You're afraid of Molyneux, but you're not afraid of me?" Beatrice's gloved hand went around his neck. She pressed, every calmly.

His eyes widened. "What..."

Beatrice pressed. She wondered how much she could press before he couldn't breathe, but so far her words had scared him.

And herself too.

She wanted him to answer her before she started to get nervous. "Speak."

"Cabin." The man looked defeated. "They're looking for the cabin."

Beatrice noted the subtle shift. The man was changing sides. He had said "they" instead of "we."

They figured Jake and Earl knew where the cabin was. They were probably right. That was also why Beatrice had followed Jake.

"Get him up," Beatrice said. "Should we take him into the forest with us?"

Raynelle smiled. She seemed to like that sort of instruction. "His buddies could make him their target practice."

"No... Let me go," He pleaded in a whiny voice.

"They also want the brooches. Molly asked for them."

"Molly?" Molyneux?

If Jake had the one-amber brooch, he'd probably stashed it somewhere else, not on his person. Beatrice didn't carry the three-amber brooch everywhere with her.

However, if Molyneux's men caught up with Jake and Earl, they'd try to make Jake turn over the brooches.

"How many people are with you?" Beatrice asked.

"Two. I'm just the driver."

"Two." Assuming he was telling the truth.

Beatrice turned to her team members. Raynelle nearly laughed. Kenichi shrugged.

Beatrice guessed they were both thinking the same thing she was. They weren't sure whether to trust the driver.

"Gag him and throw him in the trunk of his car," Kenichi said.

"There is no trunk-trunk in his SUV."

"Then just tie him to a tree." He laughed. "But we don't have a rope that long to go around a big old tree. So why don't we just kill him?"

The driver whimpered. With Raynelle

pointing the bullet end of a gun at his forehead, he didn't dare make a louder sound.

Raynelle rolled her eyes at Kenichi's silly ideas. She gagged the driver and pulled him to his feet. When they reached Jake's SUV, she made him get in the back. She tied him up like he was a roped calf in a rodeo.

Beatrice thought that was enough. The driver wasn't going anywhere. And he was in the FBI agent's SUV.

Beatrice went back to the van with Kenichi. "What can we use as a splint? Jake's friend twisted or broke his ankle."

"We have the first aid kit. That's all."

Beatrice climbed into the van. She found duct tape and two travel pillows, which were quite small. She could not find any foam that was small enough to wrap around an ankle. She stuffed the pillows and duct tape into her back pack. And threw in several bottles of water.

Kenichi was suited up and weighed down with ammunition and weapons. He brought extra weapons for Raynelle, who was outside the van.

He gave Beatrice a tiny Glock and an LED headlamp.

Oh, wait. It wasn't only a headlamp. It

projected in front of her a three-dimensional map of the forest.

Kenichi locked the van and they all put on night vision goggles.

"This way." Beatrice projected the map in front of her.

As Raynelle came close to her, she quietly handed Beatrice a second firearm, the bullpup with the shortest barrel that they had in the van.

Sigh.

At least it was still a Tavor. And her brother had taught her how to use it.

"In my moment of weakness," Benjamin would tell her numerous times after that.

If Benjamin had his way, Beatrice would never leave Charleston. Sometimes Beatrice wished her older brother wouldn't hover over her.

The world might be cruel, wicked, and evil, but God was greater still.

You are of God, little children, and have overcome them, because He who is in you is greater than he who is in the world.

The verse from 1 John 4:4 emboldened Beatrice. "Let's go!"

CHAPTER ELEVEN

You know who I am.

He stared at the text message screen, but nothing else came through. He had done what that person ordered him: conserve.

Fortunately, he hadn't installed many apps on his burner phone. He dimmed the lights on his phone.

Unfortunately, he was still at five percent juice. He wished he had bought extra battery packs with him. The mapping software ate up a lot of battery, for some reason.

He could hear Earl breathing heavily.

There was no way they could move fast enough with Earl's broken ankle, so their best bet was to stay put here until help came.

There was not enough signal for him to call on the phone or google the police station number so he could text for help.

He prayed that his rescuer had called the police on their behalf.

Twigs broke. Footsteps drew closer.

He had heard gunshots earlier, but they seemed to be farther and farther away from him.

Thank God.

"Jake?" A woman's voice came on the night wind. "Jake?"

Jake debated whether to reply. She sounded like...

Beatrice Glynn.

"I called 911, Jake. We're here."

There she went, confirming that she—or her team—had hacked into his burner phone to enable her to text him. They would need to sort out the legal problems later.

He was so stunned that he failed to respond to her calling out his name.

"I think they're behind the tree." Another woman whispered. "I can't believe how big these trees are."

"Hurry up," a man said. "They might double back."

Jake thought that man's assessment was correct.

By the mercy of God, their pursuer had overshot and walked—or ran—past them under the giant redwood tree trunk with an exposed root.

"We're here," Jake finally said.

He felt someone squatting in front of him, but he could not see them. "I can't see you. My phone battery died and we have no light."

"I can see you with my infrared goggles," Beatrice explained.

Moments later, someone turned on a flashlight. In the dim light, Beatrice pushed her goggles above her head. Jake saw the same kind eyes he had seen before in San Francisco. She was wearing a bandana mask, so he couldn't see most of her face. She pulled it down to show him who she was

"We need to stop meeting in the middle of the night like this." Jake chuckled. "Beatrice, meet Earl. Earl, this is Beatrice."

"How did you find us?" Earl covered his face with his grimy hands. He winced at his own slightest move.

"We almost didn't. You're hiding behind this old redwood tree that must be at least thirty or forty feet in circumference." Raynelle patted the tree trunk.

"Thank you for calling 911," Jake said.

"Talk later. Your friends are coming back once

they figure out where we are," Beatrice said. "How badly hurt are you?"

"Ankle broken, probably." Earl pointed.

"It's a good long way out." Beatrice removed her backpack. She handed Jake and Earl bottles of water, and then went to work making a splint for Earl's ankle.

Raynelle helped her to duct tape around the two small travel pillows.

Jake's eyes were on the third person, a heavily armed man. He hadn't removed his night vision goggles or his ski mask, and he hadn't said a word.

This must be the mystery third person on Beatrice's team.

More twigs snapped.

Jake drew a deep breath. "They're back."

Beatrice's hand reached for her semiautomatic bullpup rifle strapped over her shoulder.

Jake placed his hand on her arm. "Let me."

Beatrice frowned.

"Let him have it," the silent man finally said.

"Don't side with him, Ken."

Ken.

Jake remembered now. Back at the Fisherman's Wharf in San Francisco, Beatrice had told someone named Ken to call 911 after the sniper fired into the crowd.

"Give him one of yours," Beatrice ordered Ken. And he did without a complaint.

Jake didn't have to show off that he could handle practically any weapon like a pro.

"If you want to come with us, one of your people can stay with Earl," he said quietly to Beatrice.

"Ken and Ray are better shooters than I am," Beatrice replied. "I'll stay with Earl. Please be safe."

"I will." Jake wanted to hug—or maybe kiss—her to show his appreciation, but it was probably too soon.

Still, the fact was undeniable. She had come to his rescue yet again.

If they kept crossing paths and heading in the same direction anyway, maybe they ought to work together and consolidate resources.

If they survived tonight, Jake would suggest a collaboration, if not an alliance.

After all, they seemed to be on the same side now against a mutual enemy: Molyneux.

CHAPTER TWELVE

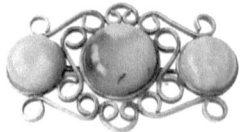

With her flashlights turned off, Beatrice sat in the dark with Earl. Her night vision goggles revealed Earl's foot sandwiched between the two travel pillows that she would have to replace for her van.

Earl closed his eyes and leaned back against the tree trunk.

All around them were giant trees that were wider than Beatrice could stretch out her arms. By eyeballing, she roughly estimated that the girths of those trees were even bigger than the one they were hiding behind.

Beatrice closed her eyes and found her other senses enhanced in this dark night. She heard the close combat battles happening on the other side of the tree they were leaning on.

There must not be much room to maneuver on the narrow forest trail. The driver they had thrown into the SUV earlier had said that two men entered the forest, but perhaps he lied. It shouldn't take Jake, Raynelle, and Kenichi this long to handle only two men.

The smell of pine was strong in Beatrice's nose, as was the smell of dirt and muddy soil after the heavy rain earlier in the night. She smelled upturned dirt.

Plus human sweat.

Very strong sweat.

Click.

Beatrice opened her eyes.

A barrel was in her face.

A man wearing night vision goggles pointed his weapons—one in each hand—at her and Earl.

At the same time, Beatrice could still hear the fighting behind the trees.

The driver had lied to them. More than two assailants had entered the forest. If the rest of them were as heavily armed as this man—

A gunshot blast.

Behind the tree.

Jake.

Beatrice had no idea why he came into her mind first.

"I don't think Molyneux would want you to shoot me," Beatrice said to the man in front of them.

The man's eyes widened, as if he was surprised by her statement. His handguns moved slightly—

And Earl took the opportunity to wrestle one weapon from his attacker.

Beatrice kicked his other arm.

He went down and Earl tackled him. Beatrice heard bones crack.

Earl pointed his newly acquired handgun at the man on the ground.

Suddenly a shot rang out and Earl fell backward, a dark blob on his stomach.

"Earl!" Beatrice gasped.

She turned to find a second gunman approaching them.

"Let's go," he said.

Beatrice had no choice. "Where to?"

"To collect my bounty—"

The man lurched and collapsed onto Beatrice.

She screamed.

Someone pulled the dead man off her. Now she could see Jake wearing a pair of night vision goggles similar to what her assailant had worn. Maybe he had confiscated them. Spoils of battle.

"You have a bounty on your head?" Jake reached for her hands to pull her to her feet.

Beatrice ignored him. It should have been obvious. Why else would she need a bodyguard if her life weren't in danger in any way?

"Earl." Beatrice crawled toward him. "He was shot."

Earl was not moving. Beatrice felt shallow breathing.

Just then, giant flashlights lit up the area.

Beatrice lifted her night vision goggles. She could only see tree trunks all around her, the top of those three-hundred-foot trees had disappeared into the night sky.

She heard dogs barking, and their handlers meting out brisk orders.

"We're here! Help! Man down!" Jake shouted.

And then the sweetest sight of the night.

Raynelle came toward them, surrounded by the local police.

Around them, lights continued to sweep the forest.

CHAPTER THIRTEEN

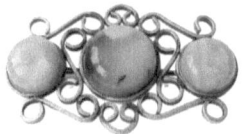

T he heroes of the Eureka Bay Police
Department had reached their battle-
ground and made short work of the
arrests.

The driver had lied, obviously, saying that only
two assailants had entered the forest, going after
Jake and Earl. In fact, five men had entered the
forest. Three battled Jake, Raynelle, and Kenichi.
And two nearly took out Beatrice and Earl as they
hid by the tree roots.

The Eureka Bay PD rounded up the rest of the
men who were still alive and read them their
Miranda rights.

Beatrice hoped they would reveal who had paid

those people to attack Jake and Earl. She had her own suspicions but no proof.

Problem was, so far she had been on the defensive—and so had Jake. It was time to turn the tables.

But first, the emergency room.

The paramedics had determined that Raynelle's right arm—her shooting arm—was broken. Beatrice couldn't get a clear picture of how it had happened, but suffice to say that Molyneux's men put up a formidable fight, and Raynelle held her own. In the scuffle and close combat, she had done more damage to the other side than they had done to her.

Still, a broken arm was a broken arm.

The paramedics loaded Earl and Raynelle into their ambulance, and off they went to the emergency room where they would treat Earl's gunshot wounds and do something about Raynelle's broken bones.

Kenichi and Beatrice waited for Jake. How else was Jake going to get back to town with his SUV tires blown out and no spare? He called the tow truck and retrieved his and Earl's bags from their SUV while Kenichi scrambled to tidy up the van and hide their laptops and equipment under the seats.

No more than half an hour later, they were at the hospital, following the ambulance.

Kenichi and Jake left the van to give Beatrice some privacy to change into clean clothes. She went with a pair of cargo pants with pockets to keep her driver's license, passport, and her debit cards. Plus the three-amber brooch.

Benjamin had cautioned her about carrying her passport everywhere, but she wanted to be ready to hop on the airplane and fly out of the country at a moment's notice.

As for the brooch, it was a replica that she and Benjamin had worked on for years. The real thing was in a safe-deposit box in San Francisco. She'd have to pick it up soon.

She wondered where Jake and Earl kept their one-amber brooch. Eventually they'd have to reconcile and she'd have to return the three-amber brooch to the authorities. With the mole inside the FBI, there was no way Beatrice was going to give it to them now, even if they had an FBI Art Crime Team.

The hospital waiting room wasn't crowded. Beatrice didn't have to sit around, but she was waiting for Raynelle to see the doctor.

As for Kenichi, he returned to the van to wait for them. He'd rather be working on his laptop inside the van—away from people, he said. He texted Beatrice, saying he would need about half an hour. Beatrice replied that they'd probably still be in the hospital for the next hour, at least.

And no, he couldn't go to the cabin without them.

Beatrice knew it was hard for Kenichi to sit and wait, but she was sure he'd make himself useful.

Meanwhile, Beatrice had booked two rooms at a hotel. She wanted her own room, but Kenichi insisted that Raynelle not leave her side. Something about not wanting Beatrice to have to kill any intruder herself. Sigh.

It sounded like what her brother would say. It also made Beatrice wonder if Kenichi was working for Benjamin rather than for her.

In any case, they would stay one more day here in Eureka so that Beatrice could check out Philomena's lakeside cabin.

They had Jake to thank for that. Thanks to Kenichi's sleuthing—basically tapping Earl's communication with Helen Hu and Jake—they knew about the cabin.

However, they did not know where it was. That was why they had followed Earl and Jake all the way from San Francisco to Eureka and beyond.

Beatrice prayed that all this would soon be over.

Every day cost her more and more. In fact, her savings were rapidly depleting in this year alone due to her many trips back and forth from Europe to the United States.

All in search of the Amber Room with the hope of defeating Molyneux. She had to pay for her crimes.

Beatrice looked up from where she was sitting, hoping to see Raynelle. She had texted her to let her know where to meet.

Instead of Raynelle, Jake walked in. He had taken off his outer shirt, leaving an olive-green tee shirt, but there was still mud caked to his boots. He was drinking from a paper cup. He tossed it into the trash can before he approached her.

"I thought you had left," he said.

"I thought you had too."

"Are they putting a cast on her arm?"

Beatrice nodded.

"I have some questions about last night," Jake said. "Obviously, you followed us without our knowledge."

Beatrice mulled over how to respond. If she said yes, then it meant someone on her team had broken into his burner phone. Never mind that he already knew that.

If she said no, she would be lying.

"Aren't you glad we came to your aid?" She ended up saying.

"You sure you weren't on your way to the cabin?" Jake sat down two seats away, as if to give them some space. He faced her.

"Cabin? What cabin?"

"I don't know. You tell me."

"Is this an interrogation, secret agent man?"

Jake chuckled. "I'm no longer one."

"What happened?" Beatrice knew what happened, thanks to Kenichi's connections, probably via her brother.

More and more, Beatrice was convinced Kenichi had added a second boss and was now working for Benjamin. She'd have to ask him later if he was drawing two paychecks.

"Long story." Jake's eyes looked distant. "I won't bore you."

"Bore me. I'm waiting for Raynelle so we can get going. She's taking forever."

"Get going where? Back to Charleston?" Jake asked. When Beatrice didn't answer, he continued. "Yes, we know a lot about each other's business, and we seem to be looking for the same things and perhaps the same people. It's a shame we're doing things in parallel and not cooperating with each other."

"Cooperating?" Beatrice wasn't sure where he was going with it. "On what, exactly?"

Several people came in and sat down near them. This wasn't the place to talk about whatever it was Jake wanted to get off his chest. Beatrice waited to see how he would handle it.

He scooted to the seat next to Beatrice. "I'd like to talk with you about potentially working together."

"Are we on the same side?" Beatrice smiled.

He stared.

Beatrice waved her hand in front of his face. "Seen a ghost?"

"The way you smile reminds me of someone."

"Good or bad?"

He swallowed. Placed his palm on his thigh. And winced.

"Are you okay?" Had she triggered a memory?

He drew a deep breath.

It made no sense to Beatrice. How could he even suggest that they work together? Didn't he remember all the things her team had done to his team?

Raynelle had stolen the three-amber brooch from under Jake's nose.

Kenichi had hacked into Jake's burner phone.

Beatrice had typed texted messages on that phone.

And yet he wanted to team up? Would that mean they would see each other's resources? Secrets? Methods?

Jake lowered his voice. "The fact that they know we're here means they're probably at the cabin as we speak."

The cabin.

Beatrice wondered what they would find there. Perhaps Philomena had kept some photos of Dad. Those memories would be more precious to Beatrice and her brother than anything else.

Possibly even more precious than the Amber Room.

That had been more of a mission of revenge than anything, right? To get to the Amber Room before Molyneux did had been Beatrice's mission for the last ten years.

Maybe Jake could help. He was a former FBI Special Agent. Surely he could be trusted.

"What's the cabin to you?" Beatrice asked.

"A place of intrigue and history. Maybe it has secrets we don't know about."

"Pieces of the puzzle?"

"Something like that." Jake studied her.

"Maybe if we go in the late morning, we could catch lunch afterwards."

"Did you just ask me to lunch?" Beatrice acted surprised, but she was warming up to him.

Eventually, they'd have to tell each other the truth about themselves.

"Looks like it."

"A business lunch if we're working together," Beatrice said. "I said *if.*"

Still, she was grateful that Jake had come to her rescue behind the redwood tree. She and Earl would have both died because she could not pull the trigger.

She couldn't do it.

That was why she had hired Raynelle to be her security detail.

All these close brushes told her one thing: Molyneux was onto her.

Eventually they would have to confront each other.

Beatrice had so many questions for Molyneux. Why did she have to kill Dad? Why not just walk away after their divorce?

And then there was the unanswered question about Beatrice's own mother. The story had always been the same. Molyneux had killed Beatrice's mother. Was that the truth, though? Could her biological mother still be alive, considering all the lies that had surrounded their family for decades?

Another question that begged for an answer was about her brother, Benjamin. Who were his biological parents?

Beatrice might never know.

Dad and Philomena, the two people who could tell her the truth about their biological parentage, were both dead.

"Are your parents still around?" Beatrice asked Jake.

He nodded. "Why do you ask?"

"Because mine are dead."

"I'm sorry." Jake extended his hand toward Beatrice.

She didn't take it. "Well, such is life."

Raynelle entered the waiting room, her elbow in a Pepto-Bismol-pink cast.

Beatrice had never pegged Raynelle as someone who liked pink. "I thought black was your favorite color?"

Raynelle lifted her arm slightly. "It'll be under a sleeve."

"What did the doctor say?"

"Broke a few bones. I'll heal." Raynelle didn't look too confident. "I can't use my right arm for a while. At least six weeks."

"I'm sorry." Beatrice knew what that meant. Raynelle's right hand couldn't shoot. "You're still my bodyguard. You may have to stay in the van and let Kenichi run about."

"Ha!" Raynelle made a face, as if relinquishing her job to a security specialist like Kenichi was beneath her.

Beatrice didn't want to say anything in front of Jake, but she knew that Kenichi had enough training to go toe-to-toe with Raynelle, even though he was at least ten years older.

"Well, Jake, nice to see you again." Beatrice stood up and changed her mind about accepting Jake's offer to visit the cabin together.

"What about the cabin?" A slow smile appeared on his face. "And lunch with me?"

"Raincheck?" Beatrice read her watch. "It's almost seven in the morning now. I need to get some sleep and I doubt I'd be up in time for lunch. Are you staying here?"

"Yeah. I'll wait until Earl comes out of surgery." He looked a bit disappointed that she was leaving. "I'll get some breakfast at the cafeteria."

"Thank you again, Jake." Beatrice wanted to shake his hand but she did not. "Earl and I would have died if you hadn't shown up."

"I wouldn't have been able to follow the two

men if Raynelle and Kenichi hadn't taken over beating the guys to a pulp."

"Thank God we made it out of the forest alive." Beatrice smiled at him one last time before they parted.

Jake snapped his fingers. "Ah. That's what it is. Your smile reminds me of...uh...you know who."

"No, I don't know who." Beatrice shook her head.

"Are you sure?" Jake asked.

Beatrice didn't answer.

CHAPTER FOURTEEN

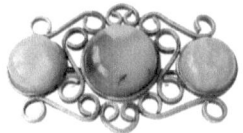

Beatrice gave credit to Kenichi for covering the van with new decals while she and Raynelle had been inside the hospital building. By the time Kenichi returned to the hospital parking lot to pick them up, the van was emblazoned with words that said "Plunging Needs Plumbers" and photos of several plungers all lined up.

"Shouldn't there be a hyphen somewhere?" Raynelle asked.

"What do you mean?" Ken looked annoyed. "I paid a lot for the decal."

"Shouldn't it say 'Plunging-hyphen-Needs Plumbers'?"

"No," Ken snapped. "It means if you have a *plunging* problem, you need plumbers."

"Who came up with that nonsense?" Raynelle rolled her eyes.

"Shut up, Ray."

"Seriously, Ken?" Beatrice climbed into the van. "Why not a cable company?"

"This costs slightly less. Single use, remember?" Kenichi handed her a cap and a brown shirt. "Look the part, Bee."

With her arm in a cast, Raynelle had a hard time taking off her shirt and replacing it with the Plunging Needs Plumbers screen-printed tee shirt.

Beatrice helped her as much as she could while Kenichi worked on his laptop.

"We can't park at the hospital too long. Cameras." Beatrice tied up her hair into a knot, and put on her baseball cap. "Give me the keys, Ken."

Ken tossed her the van key. Beatrice sat down in the driver's seat.

People entered and exited the hospital entrance. Beatrice spotted Jake. "He's leaving now."

Jake walked across the parking lot.

"Okay, I got him. Let's go." Kenichi rubbed his hands together. "The trackers I put on him work."

"Where did you stick them?"

"In his jean pocket and belt."

"When?" Raynelle asked.

"Back in the forest."

"I never noticed."

"If you did, I'd have failed." Kenichi winked at her.

Beatrice found her sunglasses and put them on. Now nobody would recognize her. "All he has to do is change clothes, and we'll lose him."

She sat down in the driver's seat. "Raynelle, get some rest. Kenichi, tell me where he goes."

Kenichi had parked the van with its rear against a wall, so all Beatrice had to do was start the van and press the gas pedal to roll it forward.

"He's walking. Can't go far," Kenichi said.

"Even with the new decals, our van is too obvious. He'll spot us following him." Beatrice frowned. "Well, strike that. I can't even see him now."

"While we were trying to get into traffic, he crossed the street."

"Is he going to rent a car?" Beatrice wondered what Jake was up to.

"Nope. Right now, he's at a motel."

"He is? Maybe he's cleaning up and taking a nap."

"We all need a long nap." Kenichi yawned loudly for effect.

JAN THOMPSON

"Yeah, and a shower. How about we circle the block?" Raynelle asked.

"How about we just check into a motel too and forget this whole thing." Kenichi told Beatrice where to turn. The roads were easy to navigate around the small hospital.

"Jake will be nice and clean and we're still smelling like the forest," Raynelle countered.

"She's right." Beatrice wasn't happy about their lack of preparation. "Besides, I booked us two rooms at a hotel some ten minutes from here."

Somewhere at the back of her mind, she suddenly wished she had gone to graduate school and then taught somewhere afterwards. Life would be so much easier than flying around the world chasing after ghosts and shadows.

Or following former FBI agents around town.

Kenichi directed Beatrice down a road. That was when she saw the dumpy motel. "Not that one."

"Let's get a room here for a couple of hours or until he leaves," Kenichi said.

"I've already reserved that other hotel. Five stars." In Beatrice's mind, the costs were escalating. "Besides, if he sees us, he might think we're following him."

106

"We have to stay close, in case he loses the tracker I put on him." Kenichi seemed adamant.

Beatrice had to agree with him. He had a point. If they left Jake, they might lose him altogether.

"Are we very sure he's going to the cabin, one way or another?" Beatrice asked.

"He's going to need a vehicle to take him there. It's fifty minutes away and he can't walk."

"Stating the obvious, aren't we, Ken?" Raynelle laughed.

"I thought you were sleeping," Kenichi snapped.

"He's going to know we're here if he looks out the window." Beatrice slowed the vehicle to a crawl. "The motel doesn't look very big. How about we give him a few minutes to check in and settle down?"

"Good idea." Kenichi pointed to a McDonald's. "Let's get some breakfast and come back. They have dollar meals."

Beatrice nodded. "I can afford dollar meals."

"I was just joking."

"You might be, but I'm not joking at all. Our Gulfstream is sitting in San Francisco waiting to take us back to Charleston. The longer we stay here, the more it will cost me." Beatrice had to be frank with him. "At some point in time, I'm going to run out of money and I'll have to sell my majority share of the company to my brother."

Raynelle groaned. "That will be bad. Your brother hates me."

"He doesn't hate you," Beatrice said. "Once he gets to know you, he'll like you."

"I doubt it."

"I'd rather work for you, Bee." Kenichi's voice was low. "Sorry I brought it all up."

Beatrice found his statement interesting. Wasn't Kenichi working for both her and her brother? Why did he say he preferred working for Beatrice?

"No." Beatrice sighed. "It's not your fault. The cost of this entire operation is on my mind, is all. It just came out of my mouth. If it makes you feel any better, you and Raynelle will still have a job, even if my brother calls the shots in the future."

Still, would she give it all up to have her father back? Yes, of course.

When Dad died, he left a fortune to Beatrice and Benjamin to the tune of several hundred million dollars each. How he had that much money was beyond her, but at least Dad hadn't spent it all.

Wouldn't Molyneux want a chunk of that fortune?

It wasn't hers to begin with, as Dad hadn't

shared his assets with Molyneux back when they were married. Molyneux walked away with nothing.

Half a billion dollars could go a very long way to funding Molyneux's nefarious projects.

No way was Beatrice going to let her have it.

CHAPTER FIFTEEN

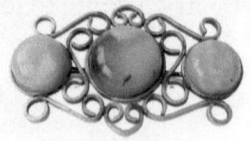

Bad news: Jake wanted to see Beatrice again. Her often faraway gaze intrigued and perplexed Jake, as though she had a secret garden no one could enter. What was in that garden? What was she cultivating?

Jake wanted to know what Beatrice was hiding and what she was searching for. He prayed that she wasn't on the other side of the law. The fact that he suspected she had stolen the three-amber brooch didn't sit well in his conscience.

And then there were certain features of hers that reminded him of Molyneux.

Could it be that he had been so enthralled by the terrorist that she was all he could see in every woman he met?

Still, it was clear that he and Beatrice were heading toward Molyneux. What business did Beatrice have with the terrorist?

Jake had to see Beatrice again.

To find out what, exactly?

Ah. Maybe his mind was wandering due to the long wait. Earl was still in surgery. Helen hadn't called. Jake had five hours to kill.

At the motel, he showered. He found a Gideon Bible in a drawer and sat down on the bed to read it. He placed a dry towel on top of the pillow behind him because his hair was still damp.

"Lord, we need all the help we can get," he prayed. "Make Earl well ASAP. Give the surgeons Your healing touch."

He tried to pray for Beatrice but he wasn't sure what to ask God for. "Maybe just Your perfect will would be enough."

Was Beatrice a Christian? Whose side was she on?

Jake brushed off his earlier suspicion that Beatrice was in any way related to Molyneux. He had been undercover in her organization for three years, and never once had Molyneux mentioned that she had a daughter or even a niece.

Then again, she also never talked about her ex-husband who had apparently run off with the nanny, Philomena, whose story ended in San Francisco.

He wondered what killed her. Who did it?

That information wasn't yet forthcoming.

He called the rental car company to let them know what happened to the SUV. The police report helped his case. The rental car company told him they'd take care of towing it back to San Francisco.

Any extra charges beyond what the insurance paid would be covered by Hu Knows, Inc., out of Savannah, Georgia, since Jake and Earl had been on official company business when they were ambushed.

He lay down on the bed, facing the popcorn ceiling. The room smelled musty. He could hear the water still running in the commode but he was too lazy to get up to jiggle the handle.

His damp hair soaked into the towel on the pillow as he nearly dozed off.

Everything could wait but sleep couldn't—

No. I have to call Helen.

"The autopsy revealed that Philomena died of a cardiac arrest," Helen Hu said via secure video on the laptop screen. It was evening in Greece, and behind her were large windows and drapes on both sides.

"Was there poison in the coffee?"

Helen nodded. "Just as we suspected, but they're doing more tests to find out who did it."

"Interesting." While listening to his new boss, Jake popped a new, hopefully untraceable, SIM card into his burner phone. It was his practice to carry spare burner phones and spare SIM cards. Just in case.

As for his old compromised SIM card, he had tossed that one in the trash can back at the hospital.

"I received word that the SFPD has finished interviewing the waitstaff and kitchen crew," Helen added.

"Any persons of interest?" Jake's hair was still damp. He sat crossed-legged on the bed. The laptop in front of him balanced on top of a pillow.

"They want to talk to all the customers there at that time, but the restaurant kept no record of people paying in cash."

"Including the woman at the table next to ours." Jake didn't want Beatrice to get into trouble, but he couldn't be sure she wasn't involved in Philomena's death.

"No one has any idea who that person is. Grainy camera. Possible wig." Helen shrugged. "However, the woman at the other end of the room is ex-CIA."

"Raynelle Dryden, who works for Beatrice Glynn." Raynelle had been how Jake spotted Beatrice in the crowd at the Fisherman's Wharf. "I suspect Beatrice was at the table next to me."

"Did she admit as much when you met her at the wharf?"

"She didn't say."

"Maybe she has several women working for her."

"Her team in town seems to have only three people on it. They're always together." He recounted the forest fight. "Which leads us back to the café. Kenichi was probably in the van. Raynelle is Beatrice's bodyguard so she goes where Beatrice goes."

"You think it's Beatrice Glynn."

"Yep." Usually his instincts were right.

"That's all I have for now." Helen hesitated. "Look, Jake. With Earl in the hospital, I don't have enough manpower to send you a new partner. Can you go solo for a little bit?"

"How long?"

"A couple of weeks."

"All expenses paid?" Jake studied her demeanor on the laptop screen.

"Please don't be high maintenance," she said.

"Me? Nah." He laughed, even as he recalled how much it had cost Helen to rescue him at sea and fly him back to the States to chase after informants.

"Make sure you fill out the expense reports twice a week," Helen said.

"That often? Am I going to spend that much?"

"Oh, I don't know. You tell me. Two flat tires. One tow truck. Gunshot wounds—"

"That's Earl, not me."

"Lost brooch. Dead informant. I could go on."

"Speaking of informant, I need to go over everything we know about Philomena."

"The fact that she showed up means we're getting close to the fire. I've gone over your phone conversations with her so many times, but I can't tell if she was telling the truth about Chisolm Wright."

"What she said makes sense though." Jake leaned back on a couple of pillows. "They lived a quiet life in the cabin for years until Chisolm received some sort of letter in the mail. He left and never returned. It has been two years. Without any income, Philomena started selling what they had in the cabin."

"Including the brooches." Helen made a face. "Since Chisolm had been hiding from Molyneux, I don't think he would have kept all three brooches in plain sight in his cabin."

"Philomena said he hid them in a safe in the basement."

"Still..."

"I hear you. You'd think he'd split up the brooches if they held the map to some of the Amber Room panels."

"Exactly."

"In any case, I'm sorry we lost the three-amber brooch." Jake knew he had to go back to San Francisco to retrieve the one-amber brooch he and Earl had kept in a safe-deposit box at the bank.

"Yeah, that was super careless of you, Jake." Helen didn't mince her words.

"You blaming Earl too?"

"Both of you should be reprimanded."

"You wouldn't believe how sorry I am."

Helen didn't smile. "I forgive you."

"You're not smiling." Jake recalled someone else who did smile. "Let's talk about Beatrice Glynn. Who is she? Why is she here? We're working in parallel so much that I'm getting a bit suspicious."

"You want to hold her close?"

"What?" Jake would have fallen off his chair if he were on a chair. But he was on this sagging motel bed.

"I meant you want to keep your enemies close."

"Right. But I don't know if Beatrice is an enemy."

Helen raised an eyebrow. "Beatrice, huh?"

"That's her name. I told her to call me Jake."

"Tired of living undercover?" Helen asked.

"Maybe." In many ways he was. "Tired of being tired, to tell you the truth. I've been chasing Molyneux for so many years that I just want to be done."

"Don't we all? The sooner the better, before she kills again."

"About that, doesn't it strike you as weird that she hasn't bombed any city in a year?" Jake could not recall any news reports.

"It just means she's gathering her troops."

"Or she's short on funds."

"If she finds the Amber Room, she will sell the panels on the black market. Even though Mr. Buchanan is gone, there are other arms dealers who would take his place."

"If she sells such a historic masterpiece in the underground, the world will never see the original Amber Room again," Jake said.

"Those pieces they found in Crete are all they have left of it," Helen said.

"I remember your story."

"It didn't end there. There were so many unanswered questions."

Jake nodded. "Which is why I think I need to work with Beatrice."

"What do you have to offer her?"

"That's the million-dollar question." Jake yawned. "Let me decompress for a little bit, and I'll think of something."

"In other words, you're going to take a nap while Beatrice and her merry people raid the cabin."

That had crossed Jake's mind, but somehow he wasn't worried about Beatrice and her team. They had come to his rescue, and he had reciprocated, saving her life. They were equals.

Aren't we?

"While you nap, Prince Charming, I'm going to dig around for more information about Beatrice Glynn."

"Raynelle is her bodyguard. She broke her arm

in the fight, so you might be able to get some hospital records about her name and such."

Jake gave Helen the hospital name and their approximate arrival time.

"Kenichi is the silent one," he continued. "From the way he fought in the forest, I think he used to be in Special Ops. Or at the very least, he had martial arts training."

"Never heard of him. Or Raynelle, for that matter."

"I had never heard of the three of them until San Francisco. However, they know a lot about us."

"I'll see what we can do. Okay. I have to go. Reuben wants to take a walk in the moonlight."

"How romantic."

"That's what married life looks like, Jake. Don't wait too long."

"Ah, Helen. You're turning into Mama Hu." Jake recalled the matriarch of the Hu family telling everyone what to do with their lives. Earl avoided her at all costs.

"Am I? So sorry. I try not to be." Helen laughed.

"Speaking of whom, how's she doing?"

"Normally I'd say Mom is languishing in prison, but she found the Lord a couple of months ago, and she's in a small Bible study with some missionaries who visit the prison."

"Wow. I didn't know she got saved." That was truly great news for Mama Hu. Jake hoped that she had turned a corner both mentally and emotionally. Must be awful to get convicted of a crime and sentenced to jail in a foreign country. She would be in her seventies by the time they let her out on parole.

Helen wiped her eyes. "I know, right. God is good."

"Amen. So she's studying the Bible now. That's positive."

Helen nodded. "And Greek. She's learning Greek. I told her it's not the same as the New Testament language since that's ancient Greek. But she said she'd feel closer to God if she could pray in Greek."

"God speaks all languages, though."

"Well, it gives Mom something to do. She's not getting out of prison any time soon."

"True. So she's learning Hebrew next?"

"You bet. By the time they release her, she'll speak at least four or five languages."

On-screen, Reuben appeared. He waved to the camera. "Hello, Jake."

"Hey, man. Well, I better let you two go so you

can take your midnight stroll or whatever it is you married couples do."

Reuben chuckled. "You'd be surprised at what we don't do. When are you coming back to Santorini?"

"When this is over, I might," Jake said.

"Come over and we'll go sailing."

"You got it, man."

CHAPTER SIXTEEN

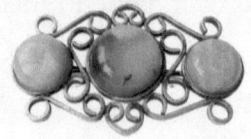

After they hung up, Jake plugged in the laptop to the wall to charge it up while he thought of Helen's husband, Reuben, who had come a very long way from being a convicted art thief to a consultant for law enforcement.

Jake firmly believed that it was possible to reform criminals. And yet, he wondered if it was too late for Molyneux.

Could she really be Imogen, the second wife of Chisolm Wright, the woman he had met while they were both at Oxford University, studying history?

How could two history students have veered so far away from lessons of history? Instead of avoiding the foibles of past wars, they had embraced them. Imogen more so than Chisolm.

Was that why their marriage had fallen apart?

Jake read that their divorce had been bitter. In the middle of their brawl were two young children, a boy and girl, who stood to lose the most.

The divorce papers had stated that neither Chisolm nor Imogen was the biological parent of the two children, which they had raised as their own. However, with Imogen gone a lot, they hired a live-in nanny, Philomena Caddock, to watch the kids.

Somehow Chisolm had fancied the nanny more than his own wife.

The fallout of the Wright divorce was bad. Chisolm threatened to testify that his estranged wife was Molyneux in real life. That didn't happen. Multiple threats to his life made Chisolm take his two children and flee to his native country of the United States, where he entered the federal Witness Security Program.

For all practical purposes, they had been gone for twenty-five years.

That was, until the nanny surfaced, insisting that Chisolm had continued living until two years prior when he disappeared for good, leaving her with no means of supporting herself. As an illegal immigrant to the United States, she could not get a proper job nor could she draw on social security or get a welfare check.

Falling through the economic cracks, Philomena drained their bank account and then began going through the valuables that Chisolm had left behind.

Etsy or eBay wasn't good enough for her. Nope. She attempted to reach Chisolm's old buddies in Europe, perhaps hoping that she could get a higher black-market price for her finds.

When buyers and brokers began to ask about a particular set of brooches, it went downhill from there for Philomena. The unwise move was probably how she ended up in the morgue.

Jake felt sorry for her.

And for himself. Philomena had wanted to meet Jake in Cannes to tell him where Chisolm's son and daughter were. The cost of that information was twenty thousand dollars, a price that Helen Hu had been willing to pay after the FBI refused the offer.

Unfortunately, Philomena had been a no-show the same day Jake ended up in the ocean.

"And here we are." Jake scooted off his bed and put the laptop on the only table in the room.

He yawned and nearly climbed back into bed.

"No," he told himself aloud. "Get some coffee and get thee out to the cabin!"

He called a local rental car place. They offered to deliver the car to the motel, but Jake said no. Instead, he took an Uber over to pick up the car.

He decided to check on Earl later. More to tell him if Jake had made it to the cabin today.

Jake had a feeling he was already late getting to the cabin. By now the whole place would have been picked over by that treasure hunter, a woman of mystery.

Who just might be the key to this whole affair.

Or not.

CHAPTER SEVENTEEN

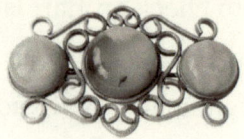

Beatrice could not believe that Dad had a cabin in the woods some three thousand miles away from where she lived in the same country. It didn't show up in the will after he supposedly passed away because he had been still living in the cabin until recently.

By the mercy of God, Dad's friends in Charleston had adopted Beatrice and Benjamin, eventually bequeathing to them several hundred million dollars on top of what Dad had left them. Sometimes Beatrice wondered where all that money had come from, but she had been taught not to look a gift horse in the mouth.

"The cabin is problematic," Kenichi announced when Beatrice parked the van by the side of the road, somewhere behind Jake's rental car. They knew it was his because Kenichi tracked the Uber that had taken Jake to pick up the car.

They had followed Jake from a distance. Vehicles were exposed to any passersby.

"Why did Jake stop here by the side of the road?" Beatrice asked. "It's too obvious."

"I think we should forget this expedition." Raynelle. Her voice sounded like she had just woken up.

Beatrice stared ahead. Through the windshield, she could see the sunlight every now and then when the wind blew the leaves to let the sunshine through.

"I love the woods and all, but something seems off," she said. "I'm beginning to think that this is not the right place. Someone tell me how Philomena could live here when there's no driveway to her cabin?"

"Good point." Kenichi surveyed Google Maps to see what they were up against. "Okay. I see a lake—or pond—near the cabin. There seems to be a parking space on the other side of the lake."

Raynelle rolled her eyes. "Please don't tell me they parked their car and rowed a boat."

"You don't necessarily have to row a boat if you have a motorboat."

"Smarty pants, Ken. I'm saying it's just a lot of trouble to get to and fro. Is that a vacation home, perhaps?"

Beatrice drew a deep breath. "Jake's parked in front of us, and he's going to see us. We have no kudzus—like back home—to hide our big van."

"So we're going to sit here and do what?" Raynelle was in a bad mood.

Kenichi laughed. "She needs more painkillers."

"No, I don't. I need my right arm to not be broken, is all. I can't protect you, Bee. I feel so useless."

"I can take care of myself," Beatrice said.

"No. Your brother is going to kill us if something happens to you," Kenichi said.

"Speak for yourself, Ken." Raynelle sat back and winced. "I don't work for Benjamin."

Beatrice was about to get out of her driver's seat when a loud rap on her window startled her.

She spun around and screamed.

Outside the window, Jake laughed. He motioned for her to roll down the window.

Beatrice hesitated before she decided to do what he asked. "What do you want?"

Well, that came out wrong, but whatever.

"We could've carpooled." He grinned.

Beatrice noticed the dimple on his cheek. She

hadn't been paying attention, really. But Jake kept showing up everywhere she went. It didn't help that she was following his trail, having no trail of her own.

She felt helpless.

In her last project the year before, she had recovered five oil paintings dating all the way to the nineteenth century. They belonged to a prominent Jewish family who perished in the Holocaust during World War II. The artwork collection was sent to Jerusalem, where their relatives eventually loaned them to a holocaust museum.

It had taken Beatrice and her team three years to find those paintings. Yet they had good fortune all the way. Each week was an adventure for her as they were met with success after success.

From that mountaintop celebration, she fell down the hill into this pit of repeated failures. At the bottom of the valley, she found herself having to follow a former FBI Special Agent who might not know what he was doing either.

After all, she had to call for help on his behalf six months prior.

He was almost shot the other day at the Fisherman's Wharf.

Now he had lost his partner, all laid up in the hospital from broken bones and gunshot wounds.

And here they were following him.

Yep, the same dude.

"Following me again, aren't you?" Jake asked.

Beatrice didn't reply.

"Thank you for your vote of confidence." He chuckled. "You're assuming I know where I'm going."

"Do you?"

"To be honest, I'm not sure. There's no path through there. Even with GPS." He held up a phone.

It wasn't his burner phone. In fact, it might be his partner's phone—the one that Kenichi couldn't track.

Beatrice didn't want to tell him about the dock.

In fact, she wasn't sure if Jake wanted to get in a boat after his harrowing experience. Then again, he wasn't her.

"The cabin is owned by a trust fund," Jake added. "Not Philomena."

Or she could own the trust fund. Either way, it was a long shot.

"Are you plying me with information so that we invite you in for coffee?" Beatrice asked.

"You have coffee? Fresh?"

"Ken made it somewhere between Eureka and here."

At the back of the van, Kenichi made a loud noise. Like he didn't approve the invitation.

Oh yeah. They had to hide everything in the van again.

"I'll just stand right here and talk to you," Jake said. "But I'd like a cup of coffee, if you don't mind. I ran out."

"Ken, please?" Beatrice didn't look away from Jake.

"I hope there's no poison in the coffee," Jake joked.

Or at least it sounded like he was joking.

Beatrice almost smiled.

Jake was looking intently at her.

Inside the van, Kenichi made an even louder grunt. "No coffee for you!"

"What now?" Beatrice asked.

"I'll live." Jake seemed amused.

"I mean what are you thinking about right now?"

Jake stepped closer to the van, lifted his sunglasses above his head. "So what's all this plumber getup?"

He must've noticed the embroidered company name on her shirt. She couldn't remember what it said, so she glanced down to make sure she had the name right.

Plunging Needs Plumbers. No hyphen.

Kenichi had thought of everything. What would they do without his brain?

"If you have to ask..." Beatrice said.

"Tell you what. If you have an extra shirt my size, I could be part of the team."

Jake surprised her. What was she going to say about that?

"No!" Kenichi yelled. He was still at the back of the van, out of sight. Apparently, he had heard the conversation.

"Who is he? The Wizard of Oz?" Jake made Beatrice laugh.

Sigh.

The whole expedition had been a failure as they were now stuck by the side of the road in the middle of nowhere, looking for a cabin that may not have plumbing needs.

"I know your bodyguard is injured. Broken arm. Can't shoot—unless she's ambidextrous." Jake waited.

Beatrice didn't say a word.

"No? Well, then you have a problem. The Wizard over there, as far as I remember, usually stays in the van. I saw him fight in the forest, so he's got training. But you could use extra protection."

"Extra protection?"

"You didn't want to tell me anything, but I looked you up, and I suspect you're not a random stranger I met in San Francisco."

"Maybe people go there for vacation though."

"Yeah, but only one person is Chisolm Wright's daughter."

Beatrice kept calm. How could he have guessed? Had Philomena told him enough to set him on her trail?

"You followed me all the way from Paris to Cannes and then from France to the States because you think that I could lead you to the Amber Room —the very thing that Molyneux wants to find." He paused. "Am I right?"

He's guessing.

Beatrice remained silent. Then nothing could be used against her. However, maybe it was a bad mission to begin with. She should have gone as far away from Molyneux as possible instead of trying to beat her to the Amber Room.

"Someone must have told you that your deceased father kept a map to the whereabouts of some of the panels of the lost Amber Room," Jake seemed to suggest.

And that person who told her everything about the Amber Room would be Benjamin, the armchair treasure hunter who knew more about Molyneux than anyone Beatrice knew.

The brooch collection was his specialty.

"When Philomena resurfaced, you thought she could lead you to your dad's map. You knew they were in a brooch collection of some sort. Perhaps it is your only connection left with him. Memories?"

"My father died twenty-five years ago."

Oops.

She hadn't meant to say anything.

Jake grinned. "Now that the truth is out, go on."

"I was a child and have few memories of him." However, Beatrice was impressed with Jake's deductions. Did he get any help from Hu Knows, Inc.?

"So you are Chisolm's daughter, after all. How did you go from Amberlyn Peterson to Beatrice Glynn?"

He had been fishing and Beatrice fell for it. She looked into the distance. A bird flew in the forest. The leaves rustled. The sunlight came through again.

Life goes on.

Her eyes moistened.

"Hey," Jake said quietly. His hand reached through the window and touched her shoulder. His fingers were warm and gentle. "I'm sorry."

Kenichi appeared. "Get your hands off her."

His snarl surprised Beatrice.

"Are you her boyfriend?" Jake retracted his hand.

Beatrice felt bereft for some reason.

"No. But neither are you," Kenichi snapped. "Now move along. Go. Leave."

"It's a pointless exercise," Jake said. "You're just going to follow me anyway. I say let's team up."

"You have nothing to offer us," Kenichi said.

"On the contrary, I do." Jake turned to Beatrice. "I think Philomena is bait. Which puts us all in Molyneux's crosshairs, considering she seemed to have a penchant for killing family members—you know, like your dad and his girlfriend."

Beatrice drew a deep breath. No, she wasn't related biologically to Molyneux. However, Jake might be getting somewhere.

"Then explain why we seem to be alone here," Kenichi replied. "I don't see her people coming after us right now, do you?"

"Because they're probably already in the cabin."

That made everyone quiet.

Beatrice couldn't imagine what she was going to miss if Molyneux's men ransacked the cabin before her team arrived. What if there were clues in the cabin about how Dad had lived long after they all thought he was dead? Why hadn't he reached out to her and Benjamin at all for over twenty years?

"They might be waiting for us," Beatrice said. "An ambush we cannot win. If we call 911, it would take forever for the police to show up."

"They can send a chopper," Jake said. "I'm in contact with my associates and they are on standby if anything happens to us."

"How far away are they on standby?" Beatrice asked. "San Francisco?"

Jake rolled his eyes. "Someday, we'll learn to trust each other."

"Not any day," Kenichi snapped. "Her standards are too high for you to reach."

What? Beatrice didn't know how to respond to Kenichi.

There was something else more urgent. "Boys, pay attention. We might be able to get to the cabin, but we might not be able to get out again if Molyneux's people are there."

"I've already worked out that scenario," Kenichi said.

"You have? We're a team here," Beatrice reminded him. "I don't recall approving anything."

"You were driving. Ray was napping. I was *braining*. You're welcome."

Beatrice did not like Kenichi's answer at all. She was in charge. She paid the bills. What was Kenichi doing behind her back? Who was ordering him around?

"Can you get backups in fifty minutes?" Beatrice asked.

When Kenichi didn't answer, Beatrice knew that he had been working on something long before they left Eureka. "We'll talk about it later, but I expect you to answer only to me."

Not to my brother also.

"If they come for us, they'll be in a group," Jake said, diffusing the tension.

Beatrice wasn't happy at this point, but she decided to deal with Kenichi later. Perhaps she would also call her brother to tell him what she thought about him running interference.

Hopefully, it was only Benjamin giving extra orders—and not the other side.

"I'm not the enemy here." Kenichi's voice softened.

Surely he hadn't read her mind.

"I have to see the cabin," Beatrice said. "Give Jake a spare uniform."

CHAPTER EIGHTEEN

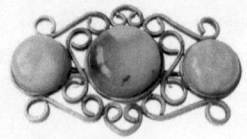

Something was terribly wrong.

Jake knew it and he sensed that Beatrice knew it too. They were probably walking into a trap.

At the moment they were parked near the dock. There was only one boat. It looked like it hadn't been used in a while.

Across the pond—filled with green scum—a small cabin stood. Its windows were closed, the curtains inside drawn. Behind the cabin, tall trees stood guard.

Truth be told, none of them knew the size of Philomena's cabin.

"What if this is the wrong cabin?" Beatrice asked.

Jake nodded. "We'd be wasting time."

"Who on earth would build a cabin there?" Raynelle ate a sandwich. She seemed to be in her own time zone or something.

Jake wondered if she was putting on a show of indifference or if the painkiller was doing a number on her. Put her in a daze, perhaps.

Inside the van, it was stuffy. Jake regretted asking for a plumber's uniform. It was made of polyester that didn't go well with the stuffy van.

Kenichi was sweating buckets as he programmed his drones.

"That's your plan?" Jake asked.

Kenichi ignored him.

"If the drones find something weird, we won't go in, okay?" Kenichi asked Beatrice.

When Beatrice didn't reply, Kenichi asked again, "Okay?"

Beatrice nodded.

She was the only one not sweating in her uniform. She was drinking cold water. Maybe that was the trick.

"I'm going outside. Everyone stay here and watch my back." Kenichi exited the van.

Through the passenger side window, Jake watched Kenichi go until he disappeared behind the trees. Pretty soon, the drone took off across the pond.

It was loud.

Since the forest was quiet, Jake was sure everyone could hear it. He glanced over to see what Beatrice was doing.

She was at the laptop, watching the live camera attached to the drone. She scooted over the bench seat to let Jake have a look at the laptop.

"If the windows are closed, there's no way for the drone to get inside," Beatrice spoke into the microphone.

"I'll send it around the back and see what we can find," Kenichi replied over the speakers.

"What do you hope to find in the cabin?" Jake asked.

"You said it. Memories."

"I don't think the third brooch is there." Jake realized he had brought up the brooch collection with that thoughtless statement.

"Are you looking for the third brooch then?" Beatrice asked.

He could smell a light fragrance that reminded him of springtime and flowers in the meadow. "What is that perfume?"

"Is that how you avoid answering questions?"

Beatrice shook his head. "I don't know you from Adam, but you're something else."

"On the contrary, I think you know me a lot more than you're saying."

"I meant what I said, Jake. I don't know you personally. Data on paper is not the same as in person, but you knew that."

"May I ask you something?" Now was as good a time as any.

"What?"

"Were you the person who called Helen in Cannes?"

Beatrice didn't reply.

"No comment? Or pleading the fifth?"

"Why are you asking me all these questions?" Beatrice turned her attention back to the laptop screen.

"I think that answers it. You didn't want me to die at sea, did you?" Jake asked.

Beatrice drew a deep breath. She looked at Jake directly and said, "My regret is that we couldn't find you sooner."

"Thank you." Jake's heart warmed. He had met his rescuer. "You didn't have to help me."

"We're on the same side, aren't we?" Beatrice asked.

Jake nodded. "We are. Someday, I'll return the favor."

"No need. You helped many by infiltrating Molyneux's camp. You sacrificed three years of your life doing that for the benefit of the world at large."

"How did you know all that?" Jake's mind went everywhere.

Beatrice seemed hesitant to answer him. Then she sighed. "You have a mole in the FBI."

"Who?"

"I don't know."

"Does your brother know?"

"I don't speak for my brother. You can ask him, but he may not speak with you." Beatrice drank more cold water. "All I can say is that you need to find that mole or you will always be one step behind Molyneux."

"Okay, lovebirds," Kenichi said through the speakers. "No more chatting. Class is in session. We're going around the back."

They watched the drone circle the cabin. There was dense forest by the back porch. The deck floor looked damp and was rotting in some places.

"I don't think anyone's lived there in a while," Beatrice said. "Are you sure it's the right cabin?"

"Unless Philomena gave us false information—which can happen," Jake said. "After all, why would she tell us where she lived if she didn't have to?"

"Yeah. Treasure hunters like us might want to check it out—Whoa! Did you see that?" Kenichi navigated the drone back to one of the windows that was less clouded over.

The camera zoomed in.

On the kitchen floor, next to the butcher block, was a body. Very dead.

Still sitting next to Jake, Beatrice shrieked, and the bottled water fell from her hand.

Cold water spilled all over Jake's lap.

CHAPTER NINETEEN

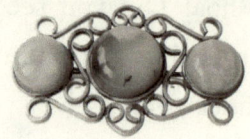

Kenichi hightailed it away from the pond like a bat flying out of a cave. He leapt inside the van, still clutching his drone. Sweat had drenched his shirt. He slid the door shut. "Go go go!"

"Someone call 911." Beatrice sat down in the driver's seat and fastened her seatbelt.

"Not staying to talk to the police?" Jake asked.

"They will ask why we're here. A plumber's van just passing through, huh? That's going to raise more questions—especially when they find out we're the same people who were in the forest last night."

Raynelle must've stirred from her painkiller-induced nap because she started talking. "What's happening?"

"I saw a ghost," Kenichi said.

"No, you didn't." Beatrice shook her head. "You saw a dead body."

"It was dried up." Kenichi raised his voice. "Mummified."

"We don't need details." Although an old body would mean it wasn't anyone they were looking for. Beatrice felt better. "Who's calling 911?"

"I am," Jake said. "I have a burner phone. They can't trace me."

Kenichi laughed. "All phones are traceable."

Except Earl's phone. Beatrice didn't say it aloud. "Ken?"

"Yes, ma'am?"

"Was it a man or a woman?" Beatrice prayed it wasn't a man—because it could be her dad. A long shot, yes, but there had been no evidence that his body was ever found.

"Woman."

Whew. "Age-wise?"

"I don't know."

"I don't expect you to know. I was just asking, is all," Beatrice said. Ahead, the road forked. "Which way should we go?"

"Let me check my laptop," Kenichi said.

Beatrice slowed down the van.

"Go right," Kenichi finally said. "I think."

"That doesn't sound good." Beatrice put the blinker on. It was then that she spotted a vehicle in the rearview mirror. "We have company."

Beatrice heard Jake ask Kenichi if there was a window they could use to look out the back.

"No, but we have a camera on the back of the van. See here."

"I don't think it's a family on vacation," Jake said. "Unless it's a family thing to carry shotguns."

"What?" Beatrice wished she wasn't driving.

"Here we go again." Raynelle's voice sounded groggy. "Next time we hunt for something more benign than the Amber Room, all right?"

"Charleston, we have a problem," Kenichi said.

"Should I go faster?" Beatrice asked. "I need some directions too. There's another fork in the road coming up."

"Go left. There's a big road—"

Boom! Boom!

Flap! Flap!

Beatrice lost control of the van. She wanted to slam on the brakes.

"No! Keep your foot on the gas," Jake said. "Sounds like they blew out a couple of tires—"

"Help!" Beatrice lurched forward as the vehicle behind them rammed the van and pushed it off the road.

The van flipped over on its side.

Everyone screamed.

CHAPTER TWENTY

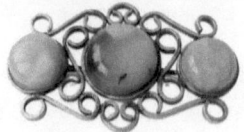

Beatrice squinted, adjusting her eyes to the dim light of the space that looked like a musty basement. She found herself tied to a chair so tightly she couldn't feel her arms and legs. Some sort of tape sealed her mouth shut.

In another chair, Jake seemed to have passed out. His face looked bloodied. His shirt was soaked through with something. Water? Blood? The tape over his mouth looked like duct tape, which made Beatrice think the same type of tape was also over her own mouth.

In front of them, a flight of stairs led one floor up to a closed door.

Where were Raynelle and Kenichi?

Beatrice tried to remember what happened to

them after the van flipped over on the side of the road. She recalled trying to crawl out of the van, only to be met by armed men, who sprayed her face with something.

Beatrice had passed out and had woken up here.

The door at the top of the stairs opened, creaking on its hinges.

A man in black leather pants and vest came down the stairs, brandishing a dagger in a sheath. He was accompanied by another man.

Ignoring Beatrice, the man went straight to Jake. "Wake him."

They splashed water on Jake.

He stirred. Gasped.

"Grady Northcutt, what a surprise," the man said to Jake. "I've been wondering what happened to you since we left the Smoky Mountains."

Of course, Jake couldn't answer with the duct tape over his mouth.

"You infiltrated our team to get to Molyneux. How did that work out for you? Ah, I forget. You can't speak." The man pulled the dagger out of the sheath. "Recognize this?"

Beatrice saw Jake's eyes widen. At the dagger or at being called by another name? She wondered if that had been his undercover name.

"Molyneux told me to finish you off." He flashed the dagger in his face. "This dagger wants to scrape your bones."

Jake's body shook.

Beatrice made noises under the duct tape. "Mmmm! Hmmmph!"

The man turned to her. Ripped the duct tape off her mouth.

"Oweee!" Beatrice winced.

"What?" His face was awfully close to hers. So close that she could smell his breath.

"You can't."

"Can't what?" The man plunged the dagger into Jake's thigh. "Here we have a doomed man—once a hero, now a zero."

The duct tape muffled Jake's scream.

"No!" Beatrice didn't know what else to do. She prayed for God to deliver them. "It's me she wants, not Jake."

The man turned to her again. "Who are you?"

"Molyneux has been looking for me for twenty-five years," Beatrice kept talking, hoping to distract him away from Jake.

Jake stared at her, as if to say something to her—to stop her, perhaps.

"I'm Chisolm Wright's daughter."

"Who?" Slowly, he pulled the dagger out of

Jake's thigh. "Next thing you're going to tell me that Molly's looking for him too."

He pointed his dagger at Jake. "How did you end up with him? He should've been dead six months ago."

"We're together." Poor choice of words. Then again, businesswise, it was true they were both on the same side.

"Together how?"

"God brought us together," Beatrice said. That was true, she felt.

"Like marriage?" The man looked baffled.

Beatrice blushed. "Business."

"What sort of business?"

"We're treasure hunters."

"Really?" Dagger pointing toward Jake again. "I thought he was a bona fide FBI agent."

"Was. He got fired."

"They don't want him either."

Beatrice tried not to look at Jake.

"You want us to let both of you go?" the man asked Beatrice.

The fact that he said *us* instead of *me* told Beatrice that he wasn't in charge. "On the contrary, take me to Molly."

Now Jake's grunts got louder and more intense. He was shooting daggers at her with his stare.

She ignored him. "We're due for a cup of tea."

"You're as crazy as..." The man lost his words.

"Molly?" Beatrice tried to help.

"No. no."

"I'll tell her what you said."

The door opened again, and sounds of boots hit the stairs. Emerging in the light was a big man with a small goatee.

"What's going on in here?" Big Man said. His voice was surprisingly low.

Beatrice had never seen him before. "Having a chat."

"Finish the job and send the video to Molly," Big Man snapped. "How hard can it be?"

The first man pointed to Beatrice, his dagger dripping with Jake's blood. "She says she's Chisolm Wright's daughter."

"Seriously?"

Beatrice realized that she had outed herself. All this time, Molyneux had been after Jake and Earl, sending assailants to Northern California after those two men. It was entirely possible she had no idea that Beatrice and her team had also been following Jake.

Soon, Molyneux would know the secret that had been kept from her for twenty-five years.

And it would be Beatrice's fault.

However, if Beatrice hadn't stopped Mr. Dagger here, who knew what he'd have done to Jake?

"She wants to have a cup of tea with Molly," Mr. Dagger added.

Big Man laughed. "Take me to your leader and all that?"

Beatrice nodded.

Roll with it. All I can do.

"You've got to be kidding me."

"Call her." Beatrice maintained a calm voice. "Let her decide if she wants to see me."

"No one who sees her lives to tell the story," Big Man said. "Unless you work for her."

"We don't, but my business partners and I have two of the three brooches she's looking for," Beatrice replied. "However, if any one of us dies, the secret is lost with us."

"I don't believe you."

"She will."

CHAPTER TWENTY-ONE

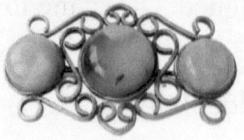

W as Molyneux trying to soften her up for the kill? It felt that way as Big Man led Beatrice up the stairs and through what turned out to be a log cabin. Two armed men flanked them.

Her hands were tied behind her back, but she was grateful for the opportunity to stretch her legs, although she did not want to leave Jake behind in the basement with Mr. Dagger there.

The afternoon sun shone in through the clearing on the side of the house, casting shadowy lights into the family room and on furniture that looked like it hadn't moved in years. Mostly leather, the brown and terra-cotta earth tones of the decor shouted male, from the pictures on the wall on one side to the stone fireplace against another wall.

On the stone fireplace were photographs.

Beatrice drew a deep breath. "May I take a look at the photos?"

Big Man grunted.

"Please? Aren't you the least bit curious why Molly picked this cabin in particular?"

Big Man raised his bushy eyebrows. He motioned for one of his men to take Beatrice to the fireplace. "Let her have her last request."

There were old photographs of teenagers whom Beatrice did not recognize, but she recognized one photograph.

Philomena without the scar on her face. Sitting on the lap of...

Chisolm Wright.

The air whooshed out of her lungs. She wanted to cry but no tears came.

She reminded herself that it might not be Dad. After all, there were few photographs of Dad, and they were all at least twenty-five years old. Some years before, Benjamin had tried putting Dad's photographs through an aging software to see how he might look.

Well, he looked like the older man in that photograph.

"Whose house is this?" Beatrice asked.

"Why don't you ask Molly?" Big Man said. "This way."

He yanked her back in line, and they marched down the hallway. Outside the bank of French doors, a wraparound deck spread out with Adirondack chairs facing the sunset.

Beatrice wondered how many times Dad had sat there in the evenings with Philomena, looking at that lovely view of tall trees and California skies.

And without his children.

Beatrice felt abandoned.

So abandoned.

Quietly, she felt a warmth in her heart. A light feathery touch and a reminder that she wasn't truly alone. Her heavenly Father God was still with her, even if her earthly father had forsaken her.

Let your conduct be without covetousness; be content with such things as you have. For He Himself has said, "I will never leave you nor forsake you."

That Hebrews 13:5 should pop into her mind at such a time as this!

Beatrice blinked as she stared at the distant sky where the sun was about to set.

And God was still there.

She hung her head.

"Move, woman!" Big Man jerked her forward.

Beatrice's shoulders slouched, as tears pooled in her eyes.

Why am I like this?

How many times must I grieve my dad?

She thought he had died twenty-five years prior. Come to find out, he had lived on for another twenty-three years or so—according to his long-time girlfriend. And now was he truly dead?

A heavy wooden door opened into what looked like a home office. More earth tones. Right in the middle of the octagonal room was a heavy desk.

Big Man jerked her forward. He motioned for someone to untie her.

Beatrice ran her finger along the smooth wood on the surface of the heavy desk. It was redwood, probably hewn from the forest nearby.

Beatrice felt sorry for the trees that fell to make this desk and the entire house.

"Sit down." Big Man pointed to an old chair on the other side of the desk.

"Why?"

"Molly wants you to sit down at the desk when you talk to her."

Over the years that she had hunted down treasures to return to their rightful owners, Beatrice had met numerous eccentric people. Thus, she wasn't surprised by this request.

From her knowledge of Molyneux, she had her own tics and quirks.

As long as none of them caused her death and that of her team, she would put up with her eccentricities.

Beatrice sat down at the chair.

Was this Dad's desk?

The desk was practically empty except for a blotter that took up half the desktop. It had ink stains on it. The way the blotches spread on the blotter, Beatrice suspected that the ink had come out of fountain pens.

Benjamin had often told her stories of how their dad liked to write with fountain pens. Sometimes the ink wells spilled and stained the table and his fingers.

No, they were not tall tales. After all, Benjamin had been ten years old when Dad disappeared the first time, shortly after Dad gave Benjamin one of his old fountain pens.

Was this where Dad sat through all those missing years?

She looked past Big Man and his cohorts. There were books on the shelves, sculptures, an old radio from the 1940s, and several closed boxes. She wondered what was in some of the lacquer and mother-of-pearl boxes, but she was afraid to provoke anyone by rushing there to peek in.

Yes, she would like to survey the house, to see what was left of it that Philomena hadn't sold.

Another man came into the office and placed a laptop on top of the desk.

Beatrice held the chair and scooted forward. As she was doing so, she glanced under the desk to see where her legs and feet were going.

That was when she spotted it.

No one would have seen it except that the waning sun was shining into the room. To begin with, if a person worked here in the afternoon, they'd have to close the curtains to prevent glare on the laptop screen.

However, thanks to the sunshine, Beatrice spotted a distressed leather pouch hanging down from underneath the table. Perhaps it had loosened from its position or something.

Surely this wasn't a big find.

Still...

Curiosity got the better of her, and she palmed the leather pouch as she pretended to adjust the office chair so that she was comfortable in it. She slid the pouch into one of her cargo pockets.

Oddly enough, Big Man hadn't emptied out her pockets. That told Beatrice that they had something bigger in mind.

The lost Amber Room, perhaps?

The audio on the laptop crackled.

Okay, it didn't crackle like in the days of old, but Beatrice imagined it could have, considering the old-world ambiance in this office.

The video screen was blank. Only Beatrice's face showed up on a rectangle in the top right-hand corner of the laptop screen.

"Amber Wright," Molyneux said.

Beatrice didn't answer.

"I'm still Imogen Wright to you."

Was that a confession?

Beatrice hadn't spoken to this woman in twenty-five years. At five years old, she could hardly recall the adoptive mother who was never home. In fact, she remembered Philomena more than anyone else. The nanny was always with Beatrice and Benjamin—even as they had different names then.

When Beatrice still didn't answer, Molyneux continued. "Your father wanted to name you 'Beatrice.' We fought over what to name you, and he finally saw things my way."

Did he?

"Looks like once he entered WITSEC, he named you what he wanted." The Witness Security Program had provided shelter for the Glynn family for many years.

"You could have tracked us down. Why didn't you?" Beatrice asked. "Twenty-five years."

"I made a promise to your father to leave you children out of our quarrels."

"A promise among thieves?" Beatrice asked.

"Look who's talking. You stole the three-amber brooch from Philomena right under our noses."

Technically, Raynelle took it. But Beatrice kept it.

Yeah, she had to return it soon. Her conscience wouldn't permit it.

Beatrice wondered what would happen to her and her team if they discovered the brooch in her cargo pocket.

"What do you want from me?" Beatrice asked.

"Nothing. You were in the way."

Who was she after? It could not be Kenichi and Raynelle since they had come in late in the game.

Jake? "In the way of what? Of whom?"

"I won't take betrayal sitting down," Molyneux said.

"Someone betrayed you?"

"Let it be a lesson for everyone." Molyneux's

tone was one of disappointment.

Beatrice wondered if that was meant more for Big Man and his people rather than for Beatrice sitting there, chatting with her long-lost adoptive mother at large.

Was it theatrics?

"Why don't I just shoot him already?" Molyneux asked.

"I don't know." Beatrice wasn't sure where the conversation was going, but she was almost sure she knew who Molyneux was taking about.

"Too quick and painless. Did you hear that, Oswald?"

"Yes, ma'am." Big Man nodded.

Oswald, huh? Beatrice filed that away.

"So you torture him?" Beatrice asked.

"The visuals are astounding."

With Dad's dagger. Beatrice frowned.

"You don't approve?" Molyneux asked.

"Of any killing, no."

"But of torture?"

"Not my cup of tea."

Molyneux laughed. "You're so grown up. Sorry I didn't check on you. Been busy, you know. In fact, I would've left you alone if only you'd stopped following that FBI agent."

"Former. He was fired."

"Thanks to me. Good. Now I won't feel bad if we work him over some."

"Work him over how?" Beatrice asked.

"You'll find out. Meantime, let me ask you one question. Why are you looking for the Amber Room?"

Beatrice wasn't sure how to answer that. She didn't want to give away anything that would cause Molyneux to go after Benjamin.

"Are you trying to finish what your father and I started?" Molyneux asked.

"Well..."

"Then join me."

Thought you'd never ask. "I'd rather be independent. Thank you, though."

"You are your father's daughter."

"I was adopted." Beatrice knew Molyneux didn't need the reminder, but she said it for her own assurance that she hadn't inherited any genetic traits from them.

"Yes, but sometimes children take on the characteristics of their adoptive parents."

That did not sound good to Beatrice at all. The last thing she wanted was to take after Molyneux—even if she had once been Imogen Wright, history scholar.

"Maybe I'll be ahead of you, retrieve those

amber panels first, and then I can offer to sell them to you for a price," Beatrice said.

At first Molyneux was silent.

Was she stunned?

Then Molyneux broke into a laughter so care-free and wild. "If Chisolm couldn't find it after all those years, would you be able to?"

"Speaking of Dad, what happened to him?"

"I killed him two years ago."

"You..." Beatrice couldn't speak.

Somewhere deep in her heart, she had held out hope that Dad was still alive, hiding somewhere in the world, keeping an eye on Benjamin and her.

"I don't believe you," Beatrice said.

"You don't want to believe me. I'm your only parent left. But I tell you, he's dead."

Somehow, the way Molyneux said it seemed mendacious.

Beatrice decided to try another angle.

"All those years when he was alive, he never called." Beatrice wanted to get Molyneux's sympathy, but the grief in her heart reminded her that it was her own pain that was exposed right now.

What if Dad is really dead?

"What kind of father would disappear for over twenty years and start a new life with someone else?"

"Do they have children?" Beatrice asked.

"Not Chisolm's. Don't worry, dear. He didn't share his fatherly love with other people."

Beatrice remembered the photos on the mantelpiece. Perhaps those were nieces and nephews.

"Besides, I took care of him. I punished him for you. He is really dead this time. End of story."

Tears pooled in Beatrice's eyes. Somewhere in her heart she was hoping—praying—that she could see Dad again.

Still, her heart felt at peace. God was with her, as He had been through her fatherless days on earth. She tried to recall Psalm 68:5.

A father of the fatherless, a defender of widows, is God in His holy habitation.

Beatrice knew she had to move forward. Looking back for a moment had caused her to grieve again, but looking forward, there was much work to be done yet.

"What are you going to do with us?" Beatrice asked.

"We'll have the cup of tea you wanted." Molyneux's voice was cheerful. "After we bury Jake Kessler, also known as Grady Northcutt when he was in my employ."

CHAPTER TWENTY-TWO

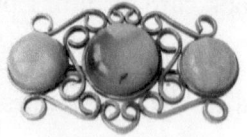

J ake prayed for Beatrice, who had been gone a long time. He had no idea where they had taken her. They had left him tied to the chair, gaping wounds on one thigh and multiple cuts on the other. What were they trying to do to him?

He couldn't even remember the man's name. Joe? Jim? John Doe then.

Oswald, he remembered, because the man had been in charge of the entire battalion who sneaked into Mendenhall Retreat some three years ago. Oswald was ex-military who ran his own mercenary militia.

Molyneux paid them well.

Still, they had abandoned the fishing vessel like

everyone else when the storm came and capsized the boat, leaving Jake to die.

Beatrice had come to his aid then. At least he believed she had been the anonymous caller.

Today, she had once again rescued him from certain death. What kind of a woman would put her own life on the line for a stranger?

Perhaps they were not strangers any longer.

They were on the same side now.

Together.

God brought us together.

He had heard what Beatrice said. What did she mean by that? She blushed at some unexpected suggestion.

If he had previously thought of her as potentially Molyneux's adopted daughter, tonight confirmed it. Something she said to Oswald.

She's been looking for me for twenty-five years.

She purposely put herself on the railroad track for Molyneux to run over. Why?

Jake wiggled his wrists to see if he could loosen the rope a bit, but the movement caused him to pull some muscles—what was left of them—in his legs, and he cried out in pain.

He wondered if he'd ever walk again with all his leg muscles so messed up.

Already, titanium rods held his legs together.

He closed his eyes to wait for the pain to subside. "Please, God."

Then he remembered his Savior on the cross, carrying on His shoulder the sins of the world. Feet and hands pierced, Jesus Christ died on the cross for him.

For me.

What unbearable pain did Jesus suffer at the cross?

At the cross, at the cross...

The old hymn penned by Isaac Watts in the eighteenth century returned to his mind. He could see himself in church as a little boy with his four brothers and one sister, singing this song with his parents.

> *At the cross, at the cross where I first*
> *saw the light,*
> *And the burden of my heart rolled*
> *away,*
> *It was there by faith I received my*
> *sight,*
> *And now I am happy all the day!*

He couldn't hear himself sing it aloud because of the duct tape over his mouth, but he hummed it until the pain in his legs went away. Or at least until he forgot about it.

The door creaked open again.

"Someone ought to oil this door." Oswald's voice was followed by multiple boots pounding on the steps.

Beatrice was not with them.

Where is she?

Jake prayed that she was still alive.

Without a word, Oswald ordered his men to untie Jake. As they headed toward the stairs, Jake felt a blow to his head.

He fell to the ground, seeing stars.

"Traitor!" Oswald spat at him and walked up the stairs first. "Get him to the driveway."

Driveway?

Were they going somewhere?

CHAPTER TWENTY-THREE

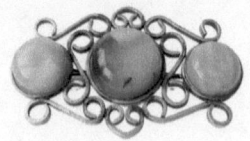

S eeing Beatrice on the driveway was like having a cool drink on a hot summer's day. Jake didn't know why he felt that way, but he just did. He wanted to say something to her, but she was facing away from him. Her hands were tied behind her back.

At least she was still standing.

On the grass nearby, Raynelle was groaning next to an unmoving Kenichi. They looked like they had been beaten up badly.

Surrounding them were Oswald, John Doe, and their merry men and women of ill repute.

Dusk was coming soon, but there was sunlight left. Jake hoped that Beatrice wouldn't be too freaked out at the sight of him. Perhaps the night-fall would cover up how bloodied he might look.

He had no idea what her tolerance level was, but he didn't want her to see him like this—

What am I thinking?

No, he wasn't falling in love with the woman who had saved his life at least three times.

Or was he?

He shuffled forward, held up by two strong men. They hadn't bothered to tie up Jake's hands because they had beaten him to a pulp. There was no way he was going to defend himself or anyone else in this state.

Beatrice must have heard him coming because she turned. Her eyes widened. "Jake!"

She tried to go toward him, but John Doe held her back.

She cares.

Interesting.

"So you are really *together?*" John Doe touched Beatrice's chin with his gloved hand. Ran his finger down her neck to her chest...

Jake tried not to react.

React? Huh. That's surprising.

But there was more. Reacting was what he had been doing of late. Reacting. Running. Hiding.

Molyneux had many steps ahead of him. Them.

How?

Was Beatrice correct when she said that there was a spy inside the FBI? Who was it?

Raynelle rose from the grass.

Immediately, weapons pointed at her.

She didn't seem to care. "You touch her. You die."

"Ooh. A rash champion." John Doe walked toward Raynelle. "Who might you be?"

Jake waited.

"Let's do a headcount, shall we?" John Doe said. "There are dozens of us. There are two of you still standing—not counting your Asian friend on the grass and Grady over there."

Jake wondered if Kenichi was playing possum. He hoped that they hadn't beaten him up too much. He remembered how Kenichi and Raynelle had helped him fight off Molyneux's other men back in the forest.

When was that?

The night before?

Then again, there were only four assailants coming at them that night. This time, Oswald had brought reinforcements.

Jake hated to think he had no control over his

circumstances, but here he was on the ground, unable to stand up on his own, let alone run to anyone's aid.

"Why are we still waiting here?" Beatrice asked.

John Doe turned his attention away from Raynelle.

Oswald spoke on his phone. "They're almost here."

"Who?" Beatrice asked.

"You wanted an audience with Molly. You got it." Oswald laughed. "You'll wish you never had the opportunity."

Being taken captive alone was one thing, but Jake could not let them take Beatrice.

"Hey, Oswald," Jake called out. "How much is Molyneux paying you?"

Oswald laughed. "More than you can ever pay me."

Beatrice glanced at Jake. It seemed to be the opening she needed.

She turned to Oswald. "Did she offer you a piece of the Amber Room like she offered my dad?"

Oswald's eyes lit up.

"No?" Beatrice smiled. "You know she will never give up any part of it. Not even a small chunk of the smallest panel."

Oswald didn't say a word.

"You know she will kill you like she killed her own husband."

"I thought they were divorced?" John Doe chimed in.

Beatrice ignored him. "My dad wanted the Amber Room too. It was going to be their nest egg. Millions of dollars earned if sold on the black market."

Oswald grunted.

"You signed a contact with Molyneux, didn't you?" Jake asked. "You'll honor your part, of course. You're an honorable man. But she won't honor hers. Look what she did to me."

"You were a traitor." They had gotten Oswald talking.

"I wasn't earning enough in the bureau. I told you that three years ago, didn't I? I wanted some extra money for a new Lambo."

"No kidding." John Doe bought it all.

Well, Jake wouldn't mind driving a Lamborghini, and it worked well as a cover story when he had applied for the job on Oswald's team.

Beatrice made a face at Jake, as though she couldn't believe he was that shallow.

Jake had to keep up the story. "When Molly found out I was pretending to be undercover, she couldn't believe I actually cashed the money and bought a Lambo."

"She doesn't believe anyone." Beatrice waited for Oswald to say something. "She's a liar all the way."

Oswald straightened up. "You may be lying yourself. Like mother, like daughter."

"Adoptive mother. Biologically unrelated. I don't know who my mother is."

"You poor thing."

"But I learned a thing or two about Molly." Beatrice straightened up. "I don't work for her. In fact, I'm her rival."

It made Oswald chuckle.

"She wants me because she wants the map to the final resting place of most of the panels from the original Amber Room," Beatrice said. "Do you know how much that is worth? And don't think you're going to get any of it. Have you ever seen anyone selfish become suddenly generous?"

Even in the small light above the driveway, Jake could see that Beatrice had cast doubt in Oswald's mind.

She seemed to be good at this.

It made Jake wonder if she might be related to Molyneux after all. Or at least, she would make a great undercover agent.

No, I'm not recruiting her.

"You do know that the map is hidden in a three-piece brooch collection," Beatrice continued, not that she had Oswald's attention. "One brooch is in San Francisco in a safe-deposit box. I have the third brooch in my right pocket."

"No, Bee!" Jake shouted. "Why did you bring it with you?"

"Do you know where the two-amber brooch is?" Beatrice asked. When Oswald's face changed slightly, she continued talking. "I see you do. I told you I'm her rival. I will split it with you."

Oswald pointed to Jake. "You forgot your boyfriend."

"You made mincemeat out of him. You think he'll live? So let's discuss our business transaction here. Do you want a share or not?"

Oswald turned to Jake. "She's cold. My kind of gal."

Jake winced. Gritted his teeth.

"I have the three-amber brooch in my right pocket," Beatrice said. "I can't reach it since my hands are tied. I need some assistance."

"Let me help." John Doe was quick on his toes. He took off his glove and reached into Beatrice's pocket, moving in an excruciatingly slow manner.

It made Jake's blood boil.

Beatrice remained calm, as if a snake was crawling over her.

John Doe produced the brooch.

Under the lamp, it looked like the same brooch that Philomena had tried to give Jake at the café in San Francisco before she was murdered by coffee.

Did this confirm that Beatrice or her team had stolen the brooch off Jake's table?

"I could take this from you and kill you and keep everything to myself and my team," Oswald said.

"If you ask me to choose between my life and the Amber Room, I would tell you that I'd rather live. I value my life more than all the treasures on earth."

"Oh, so philosophical." John Doe stood awfully close to Beatrice.

"I'm being realistic."

"You are so unlike your mother, then. She's idealistic, not realistic." Oswald thumbed the three-amber brooch.

"Be careful," Beatrice said. "She'll cut off your head like a praying mantis."

Oswald laughed. "And you wouldn't?"

"I told you we're not related. Otherwise, why would she want to kill me? Would a mother kill her own child?"

Barring insanity, Jake thought.

He was impressed that Beatrice had put Oswald at ease. Maybe she had taken acting classes in college.

Oswald put the three-amber brooch in his vest pocket. "You talk a good talk, lady, but you're still going on the chopper."

Jake listened but could not hear any helicopter blades. All was quiet beyond the sound of nature and impending doom.

Regardless, he did not want Beatrice to go.

"Before we go..." Oswald smiled. "You made a deal with Molyneux."

Beatrice looked stunned. "What deal?"

"Which deal, you mean?" Oswald extended his palm toward John Doe. The latter handed him the dagger. "You get to have that cup of tea with Molyneux if you kill Grady here—also known as Jake Kessler."

Beatrice's knees went weak. John Doe held her up by her arm.

"Just take this pointy end and push it into his chest."

"No." Beatrice shook her head.

"The deal is sealed. The chopper comes and you go."

Jake tried to read Beatrice's face, but in the

waning light he couldn't make out what she might be thinking.

Somewhere, he heard a distant sound of...drones?

Sure enough, two drones appeared above them.

"This is the Eureka Bay Police!" The loud voice came through the loudspeakers attached to the drones.

Oswald cursed.

"You're surrounded. Put down your weapons!"

Oswald and his people held on to their weapons. Jake noticed movement around him. He was surrounded by two of Oswald's men.

Beatrice turned to him. "Stay down, Jake!"

Her mouth opened as if to say more, but she seemed to hesitate.

Jake hugged the ground and covered his head with his free arm. He heard someone.

"How now brown cow!" Kenichi yelled in a strained—and pained—voice.

Then Jake heard an explosion. When it was over, he looked up to find Oswald splattered on the driveway, his torso and head gone. Two or three other people were also down on the driveway with him.

Blood and body matter were everywhere.

The remainder of Oswald's militia slowly

placed their weapons on the ground and put their hands in the air in front of the drones.

Jake dragged his body on his hip and good leg toward Beatrice, still crouched down on the concrete driveway. He called her name softly.

She looked up. Her hands were still tied.

Before Jake could reach her, a much louder explosion rocked the property. Part of the roof flew over Jake and Beatrice and landed on the driveway and the grass front yard.

The heat nearly seared Jake's back. He turned to see what had happened, and found the entire cabin engulfed in flames.

He glanced over at Beatrice to see her reaction.

Her face looked stunned.

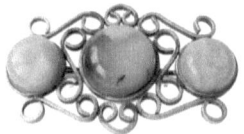

CHAPTER TWENTY-FOUR

Word would get back to Molyneux that Oswald was dead. She would regroup and retaliate fast. The world's most notorious terrorist had a reputation to keep.

That and many other things percolated through Beatrice's mind as she walked down the hallway of the Eureka hospital to find Raynelle and Kenichi. They both were treated as outpatients because their injuries were not life threatening.

Yeah, how to get a step ahead of Molyneux?

Her team had been decimated.

Kenichi had a broken leg.

Raynelle's arm was still broken.

Earl was still hospitalized for his internal injuries.

Their other new temporary addition to the team, Jake, required extensive stitches on his thigh, busted lips, and a gash on his forehead.

None of them was in any position to fly out there to Europe, track down Molyneux, and knock on her door.

Beatrice herself had bruises from the van wreck. Beyond that, everyone else had taken hits for her. She had somehow managed to talk her way out of serious injuries.

That scared her.

She had heard it told that many things in a person's life were ingrained by the age of five. That had been the age when her parents broke up and Dad had to flee England with his kids. Could it be possible that Molyneux—as Imogen Wright—had imprinted into Beatrice some of her undesirable ways?

The cabin was gone and along with it, all potential clues to the whereabouts of the Amber Room. Then again, if Dad had the clues all along, he would have found the Amber Room by now, right?

With the cabin destroyed, Beatrice had no hope of going back there to sift through what might be potentially Dad's belongings and keepsakes.

Oh well. She'd sort all that out later.

For now, she had to attend to the well-being of her two loyal employees, and pay their hospital bills. She also wanted to drop in to see how Jake was doing, but there would be no time to wait for him if the doctors decided he had to stay overnight at the hospital.

They had to return to San Francisco as soon as possible to fly out. She might have to drop off Raynelle and Kenichi in Charleston to rest and recuperate.

Benjamin could send some of his people to Eureka to inventory the cabin.

Hmm... Benjamin.

Perhaps she could persuade Benjamin to leave his Charleston mansion and help her finish the project. She texted him as she walked down the hallway.

> Benjamin: Nope. You come home right now and we'll discuss what's next.
> Beatrice: Come on, Ben. No time to lose.
> Benjamin: Do you have the map?

Beatrice: No. Missing one brooch.

Benjamin: I've already lost a father. I

don't want to lose my sister too.

Come home.

He could not be persuaded. Benjamin went on to say that all his resources would be hers when they made their next move.

Sigh.

She must have walked down the wrong section of the hospital. She could not find Kenichi or Raynelle. Where were they?

She texted both of them.

Kenichi told her where to go. All the way to the other end of the small hospital.

When she arrived, Beatrice could hear Kenichi laughing. When she entered the room, all three of them were there, including Jake sitting up in bed in a hospital gown. He seemed to be in the middle of telling a story, something about his Quantico training days.

Beatrice could not see his thigh where the stab wounds were. However, she could see the stitches on his forehead and lips.

Would be hard to kiss...

Beatrice caught herself. She cleared her throat.

"Hey." Jake extended his arm.

Instinctively, Beatrice went to him, but did not touch his hand. "You cleaned up nicely."

Jake dropped his arm back on the bed. "I check out at four."

"So quickly?"

"No broken bones. Not too much. They cleaned my wounds and sewed them up. I'll have scars on both thighs forever, but nothing too serious —unless my future girlfriend has an issue with it. My tetanus shot is up to date, so no worries there."

Beatrice nodded. "Thank God."

"Yeah. Thank God indeed. I'll just need to pick up some antibiotics and Tylenol from the pharmacy and I'm out of here. As long as I don't develop a fever next week or something."

"Good."

He turned pensive. "If you hadn't talked to John Doe back at the cabin, stopped him from doing more damage, I might have lost a leg. Thank you."

"Don't mention it." Beatrice turned to Kenichi and Raynelle. "You two make quite a pair. One broken arm and one broken leg."

"I'm sorry I couldn't do more," Raynelle said.

"I knew you'd say that. Don't. We did the best we could, given the circumstances." Beatrice drew a deep breath, hoping she wouldn't cry over Dad again. "We keep moving forward. By the way, I talked to Benjamin. He wants us to go home."

"May I come along?" Jake asked.

"What about your partner upstairs? When are they releasing him?" Beatrice didn't want to invite him to continue the mission with her without a contract for him to sign. She hadn't thought about liabilities, compensations, and all the other things that would make him a permanent member of her team.

"In a couple of days."

"Don't you want to stay with him?"

"Nah. Helen is letting him fly first-class home as soon as he can, but Earl seems to think he needs to stay here a bit longer. He has some internal damage to his stomach from the gunshot wound."

"I'm sorry." Beatrice meant it.

"He'll recover. As for me, I think I can keep going, like you said just now."

"I meant my *team* would keep going forward."

"Am I not on your team? I wore the plumber's shirt, didn't I? We're practically friends. Or maybe more than friends."

He said it so casually that Beatrice wondered what he was thinking.

"I could sweeten the deal," Jake said. "Helen is offering a jet to fly to Europe."

"We have our own."

"Don't you want to save on fuel cost? Let someone else pay for it?"

"My jet, my schedule."

"Okay. Makes sense." Jake seemed to be in deep thought. "What about access to data?"

"What kind of data?"

"Helen's team has been tracking Molyneux for a couple of years. We could combine forces."

Beatrice waited for her people to comment.

Raynelle was nonchalant.

All Kenichi did was widen his eyes.

"You got something to say about it?" Beatrice asked.

"I don't want to sway your decision, but I want to see what Helen has in their tracking system," Kenichi said. "They hunt for treasure too sometimes."

Beatrice turned to Jake. "Would Helen allow us access to the system or is she just sending us reports of her findings?"

Jake moved his leg and winced. "Well, I'm non-tech, so she just sends me stuff. But I'm sure we can talk about access."

"Even limited access is fine," Kenichi said. "We can reciprocate at whatever level she offers."

"Benjamin's computer database is off-limits,"

Beatrice reminded everyone. "Besides we're already reciprocating if we let Jake here get a ride with us."

Jake cheered.

"I've rented a sleeper coach, and it'll be here after lunch," Beatrice added.

"I can't leave without my equipment from the van," Kenichi said. "They towed the van. I'm going to need some help carrying stuff."

"We'll stop," Beatrice said. "They also have our suitcases and whatever else we left in the van."

Beatrice made a mental checklist of the things they would need to do in San Francisco before they boarded the Gulfstream. For instance, she would have to stop at the bank to retrieve the three-amber brooch from their temporary safe-deposit box.

Speaking of which...

"Where's the one-amber brooch?" Beatrice asked Jake.

"Well, the price of that is team membership."

"You drive a hard bargain. Yet we're nowhere without the two-amber brooch. Where do you think it is?"

"Maybe if we combine Helen's system with Kenichi's system, we could find that brooch," Jake replied. "Perhaps the reason we haven't found it in the last three years was that we didn't have enough resources to do so on our own."

"You also make a good point."

"I aim to please." Jake winced again.

"Tell you what, Agent Kessler. Why don't we let you rest until it's time for you to check out? Meanwhile, we're going to the tow truck company to get our stuff. Be ready to sign a contract when we come back for you."

"A contract for what?"

"Liability. I don't want to be responsible for your well-being or lack thereof. That's Helen's problem. We're working together in this collaborative effort and that is all."

"Together. I like that word."

So do I.

But Beatrice wouldn't say it aloud.

CHAPTER TWENTY-FIVE

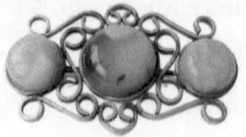

By the time the rental entertainer coach left Eureka for San Francisco, it was past Beatrice's bedtime, but she could not keep her eyes closed. Three hours of tossing and turning later, she was still wide awake.

They'd be in San Francisco in a couple of hours.

She had her own bunk bed across from Raynelle, who slept like a quiet baby. Adjacent to them, no sound came from the rest of the sleeper coach where Jake and Kenichi were.

In the quiet of the night—except for the sound of the vehicle moving—Beatrice ran through the events of the day before, and blinked away a tear.

Dad's cabin—if it had been really his—was

completely destroyed by the firebomb. None of Oswald's militia confessed to setting it. The arson investigator had not completed her investigation.

For all practical purposes, there was nothing left for them to comb through in Eureka.

Except the old leather pouch she had picked up from what she assumed to be Dad's office.

It had an old golden key and postcard of San Francisco in it. What did they mean?

She had sent Benjamin a photograph of both items. He told her to run through the database—something she planned to do once on board the Gulfstream.

Maybe it made sense for her to return to Charleston. She needed Benjamin's knowledge of antiquities right now.

Nonetheless, they had to go back to San Francisco to pick up the brooches and the Gulfstream. She had offered to give Earl and Jake a free flight to Charleston. The two could then get a ride back to Savannah—unless Jake stayed on with her team.

Earl was still at the hospital. He would check out the next day. He had asked the hospital to send his records over to Savannah Memorial, where he expected to do the next surgery on his stomach. The poor dude had much damage from the gunshots in the forest.

Fortunately for him, every bullet missed his spine.

As for Jake, he had tried not to show pain, but Beatrice saw that he had a hard time walking fast. She wondered if he could keep up with her on the next leg of their adventure.

Together.

She closed her eyes and recalled the moment he reached out to her. He nearly touched her just before Dad's house exploded in a fireball.

Beatrice tossed aside the thin blanket in her bunk bed. She found her flip-flops and made her way to the bathroom at the end of the tour bus, passing by more bunk beds with curtains drawn.

She splashed warm—almost hot—water on her face and brushed her teeth.

Even before she reached the small galley kitchen that separated the sleeping quarters from the dining and sitting area, she smelled fresh coffee. Someone else was awake.

"Good morning." Jake looked up from his iPad.

"Morning? More like the middle of the night. You up early?"

"I had two hours of sleep."

"I had none."

"Have some coffee. I ground the beans myself."

"No, thanks. I want to go back to bed as soon as

I feel sleepy. Caffeine will keep me awake past my ability to stay awake."

"Isn't that the whole purpose?" Jake offered her a seat across the table.

Beatrice opted for a bottle of mineral water from the refrigerator.

"What are you working on?" Beatrice noticed the five o'clock shadow on his chin. He looked cute that way, but she preferred clean-shaven men.

"Making a list of everything we know and everything we don't know."

"Everything we don't know? From the beginning of time to the end of time?"

"Aren't you the genius." Jake laughed. "Sorry. I'm not in a very good mood because I didn't get enough sleep and I can't figure out why we're constantly behind Molyneux."

"You're thinking that the three years you were with her organization would have afforded you some sort of hidden cards."

Jake nodded. "Unfortunately, I have nothing and we're back to square one."

"*We* have nothing. We're in this together, aren't we?"

"Yeah, you keep saying that but are we really being transparent with each other?" Jake asked.

"What do you mean?" Beatrice really wanted

to know.

"For instance, are you or are you not the adopted daughter of Imogen Wright, also known as Molyneux?"

Might as well come clean. "Yes, but you knew that already."

"I had my suspicions. Yet back at the cabin I did not recall you saying you were—not a single time."

"I wasn't sure myself."

"What makes you think you are now?"

"When I talked to Molyneux in Dad's office." Back in Eureka the evening before, Beatrice had told her team about her conversation with Molyneux in the office, but she did not mention the leather pouch in Jake's presence because she wasn't sure how much she could trust him.

"Were you surprised she talked to you?" Jake asked.

"I thought she wasn't going to kill my brother or me. However, she confessed to killing Dad. So I'm not sure we're safe anymore." Beatrice groaned. "What a messed-up family."

"If you need support, I'm here." Jake extended his hand across the table, palm up.

It reminded her of the driveway scene at the cabin, when he was trying to get to her.

Beatrice placed her hand in his. His fingers and palm were warm to the touch.

"The good news is that I'm not her biological daughter." Beatrice retracted her hand. "I was afraid I might be. I don't know about Benjamin, though he's supposed to have been adopted."

"And yet I've said before that your smile reminded me of Molyneux. Maybe it's possible for adopted children to take after the traits and characteristics of their adoptive parents."

"I don't know." Beatrice dared not entertain the idea that Molyneux and her dad might have lied about her parentage.

"Sometimes God brings families together in ways we don't understand."

Beatrice laughed. "I don't understand why my parents are thieves, robbers, killers, murderers."

"We can't choose our parents, but we don't have to be like them."

Beatrice nodded. "I should like to think we're not like our parents, but I have a confession—or a few."

"Uh-oh." Jake put down his iPad and waited.

"I took something from the cabin office before it blew up," Beatrice said.

"What?"

"It's a small leather pouch. Inside, I found an

old San Francisco postcard and a golden key—maybe medieval, but I need to have it analyzed."

"How old is the postcard?"

"Maybe from the fifties."

"When your dad was a kid? Where was he born?"

"He was born in Connecticut to diplomat parents who then returned to Britain."

"Has he been to San Francisco a lot?"

"He would have lately, but the postcard was old —although I buy old things all the time."

"Right. So the age might not mean anything."

Beatrice didn't tell him that she had planned to scan the postcard soon.

"Where are you going to stay in Charleston?" Beatrice asked.

"Near your office so it won't take too long to get there when we plan our next move."

"I don't think we'll be in Charleston long. I hope my brother will come with us, but he's such a homebody."

"You seem to look up to him."

"I love him with all my heart. I feel that I need to protect him, even though he's five years older. I suspect he's been looking out for me in more ways than I know." She didn't say that she also believed that Kenichi worked for Benjamin.

"Your brother sounds like a nice guy. I'd like to meet him."

"He doesn't like to meet people."

"A recluse?"

"You know, sometimes parents don't realize the repercussions they leave in their children's lives." Beatrice sighed. "Ten, twenty years later, we still feel it."

"God can help us to rise above the chaos." Jake smiled. His dimples showed again. "We look to Christ, the author and perfecter of our faith."

"Hebrews 12:2. You know your scripture." Beatrice was impressed. He wasn't the only one who knew the scripture passage that made up the complete thought in that verse.

> *Therefore we also, since we are surrounded by so great a cloud of witnesses, let us lay aside every weight, and the sin which so easily ensnares us, and let us run with endurance the race that is set before us, looking unto Jesus, the author and finisher of our faith, who for the joy that was set before Him endured the cross, despising the shame, and has sat down at the right hand of the throne of God.*

"Are you a praying person?" Beatrice asked.

"Yes, ma'am. Without God, I wouldn't have survived all those years of being undercover."

Beatrice studied him. He seemed to have said that with confidence—or he had been compartmentalizing his undercover work.

"How do you live like this?" she asked. "You're one person in real life, and another undercover as part of your job."

"If I look at myself as an actor on a stage, I can see that my undercover job is a role I play. When the curtain falls, the job is done. I go to another play."

"Interesting. Are you in theater right now? Are you playing a role with us? Infiltrating my team?"

Jake looked surprised. "No. I'm all me here. Jacob Gavin Kessler. Look it up. Take my fingerprints. DNA."

"Why do you keep wanting to go after Molyneux—spare me the save-the-world talking points—when you've lost your badge, your job, your salary, due to her?"

"Are you saying I'm an underdog and I have no chance against Molyneux?"

"At this point, none of us seems to be making progress."

"So we pray for success." Jake offered his hand again.

She did not take it.

"Prayers against my wicked adoptive mother." Beatrice finished her bottled water. "Enough about my broken family. Tell me about yours."

"I come from a big family of five boys and one girl. My parents have been married for almost fifty years. They still live in Florida where they grew up. They farm the land their grandparents left them."

"Really? What do they farm?"

"Strawberries."

That surprised Beatrice. "How did a farm boy end up as an FBI agent?"

"Florida is a tourist place, as you know. Being exposed to the world at large opened our eyes to all kinds of job options. My siblings are in many professions. One missionary, one soldier, one tour guide, one teacher, one farmer—and then there's me."

"The runt?" Beatrice laughed.

"No, no. I meant that not only are my siblings happily working in the jobs they like, they are also married, and some with kids. I'm thirty-eight and single and—why am I telling you this?"

"Let me take a stab at it."

"Ouch." He winced.

"Oh sorry. I didn't mean..."

"Don't worry about it. I was only kidding. You

were saying?"

"Your family sounds like it's intact. You don't have drama or disasters. Yet you're trying to say that you have problems too."

Jake nodded. "No matter what your family is, there are always problems because we live in a world where there's sin all around us. Sin causes trouble for everyone."

"Sin nature, you mean."

"Yeah, that being the root."

"It's a good reminder for us that the battle is bigger than flesh and blood. There are forces of good and bad just duking it out."

"And we're in the middle of the warfare." Jake brightened up. "But if we can send Molyneux to jail, maybe the world will be a safer place."

"Someone else will simply fill her place."

"Not if we can help it."

"We?" Beatrice raised her eyebrows.

"We're together, remember?"

Beatrice shrugged. "I had to say something to prevent the man you called John Doe from killing you back at the cabin."

"For that, I thank you. However you meant it, don't you agree that we are indeed in business together?"

"Technically speaking."

Jake got up slowly, carrying an empty coffee mug. He shuffled on his good leg. That knife wound in his thigh must still be raw, in spite of the stitches and painkillers.

"Going for a refill?" Beatrice asked.

Jake nodded.

"Sit down. Let me get it for you." Beatrice was on her feet. She took the cup from him.

And she felt something warm on her free hand. His fingers wove into hers. His other hand reached up to touch her chin, then her neckline.

He dipped his forehead toward hers.

He smelled like fresh soap.

They stayed that way for a while, forehead to forehead. Beatrice wondered if he was asking for permission.

She lifted her lips and touched his briefly. He tasted like coffee with cream.

He took that as a "yes, you may," and bathed her with warmth that spread from his full lips to hers. The warmth lingered across her face, through her chest, and down to her toes.

Beatrice had never felt this way before with any other man. Well, it had been a while since she had a date, let alone a boyfriend.

And here was Jake, tugging at her heart.

Most unexpected.

CHAPTER TWENTY-SIX

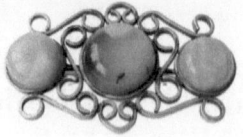

S an Francisco had been where Beatrice and Jake first met, albeit under less than ideal circumstances. Secrets hidden from each other made it hard for Jake to take Beatrice at her word.

He looked out the passenger side window of the rental car, wondering how to respond to what she had just told him to do. Maybe he was tired from the lack of sleep in the sleeper coach. Maybe his growing feelings for her interfered with his train of thought.

After arriving at the San Francisco Airport, they had moved their luggage from the entertainer coach to the Gulfstream. Beatrice and Jake rented a car to go back to the city to retrieve their brooches while Kenichi and Helen Hu's team began collaborating.

Jake's bank where he had kept the one-amber brooch was their first stop. As soon as it opened at nine o'clock, he went in. Wearing a wig under a baseball cap, Beatrice waited in the lobby.

Then they went to Beatrice's bank. This time, she did not want him to go with her.

"You want me to sit out here while you open your safe-deposit box?" he asked.

"They won't let you inside the vault anyway."

"I could sit in the AC." The weather was warm this May, although not hot. The breeze from the Pacific Ocean helped.

Yeah, Jake could sit out here and wait.

Beatrice unbuckled her seat belt. She handed Jake the car key.

"Technically, Philomena meant to give the three-amber brooch to me." Jake rolled down his window.

"Technically, she stole it from my dad. His will stated that all he ever owned belonged to my brother and me—including the one-amber brooch you now have in your pocket."

"Apparently, your dad didn't die twenty-five years ago. Does that make his will null and void?"

"Why don't you tell me, Mr. Kessler?"

"So it's Mr. Kessler now, huh? I thought we were getting to know each other on a first-name basis." Jake grinned. "Tell me one thing before you go."

Beatrice waited.

"Did our kiss last night mean anything to you? Or were we caught in the moment?"

Beatrice leaned toward him, placed her palm around his neck, and gently pulled him toward her. She touched her lips to the edge of his.

It was feather light, but Jake felt it down his spine.

Wow. "Should I be careful about you, Miss Glynn?" He smiled giddily.

"Always. If you know anything about our family, you know we love passionately."

"Then why are you still single?"

"Because I haven't found the right man. I don't want to make the same mistakes my parents did. I'm waiting for the right man God sends my way."

"Am I the one?" Maybe Jake shouldn't have asked that. A kiss did not a relationship make. Not one, not two.

"We just met—sort of. So I don't know. I need to pray about it some more. We both need to pray."

"Sort of?" Jake's eyebrows shot up. "Have we met before San Francisco?"

Beatrice pursed her lips. She got out of the car, shut the door, and joined the crowd of pedestrians on the sidewalk.

Jake watched her go.

Sort of how?

It gave him food for thought. On the sidewalk outside the car windows, a couple of homeless dudes were panhandling. One tall man was wearing too-big jeans and scruffy boots with broken shoelaces. The other man was shorter, but more muscular—like he was perhaps newly homeless and hadn't starved off those muscles yet.

Up and down the sidewalk they went. Somehow, they knew who looked like tourists and who were locals.

Ten minutes.

Twenty minutes.

The bank door opened two doors away.

Beatrice came out carrying a colorful floral crossbody bag and wearing a different baseball cap. Jake wondered if those two items had been in the safe-deposit box alongside the three-amber brooch.

She looked to her left and right, and made her way toward their parked car.

As Jake watched her, he noticed the two homeless men ambling her way. They brushed past her, and one of them produced a pocket knife—

"Watch out!" Jake yelled from the car. A sharp pain seared his thigh and he could not get out of the car quickly enough.

The man with the knife took off running with the bag as Beatrice shouted for help.

Jake pulled himself out of the passenger seat. He leaned against the car and winced. When he looked up, Beatrice had the other homeless man in a chokehold as she kicked him in the groin.

The homeless man doubled over on the sidewalk and moaned.

"Help! He stole my purse!" Beatrice sprinted after Mr. Knife.

Hobbling toward the homeless man on the sidewalk, Jake called 911. He had never felt so helpless in his life. Fortunately, several tourists saw the situation and came to his aid.

They pinned down the homeless man until the SFPD arrived mere minutes later.

"He and his buddy tried to steal that lady's purse." Someone pointed toward Beatrice, who was jogging back.

"Lost him. My purse is gone." She leaned against a pole to catch her breath.

After they gave their statements to the police office, Beatrice and Jake left for the airport.

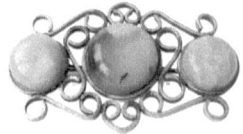

CHAPTER TWENTY-SEVEN

" **I** should have gone into the bank with you."
It might be one of the few things he
regretted in life, but Jake felt it all the
more now that his feelings for Beatrice had grown
stronger. "Next time don't tell me no."

"It's my fault now?" Beatrice kept her eyes on
the road as she drove the rental car.

"I'm not blaming you. After what happened at
the cabin..." Jake shook his head. "I should have
gone with you."

"Like you said, I told you no."

"Thank God you're okay."

Beatrice nodded.

"Tell me your three-amber brooch isn't in the

stolen purse," Jake said as Beatrice stopped at a red light.

"In my jeans pocket." Beatrice didn't show him, though.

He didn't press for it. "Whew."

"You don't trust me? Did you assume I put it in my brightly-colored crossbody bag?" Beatrice talked as she listened to the navigator on her phone telling her how to get to the private airport.

Jake sighed. "I'm guessing there's more."

"There's something valuable in the crossbody bag." Before she could continue, her hands-free phone rang. It was Ken.

"Got it, Bee." Ken hung up without fanfare.

"Isn't it nice to have employees who instinctively know that I'm driving and can't read text messages so they call me to tell me three words and then hang up?"

Jake brushed aside Beatrice's question to ask one of his own. "What did he get, exactly?"

"There are two brooches in a pretty box inside the crossbody bag. That's what Molyneux wants."

"A box? The brooch box that no one could find?"

"I didn't spend the last five years looking for that box for nothing." She paused. "Let me correct that. My brother, my team, and I. I don't usually operate alone."

"The real box?"

"Yes, with some modifications."

Jake understood. "You inserted a GPS tracker into the box."

"Ken did."

"The two brooches in there, though..."

"Are fake, of course."

"Will it blow up?"

"No. You can't board a plane with an explosive."

"I knew that, but how sure are you they will fly out of the country?" Jake asked.

"Because the rest of the Amber Room is not in the United States. At least we hope not."

So many unanswered questions. "Let's backtrack a bit. Did you know those two homeless men were fakes?"

Beatrice shook her head. "I figured as soon as Molyneux knew I was here, she would deflect her personnel toward me."

"I don't want you to get hurt."

"It's a bit late for that, isn't it?"

What did she mean by that? Jake waited for an explanation, but Beatrice drove on in silence.

Jake did not push her. He could be a patient

man. He had been hunting for Molyneux for a few years now. He had been trained to wait patiently—for a few more minutes.

"I saw those two men as I was entering the bank." Beatrice went in another direction with the conversation. "However, I could not assume they were not genuinely homeless, you know?"

"I'm sorry I wasn't nimble on my feet."

"Are you sure you don't want to go home and rest that leg for a few days? I'll text you if we find anything."

Jake laughed. "Not a chance. I'll just wrap more gauze on it, and pray to God the stitches will hold."

"I don't want you to take too many painkillers. Maybe you should switch to Tylenol or something OTC."

Jake reached for her arm. "Are you my nurse practitioner now?"

At the green light, Beatrice went straight through instead of turning right. The nice British lady on the phone told her to turn around.

"Airport is that way, isn't it?" Jake remembered their first trip there this morning on the coach.

"I think we're being followed."

Jake peeked at the side rearview mirror. "That black truck?"

"It's been right behind us since we left the bank."

"Then it's too obvious."

"I wish Ken and Ray were a hundred percent well. I could use them right now."

"What about me? I'm here." Jake realized he wasn't much help with a bad leg. "I'm sorry I'm no use until my leg heals."

"Don't sell yourself short. Not every battle requires a sword. In some cases, it's a battle of the mind." Beatrice glanced in her rearview mirror. "Is the truck still there?"

"It's gone." Jake was happy to report that. "It veered off."

"Oh. Maybe I was mistaken." She still gripped the steering wheel. She leaned forward.

"It's okay to be careful."

"To be honest, I'm freaked out right now. If Ken and Ray were here, I'd worry less. I pay them to drive and shoot." She laughed nervously.

"You and your team..."

"What?"

"...are a mystery to me."

"So are you, Mr. Kessler."

"Let's dispense with the mister and missus— oops, a slip of the tongue. I meant mister and miss."

Beatrice seemed to mull over what he said.

"Matthew 12:34 says, 'For out of the abundance of the heart the mouth speaks.' I wonder if you really made a faux pas."

"Please don't read too much into it." Even as he spoke it, Jake knew that his feelings for Beatrice were getting stronger by the hour as they spent more time together.

He prayed that it wasn't a fleeting feeling. A crush of some sort. After all, she was a woman of mystery who suddenly showed up after twenty-five years of hiding, rescued him several times, and then confessed that she was indeed the daughter of the infamous treasure hunter, Chisolm Wright, as well as the world's most wanted criminal, Molyneux.

How could any one person be so unfortunate?

And yet there were two of them: Beatrice and her older brother.

In the three years that Jake had infiltrated Molyneux's organization and rose through the ranks, he had never once heard Molyneux or the people close to her mention her adopted children. What he knew, he had learned from Helen Hu's sleuthing ability. Court documents provided the rest. How Helen had obtained those files, he could not begin to ask.

In the driver's seat, Beatrice drew a deep breath and her shoulders relaxed. She lifted a hand away from the steering wheel to wipe sweat off her forehead.

Jake saw how much her hand trembled. He reached out to hold it.

"I can't drive with one hand," Beatrice said.

"Cruise control?"

"Never used it in my life." She pointed to the highway sign. "The airport is up ahead. We'll be out of here soon."

"I can't wait for this entire nightmare to be over." Jake looked out the window.

"And I can't wait to go home. I haven't seen my brother in six months..." Her words tapered off, as if saying more would be to give away secrets.

"Tell me about your brother," Jake said. "Maybe if we talk about happy things, it will get our minds off what happened today."

"My brother is paranoid times a thousand." She laughed. "That about sums him up."

"You love him very much. I can tell."

Beatrice nodded. "We've been through a lot together. He was adopted when he was two years old, and when he was five, I joined the family."

"I'm gathering you had happy days."

"Well, they left us some old DVDs of our park days, field trips, vacations, and holidays. Do you still remember DVDs?"

"Yes. And CDs."

"Ha. Those too. Yeah, they left us DVDs of the first five years of my life in the Wright household. Turned out that Mom and Dad quarreled a lot away from our presence. Whenever they were with us, we were always happy, especially when they were filming us to make the memory DVDs."

"Did your brother have his special events recorded before you were born?"

"Yeah. He was a very pampered only child for five years."

"I have four brothers and one sister," Jake said. "I have no idea what it means to be an only child."

"Six kids, huh?" Beatrice parked the car. "You'll have to tell me more about your family sometime."

"Over dinner, perhaps?" Jake asked. No regrets.

"Perhaps." Beatrice got out of the car and closed the door. "However, at this time, my immediate problems are more than I can handle."

Jake limped alongside Beatrice as they walked to the aircraft hangar. "If there's anything I can do for you, let me know."

"You can pray for all of us, Jake."

Prayer.

That should have crossed his mind first, Jake

thought. Yet it hadn't. All he had thought of was physically helping Beatrice himself.

She needed as much spiritual help as she did physical—although all help came from God above.

Jake felt bad that he hadn't been a spiritual encourager to Beatrice. What if God had placed him there for such a time as this? Perhaps Beatrice needed reminders that God was still sovereign over all her troubles?

Quietly, Jake asked God to forgive him.

"Amen," he whispered after he finished his quick prayer.

"Pardon?" Beatrice asked. "Did you say something?"

"I was thinking that every bit of help we get is from God."

"Indeed."

"Psalm 121:1-2 comes to mind. 'I will lift up my eyes to the hills—From whence comes my help? My help comes from the Lord, who made heaven and earth.' I've tried to memorize this verse."

"Thank you for the reminder that God is my provider. I need to hear that today."

"Same here."

"I need to read my Bible more," she added, without explaining further.

"Me too, Beatrice. Me too."

CHAPTER TWENTY-EIGHT

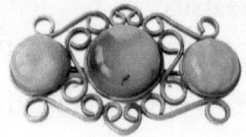

enjamin's face became increasingly redder onscreen as Beatrice explained what had happened outside the San Francisco bank. "What on earth, Bee?"

It sounded like the beginning of a rant, so it was best to let him start and finish, even though Beatrice had heard it all.

I don't want to lose my baby sister.

Benjamin was only five years older than her, but ever since they had been abandoned by both adoptive parents—one could say they had been abandoned twice at that point—Benjamin had felt a heavy responsibility for his sister.

"You keep getting in harm's way." On the other side of the videoconference call, Benjamin leaned forward on his favorite couch and stared into the camera.

Oddly enough, his voice softened. "I know you two had to get the brooches from two different banks, but you could at least have some protection. I should have sent someone."

"It's not your fault." Beatrice was surprised that her brother blamed himself. "I didn't fill you in enough to make it your fault."

"I could have figured it out."

"Yeah?"

"There was plenty of time. You had to wait for that FBI dude to check out of the hospital. It took another five hours to drive from Eureka to San Francisco. I could have flown someone there on commercial to meet you, regardless of what your situation was."

It was all true, but it was too late now. "What's done is done, as they say. Maybe you can send some extra personnel to meet us in Paris, considering that Ken has a broken leg and Ray a broken arm."

Beatrice could have made the order for additional security herself, since she owned part of Glynn, Inc. However, Benjamin had been cooped up in the mansion for years, unable to set foot outside their property line. This would give him something to do. Make him feel useful.

"Okay. I'll send Ansel and his team."

"Thank you. Of course, we don't know if the brooch box will end up in Paris, but meeting there will get us closer to wherever we need to go." Beatrice leaned back in her office chair.

She was feeling tired, like she needed a nap or something, but she wasn't going to rest until the plane took off. There was a slight delay as they waited for the extra food the flight attendant had ordered for them.

"I was reviewing your report on what happened in Eureka," Benjamin said. "Maybe you shouldn't have told them who you are."

Beatrice knew what he was referring to. "They were going to hurt Jake."

"You felt you had to stall."

Beatrice nodded.

"You felt sorry for him because they had tortured him six months ago."

Beatrice nodded again, and then realized what Benjamin was driving at.

"You felt this and that. It was all feelings, Bee."

That was another big difference between the two siblings. Benjamin was all head and no heart. Beatrice ran the risk of being all heart and...no head?

She was sure she had made each decision in California rationally.

"I should've stopped you from tracking Helen Hu and the FBI." Benjamin grunted. He did that when he regretted something big.

"That's how we discovered that the FBI has a mole, Ben. We're doing them a favor."

"And that makes it all worthwhile for you?"

Getting to know Jake was worthwhile, but she wouldn't tell her brother that. It was early in their relationship—if there was one.

"I told you before that you need to rein in your feelings. You crossed the line when you called Helen in Cannes."

"I couldn't let Jake drown."

"Listen to yourself. You said earlier that you didn't want them to hurt Jake. That's twice that you went out of your way—way out—to rescue a man you don't know."

Didn't know.

She didn't want to correct him. It would invite more questions about her feelings for Jake.

"If Dad were here, he'd probably say that we need to work on patience and not desperation," Benjamin said.

"Ben, you don't know what he would say. It has been twenty-five years since we last saw him."

"My observation still stands. Are you desperate?"

"No."

"Making yourself bait is not desperate?"

Bait.

An ugly word.

"We have hidden for twenty-five years from Molyneux." He would never call her Mom again. "If we're patient, we'll defeat her sooner or later. There's no need to rush."

"Eureka was the closest we got to her," Beatrice explained. "My best guess is that they didn't know we were following Jake, and when they realized it, they had no idea who we were. We were sort of a ragtag group in a plumber van."

Beatrice admitted that giving herself away had accelerated the problem. She didn't know whether her team had the wherewithal to handle the sudden turn of events.

"Like they say, what's done is done." Benjamin threw up his hands in the air.

Beatrice laughed.

"What's so funny?"

"We're repeating a phrase with dubious origin. Who are the *they* who said that first?"

"Yeah. We say things we don't understand fully. It could be a parody for all we know."

Benjamin drew a deep breath. "In any case, thank God that you're alive."

"I'll talk to you again before we reach Paris."

"I still can't believe all the things that happened to you in the last couple of days," Benjamin said. "Most of all, I can't believe Ken rigged the brooch. It could've killed you if it had exploded in your pocket."

"We had to use the magic words to activate it." Beatrice meant for it to be a joke, but neither of them laughed. Life and death were serious matters.

"And then the brooch box. Whose idea was it to rig that?"

"Well, it was my idea to make it a GPS, but it wasn't an original idea. I had read about the Petros eggs that Helen and her mother uncovered. You remember that? They had GPSs on them."

"Thereby destroying the value of the set of eggs."

"And saving the lives of Helen and her mother."

"So you think if it worked then, it would work now."

"No harm trying."

Benjamin made a face. "I should have been there with you to keep you safe."

"God kept us safe."

"I know, but I could have been part of the team on the ground."

"You can join us in Paris."

"Ah." He looked disturbed, as though he had been asked to do the impossible. "I'll try."

Even as he said it, Beatrice knew he wouldn't go. Something had happened to him over the years. Something had made him stay home, away from the public, for so long.

Beatrice wished she knew what had happened to Benjamin while she had been away at university.

Who did this to my brother?

Perhaps someday, Benjamin would tell his own story.

CHAPTER TWENTY-NINE

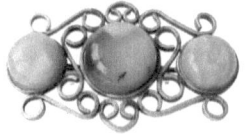

After the meal carts were loaded onto the Gulfstream G650, the jet lifted off for Paris, which Beatrice had determined to be the best place for them to wait for the signal from the brooch box.

Jake noticed that there were two flight attendants who took turns serving the meals and cleaning up afterwards. He assumed they had been properly vetted before being allowed on the private jet.

Kenichi made a remark to him that Beatrice could have hired a cook for the kitchen on board, but since everyone basically ate soup, sandwiches, or microwaved dinners on their flights around the world, Beatrice had saved the money.

Jake couldn't complain about the free ride and meals. When the flight attendant took his order, he asked for a tray of cheese and crackers, figuring he'd eat lunch later—perhaps with Beatrice.

She had gone to her private room to take a nap, leaving Jake bereft of her company. She had made him feel at ease, welcomed him into her team, as though they had been friends for a while.

In the main cabin, he kicked off his shoes and reclined on the leather seat by the window. He sat alone in this space with his burner phone. Kenichi was in the conference room with his computers. Raynelle had disappeared somewhere.

As Jake had stopped taking painkillers this morning, he felt the tight stitches in his thigh. He prayed for quick healing and for no infections to set in.

He texted Earl via an encrypted virtual private network beyond the walls of the airplane. It would have been easier to chat with Earl if Jake had his iPad, but it was way back in the sleeping quarters, and he didn't feel like limping there and back.

A small dinky phone would have to do.

Notwithstanding his injuries, Earl Young was living the life. Helen had sent a limousine to take him from the hospital to a small airport nearby. There, he would board a puddle jumper to San

Francisco where he'd fly home to Savannah in first-class.

Jake thanked God that Earl was recovering from his gunshot wound to the gut. It seemed worse than it sounded, the way Earl described it.

In spite of all that, his friend would live.

Thank God.

Sadly, Helen had removed Earl from the project. The next few weeks of his life would be spent hanging out on the beaches of Tybee Island, where he lived in an oceanfront cottage facing the Atlantic Ocean.

Jake would be alone until Helen sent a new partner—if she did at all, and if the project lasted that long. He anticipated another two weeks with Beatrice.

And then they would part ways.

He prayed that he wouldn't show poor skills in front of her.

He caught himself.

He reminded himself that he should do his best for God rather than for a woman he barely knew...

Whom he had kissed in the coach to San Francisco.

What did Beatrice think about their moment together? Did the kiss mean anything to her?

She hadn't asked for anything else. That said something, didn't it?

In fact, since then, she had talked to him the same way she talked to Kenichi, as platonic friends.

Jake wanted more.

So much more.

Perhaps he could start by learning about Beatrice. What she liked, disliked. Who her family really was. Her brother, for example.

At some time during the flight, they were scheduled to have an in-flight meeting with Benjamin Glynn. Jake looked forward to that even though he wasn't sure what his own contributions were, other than the one-amber brooch that Philomena had given him.

That posed a dilemma. How could he prepare for a meeting he was unprepared for?

He could check his email to see if Helen had anything for him. He scrolled through his email, and found a long rigamarole Helen had sent him hours before.

As the plane cruised at an altitude above 40,000 feet, Jake pored over Helen's notes about Chisolm Wright's children. The information obtained by the FBI ended twenty-five years prior.

On that note, he sent another encrypted email

to his friend inside the bureau. He wanted to know if Stella Evans had found the mole.

And he complained to himself about his phone again. The phone screen was small and he spent a lot of time scrolling through Helen's meticulous notes. The ever-intrepid private investigator had found the rest of the missing Wright years.

Jake sifted through the photographs of Beatrice at the prom in high school with a date, her years in college and the master's program, studying World War II history.

He paid particular attention to her personal life, noting that she had never been married. She spent most of her career hunting for treasures lost in world wars.

A career woman.

And he, a career man.

Jake had never married either. Almost thirty-nine, he had spent most of his adult life in the employ of the FBI. At some point, he would like to settle down, but with whom? He'd have to trust God to provide the best partner in life for him.

The door to the conference room swung open. Kenichi limped out on his crutches. "All roads lead to Paris, right?"

Since Jake was the only one there, he assumed

Kenichi had directed the question to him. "I don't know. You tell me."

"Oh no. Not this time." He limped forward, trying not to put pressure on his broken leg in a cast.

"Where does the road lead?"

Kenichi kept walking. "Let me check with Bee, and we'll know for sure."

"She's taking a nap." Jake tried to be helpful.

"I'll wake her up." He made his way toward some closed doors. "She's going to want to hear this."

Jake wondered how he knew which sleeper cabin was Beatrice's. And then he remembered that those two had worked together for years.

Still. "If she's asleep..."

"She'll let me in. I'm her second big brother. By the way, if anybody hurts her, Benjamin and I will go after them with a big stick."

That sounded like a threat.

Halfway down the aisle, Kenichi stopped and knocked on the door. Jake couldn't hear what Beatrice said from behind the closed door, if she said anything at all. But he stared when Kenichi turned the knob and went inside.

A lump of jealousy dislodged from Jake's heart and rolled onto the floor.

He heard two voices now. At least they had left the door open.

He quickly returned to his phone with a "so what" look on his face. His ears were perked, listening to what Beatrice was saying. He glanced up to find her knocking on another door. Raynelle's?

Inside the cabin there was a perpetual sound—something like a loud air-conditioner—that muffled distant voices. Even though the Gulfstream was smaller than a commercial airliner Jake had flown in, the distance between him and the two of them was still far enough away that he could not make out what they were saying to each other.

Thankfully, the voices came closer.

"Jake?"

Jake looked up, trying to be nonchalant. He wasn't sure why he was this way. If his older brothers could see him now, they'd never let him hear the end of it.

"Meeting in five," Beatrice said.

Jake barely looked at her. He couldn't help himself. Never in his life had he experienced such a feeling, as if only he could want her, have her, and no one else.

He couldn't recall his last girlfriend making him go topsy-turvy like this.

What's happening to me?

When Beatrice smiled at him, his eyes clouded over. He knew then that he would protect her at all costs.

"Jake," Beatrice said his name again, softly this time.

Without waiting for him to reply, Beatrice leaned down and kissed his forehead.

"What was that for?" Jake managed a smile even as he was all undone inside.

"A stamp of approval." Beatrice laughed.

"A what?"

She waltzed off. "See you at the meeting. Don't be late."

Jake felt all warm and fuzzy and all giddy inside.

A stamp of approval.

That woman is full of surprises.

CHAPTER THIRTY

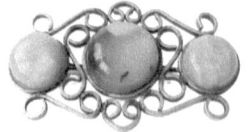

" They could have put it in a Faraday bag," Kenichi said, trying to explain why the signal was lost over the Pacific Ocean. "No signals go in and out of the bag."

Across from him, Raynelle walked in, her hair all askew. Beatrice felt bad that they'd had to wake her up. Beatrice wanted Raynelle to be in the meetings so she would know what was going on firsthand. That way, Benjamin would have nothing to say about Raynelle being only a bodyguard.

She was more than a bodyguard. Beatrice considered Raynelle an invaluable member of her team. She wished that Benjamin would at least be nice to Raynelle, whether or not he liked her.

"Where are they heading?" Jake asked.

He was sitting next to Beatrice. In fact, he had followed her to the conference room and sat down after she did so that he could choose to sit next to her. Whenever Kenichi talked, he reached over to pat her thigh.

It was most distracting.

Surely it could not be because Jake had seen Kenichi enter her cabin. Surely not that?

Perhaps Jake didn't know that there was nothing going on between Beatrice and Kenichi. They were only professional colleagues.

As far as relationships were concerned, Beatrice was open to Jake. They were two single people without any attachments.

And yet she wanted to wait for God.

Just in case Jake was not the one.

Like Benjamin said, Beatrice had to be careful about thinking with her heart and feeling with her head. She didn't want to do anything that she would regret later.

"We know that all roads lead to Paris," Kenichi said. "That's Molyneux's Rome."

"So why the circuitous route over the Pacific?" Jake asked. "To throw us off?"

"Or to show a buyer," Beatrice said. "We know from extensive research that Molyneux wouldn't pass up making a buck."

"Isn't the brooch box a reproduction?" Jake asked.

Beatrice nodded. "It is, but do you know who made it for us?"

Jake shook his head.

"The same jeweler who made the original amber brooches in 1976. He wrote down everything he did and he photographed the original."

"When we explained to him why we needed a second set of amber brooches, he became interested in redeeming his reputation—and possibly himself," Kenichi said.

"It must have cost you a fortune." Jake turned to Beatrice.

"There was no other choice. Everyone has tried to get Molyneux. What if we have a practical way take her down?" Beatrice asked. "I want her alive to stand trial. In prison, she might have more opportunities to repent and seek God's forgiveness for all the many murders she had ordered over the years."

"That's what we told the jeweler," Raynelle added.

"It was the truth." Beatrice leaned back in the office chair.

"Unfortunately, it got the jeweler killed two days later." Kenichi shook his head. "Such a waste. He was super talented."

"The good news is that before he died, he told us what we need to do next, but we need all three brooches for the hidden code to be visible." Beatrice tapped her iPad and showed it to Jake.

He leaned toward the iPad. "What am I seeing here?"

"The design of the original brooches. We're missing one." She pointed to the empty tray in the middle of the sketch. "There is a latch, and underneath is an engraved map."

"That missing brooch is the key."

"Who told the jeweler to put the map in the brooches?" Jake scrunched his eyebrows together.

"Dad. He must have thought that would get Molyneux out of his hair," Beatrice said.

"The jeweler told you that, right? Can you believe him at all?"

Beatrice wondered what was going on in Jake's mind. "Five years and ten million dollars later, the information better be good or we'll be set back ten years in our search for the Amber Room."

"Well, you've certainly done more work than my entire division combined."

Beatrice didn't answer him. Truth be told, she was weary. She wanted this to be the last job she did with Benjamin. After this, she wanted to find a community college somewhere and teach. Teaching seemed like a stable job with a stable income—not that she needed either one. The trust fund their second adoptive parents left them was enough to take care of them for the rest of their lives.

Beatrice sighed. "I'm assuming you still have your one-amber brooch?"

"Yes. In my pocket."

"What a safe place that is." Kenichi rolled his eyes.

"We have a safe in my office," Beatrice offered. "An actual safe built into the wall."

Jake didn't reply. Instead, he asked, "Where's the original brooch box?"

Kenichi looked up from his laptop. "No one knows. If Chisolm were alive today, he might be able to tell us."

"A lot of things have been lost to history," Beatrice said. "For all we know, searching for the Amber Room is fruitless. Yet all we really want is to be the first to get there for leverage against Molyneux. I pray she will be arrested peacefully."

"She wants the Amber Room so badly that it will be a trap for her," Jake said.

"Exactly."

"Did she kill your dad for it?"

Beatrice nodded. "I wonder how many times she tried."

"How do you know that Molyneux hasn't found the Amber Room, or at least more pieces of it?"

"No one could find all the panels," Raynelle said. She hadn't said much in the meeting, so when she did say something, Beatrice listened.

Kenichi nodded. "For all we know, the original Amber Room is lost. The Russians seem to think so. They're happy with their reproduction."

"I still can't imagine a chamber where the walls were made entirely of carved amber." Jake shook his head.

"The ceiling too," Beatrice added.

The eighteenth-century chamber had been a gift from the King of Prussia to Peter the Great of Russia. There it remained until Nazi Germany got wind of it in World War II. Apparently, the Russians failed to protect the room, and everything in it had been lost to the war.

Or had it?

"If we don't find the Amber Room or parts of it, will we lose our trail to Molyneux?" Jake asked.

"That's where you come in." Beatrice gently tapped Jake's arm, then wondered if she should have. "You interrupted her quest."

"I did?"

"You made her look like a fool, infiltrating her organization for three years," Kenichi added.

"Yep." Beatrice nodded. "She's going to make an example out of you. She targeted you as a lesson for everyone."

Jake's shoulders sagged. "Am I putting you all in danger?"

"We're past that." Beatrice almost reached for Jake again, but she kept her hands to herself. "You're one of us now. We're in this together. Business, you know?"

"And more," Jake mouthed.

But Beatrice read his lips.

CHAPTER THIRTY-ONE

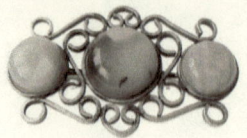

Beatrice had a late lunch at two o'clock, and Jake joined her in the galley kitchen as they heated up frozen dinners in the microwave. Beatrice went for chicken tikka masala. Jake opted for chicken pot pie.

Neither of them wanted the assistance of the flight attendant, who was loading the compact dishwasher nearby. In fact, Beatrice told her to get some rest since the flight to Paris would be long.

Jake was happy not to have a third wheel in the kitchen. He wanted every opportunity to be alone with Beatrice.

To talk.

Jake tried to contain his heartbeats—if it was possible to do so—but their proximity to each other in the kitchen made him want to wrap his arms around Beatrice's waist for some reason. At this moment in time, he didn't understand himself.

Stay calm.

He watched Beatrice press the timer on the microwave. In his mind, he wondered what life must be like living on the road—or in an airplane—all year round. He wondered if someday Beatrice might stop flying around and maybe...

Settle down?

He cleared his throat.

"You must be wondering why we're eating frozen dinners when we could afford this Gulfstream." Beatrice leaned against a stainless-steel cabinet. She pointed to the unused stove nearby.

Jake shrugged himself out of his other train of thought. "Sometimes I get home to my apartment famished. There's no time to cook anything, so I get a takeout or I pop something in the microwave or I make a PBJ."

There, he'd admitted it. There were evenings when he made do with a peanut butter and jelly sandwich only because he had no time to cook or even get a takeout. Work could take over his life, like it had the last three years.

He couldn't help it. He liked to work.

"I like PBJ. Comfort food," Beatrice said. "What's your jam?"

"Blueberry."

"Strawberry for me."

"What's your bread?" The microwave pinged. Beatrice took her food out and handed Jake the unlined paper plate that he could cover his bowl with.

He put his chicken pot pie in the microwave. "Wheat or whatever I have."

"I prefer sourdough or sprouted bread—like Ezekiel bread."

"Fancy." Jake said. He opened the refrigerator and looked inside. "What do you want to drink?"

"Water, please."

"Mineral water or plain?"

"Mineral." Beatrice stirred her food. "Still a bit cold. I'll put it in after yours."

Jake wanted to offer to take his dish out of the microwave so that she could put hers in, but maybe that was too much work. Two more minutes to go, and she could wait.

"Is there anything stronger than water and soda? My eyes are about to close on me." Jake laughed. "I need some caffeine."

"Or a nap if you feel sleepy. Just saying."

"I don't want to miss out on our meeting with

your brother." It was the truth. "Do you think he will postpone the meeting so I could get some shut-eye?"

"I doubt it."

"I figured. So where can I get some tea or coffee? Regular, preferably." Jake looked around.

Beatrice pointed to a cabinet near them and then to the coffee maker. "There's a button on it where you can get hot water."

"Would you like a cup of tea?" Jake asked.

"No, thanks. I only drink loose leaf tea and they don't have it on board today." She waited for Jake to take out his plate from the microwave.

"So why didn't you ask for it?"

"Well, here's the thing with caffeine. It keeps me awake. It gives me a false notion that I'm able to keep going, when in reality, I need to be resting or sleeping if I'm tired."

"I know what you mean." Jake swapped out the plate and put hers back into the microwave.

Just then the plane shook a bit.

"Turbulence?" Jake said just before the captain came on the PA system apologizing like it was his fault the turbulence happened.

"Do you fly a lot?" Jake had guessed the answer himself, but he wanted to make small talk with Beatrice to keep her engaged.

Beatrice nodded. "I'm tired of it, to be honest. What wouldn't I do for a home-cooked meal at the house."

"The call of work is strong." Jake put two tea bags into a ceramic mug and poured hot water over it. He stirred the water, pressing down the tea bags to extract the flavor.

"It's waning for me," Beatrice said. "After we turn Molyneux over to you—or the FBI since you don't have your badge—I will retire from the field."

This, Jake had to hear. "You're thinking of a career change."

"I can't until my brother takes my place and lets me stay home. He won't leave the house and I can't make him." Beatrice folded her arms across her chest. "If we both stay home—at the office—we don't have anyone to send to the field."

"Kenichi and Raynelle?"

"They have special skills, yes, but they're in supporting roles. No one is going to think like Benjamin or me."

Jake removed Beatrice's dinner from the microwave. Beatrice placed two trays on the counter. Jake offered to carry both of them. "Just show the way."

Beatrice grabbed a couple of apples from a fruit basket on their way out of the galley kitchen.

When they sat down in the main cabin, Jake asked if he could say a blessing.

"Go ahead. We're both Christians here."

"So you knew I'm a believer." Jake didn't reach out for her hand, just in case it sent the wrong signal.

Wrong signal?

And what might that be?

Jake had no idea himself.

"Research goes both ways," Beatrice replied.

"How much do you know about me?"

"Enough."

That was all she said.

"How about you say grace first?"

"Okay. Sorry." He closed his eyes. "Lord Jesus, thank You for this food. I pray that You will provide nourishment and healing for our bodies. I pray that You will give us a safe flight to Paris."

Then Jake went on, thanking God for their lives and their salvation. He asked for divine help to "defeat the enemy of humankind."

"Amen." Beatrice drank some water first. "Whoa. Your prayer sounded like we were marching into a battlefield against a vicious enemy."

"God is the Lord of the Army, after all."

"Good point." Beatrice started eating.

"So you travel the world to find stolen treasures to return to their rightful owners," Jake said. He could eat pretty fast but he slowed down now so that he could talk with Beatrice.

"You've done your research. Very good."

"Helen's team did, while I was trying not to get stabbed and killed."

"Well, I delegate research too. My brother and Kenichi dig up most of the information, and then I go out there to track down the artifacts. Most of the time we find lost paintings and family heirlooms. But we're limited to only World War II treasures. Did you know that billions of dollars' worth of artwork was stolen during the war?"

"Could you hire more people to help you?" Jake thought the chicken pot pie tasted good, although the chunks of white potato would surely find their way onto his waistline if he didn't exercise it off.

"We don't want to add more people—at least, I don't."

"How does it work?" Jake asked. "Do people pay you to find their lost treasures?"

"We take a percentage of the appraised value for our hard work."

"I'm sure it's very hard work. Has anyone ever attempted to kill you?" Jake asked it in jest. Surely hunting for treasures couldn't be as hard as working as an FBI Special Agent.

"Countless times."

"No kidding." Well, he took back his assumption.

"It means a lot to the heirs to see their family heirloom returned to their home."

"So you risk life and limb for them."

"It's worth it."

The afternoon sun shone in through the airplane window on Beatrice's hair. In the sunlight, there were strawberry blonde strands among the brown in her hair. Her eyes were brown too. They were soft and kind. Gentle eyes.

Like she was the most fragile woman in the world.

And yet, Jake knew she wasn't frail.

She had entered a giant forest at night to rescue him and Earl. It took a lot of bravery for her to risk her own life.

And then the dagger incident. She had distracted John Doe away from his plan. Jake was almost certain that if Beatrice hadn't done that, he would have been dead by now, or at least badly wounded.

Jake finished his chicken pot pie. He sipped hot tea. "We're very much alike in several ways."

"Yeah?" Beatrice also finished her lunch.

"Uh-huh. We both like to help people. We're happiest when we can truly help someone else."

"That's why you joined the FBI." Beatrice pointed at him.

Jake nodded. "However, the last three years have been frustrating."

"Because you couldn't help the world."

"Well, if you put it that way..."

"Maybe your goal was too lofty there. You wanted to take down Molyneux's organization. It's a formidable task."

"Not to be done alone, I know. There are many people working together." Jake sighed. "Still, it's been fruitless."

"Not altogether." Beatrice smiled. "We met. We joined forces. We can do this."

"With God's help." Jake didn't mean to correct her or anything. He merely spoke what was in his heart. If it wasn't for God, he wouldn't be here today. And neither would Beatrice.

"Of course. And at the end of the day, God gets the credit."

"Amen."

CHAPTER THIRTY-TWO

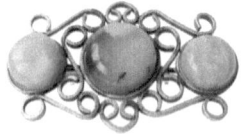

I n spite of feeling like she could use a nap after lunch, Beatrice decided to work in her office instead. It was her brother's office, but he had never used it. In fact, it had been his idea that the family Gulfstream would function as a flying laboratory with enough tools to help her get to her objective.

The jet also came with a satellite-driven ultra-high-speed secure internet connection, which enabled them to be all over the internet while cruising at forty thousand feet in the air.

While Kenichi was busy teaming up with Helen Hu's hacker associates to track the fake brooch box and find other ways to uncover Molyneux's actual physical location, Beatrice had started feeding the photograph of the golden key through their extensive worldwide database of old keys to narrow down its potential origin.

Thanks to Benjamin, they had access to many types of databases, from old doors to old roads to paintings to keys. Beatrice used to think they were trivial databases, but she had changed her mind after several successful matches in the past.

The jet was still flying over the United States, and somewhere at the back of her mind, Beatrice hoped to get a call from Benjamin asking to join the search party. If he did, they'd make a slight detour to Charleston to pick him up.

It would be a long shot, but a sister could wish.

Beatrice had been trying to get Benjamin to leave the house—even for coffee—but he had refused. For years he had been cooped up inside the sprawling ten-thousand-acre estate. Walking about in the gardens wasn't the same as leaving the gates and driving to town.

What was her brother afraid of?

All Beatrice could do was pray for Benjamin, for him to turn over his fears to God.

She looked up at her large monitor anchored to her table. Onscreen, thousands of keys appeared, one after another, an ultra-fast slide show with no ending.

"How could it be this hard to find a match?" Beatrice asked.

"I don't know. You tell me." Leaning against the doorframe, Jake looked as though he needed more sleep.

"How was your nap?"

"Too short, but I didn't want to miss out. What have you got?" He hobbled toward the desk.

Beatrice pointed to the screen. "Nothing yet. You missed nothing."

"Do you have to sit here and stare at that?" Jake chuckled.

"Probably not, but I'm a bit anxious. We have nothing to go on at this moment, and we're flying to Paris."

"With no plan?"

"Well, we have a plan. It's the getting-there we need to polish." Beatrice knew that Molyneux was waiting for them. She wasn't sure how it would end.

"Where's the postcard?" Jake asked.

"On the side table over there."

Beatrice watched Jake shuffle to the armchair. "How's your leg?"

"It's better than it looks." Jake sat down. "I just don't want to put too much pressure on it before we get to Molyneux so I don't end up sitting out the championship match, you know?"

"Hope the stitches hold."

"I think they are the heavy-duty kind."

"Still, it seems to me that you need to take some time off to heal." Beatrice hoped he didn't misunderstand her concern.

"I should, but after this is over." He flipped the postcard front and back and then checked the sides. "I don't know much about postcards from the fifties, but are they usually made this thick?"

Beatrice went around the desk. "Maybe some were? I've seen postcards made of plastic and wood."

"Maybe we should x-ray this." Jake handed it to Beatrice.

When she took the postcard from him, their fingers met. Beatrice tried not to think about it, but the touch was another reminder that she felt attracted to him.

The way Jake looked at her made her think that the feeling was mutual.

But we have here a project between us.

Beatrice sighed.

"What's the matter?" Jake asked.

She lifted the postcard to the reading light, seemingly ignoring him. It was perhaps best not to pursue this further. She had known him for a year, but he didn't need to know that.

It all came to a head six months ago when she had tracked him all the way to the ocean and called for help.

Perhaps she felt lonely. Treasure hunting could be a lonely business.

Jake tried again. "What's on your mind?"

"This postcard might have an extra layer inside," Beatrice said. "But what if I'm wrong? We'd ruin the postcard taking it apart."

Slowly, Jake got up from the armchair. He touched her arm and then interlocked his fingers in hers.

The office door was still open, but Beatrice didn't care. She liked the feel of his warm hand.

"Tell me what you were thinking just now when you sighed," Jake almost whispered.

"Nothing important." Not to the project, anyway.

After this, Jake would probably get his badge back and return to the FBI. Beatrice would continue her work.

"I'm listening," Jake said.

"Are you prying?"

"I wouldn't be if I thought there was nothing between us."

There was something. But... Where would they go from here?

"Maybe there's nothing between us," Beatrice finally said.

"Do you believe that?"

She couldn't reply.

"I didn't think so. Otherwise you wouldn't have let me hold your hand."

Beatrice smiled. "That means a lot to you, I suppose."

"I don't usually go around holding people's hands, if you must know." Jake stepped closer. "Nor do I go around doing this..."

He leaned toward Beatrice and his lips found hers.

They stood there for a while.

Then Beatrice backed away. "We'd better x-ray the postcard in our mobile lab."

Jake's eyelids opened. "Back to work, I guess."

"Yep. Back to work. We have to learn to draw some lines or we'll never get anything done."

"We'd get some things done, but they may not be work related." Jake drew a deep breath. "Although relationships do take work."

"A lot of work. Maybe more than we have time for."

Jake shook his head. "We'll find time. If God

wants us to proceed, He'll give us wisdom to find time for each other."

"Let's get the project done, and we'll see where we go from there." Beatrice sat down. The screen had gone to sleep. She tapped on the trackpad. The screen displayed a password box.

She quickly typed in her password.

The key search program was still running.

"How long is that going to take?" Jake asked.

"Maybe hours, maybe days."

"So we'll go to Paris and wait?"

Beatrice could not read his mind. His question could be taken in so many ways. She decided to take it at face value.

"We have a rental chateau outside Paris in which we can do some work." She did not mention that Ansel's team had probably arrived with tourist visas.

"A chateau," Jake repeated.

"It's not a vacation destination."

"I know."

"We may not go there if we can get all the information we need in flight."

Jake seemed to study her. "You're not afraid of Molyneux at all, are you?"

"Should I be?"

Jake shrugged. "She's only the world's deadliest criminal."

"And my adoptive mother."

"The ironies of life."

"From time to time, I'm still sad that she killed Dad. However, my brother and I have had grief counseling. If I see her face to face, I would feel sorry for her. I was angry with her for a long time, but now I only feel pity for her."

"And yet you want her to live."

"In prison for the rest of her life, yes." Beatrice spun in her chair and faced Jake. "Everyone deserves a second chance, even Molyneux."

"You have a generous heart, but I can tell you that there are many governments who want her dead."

"If she dies, she dies."

Jake's eyes widened and then his face softened. "If they recruit you to work for them, say no. Just say no."

"What are you talking about?"

"If I were recruiting for the FBI, I would ask you to join us." He hesitated. "However, I won't because it's a messy world where I work. I don't want you to... I mean, I feel like you shouldn't... Uh... I don't know what I'm saying."

"You're trying to tell me what to do with my life."

"I was just trying to..."

"Protect me from the big bad world?" Beatrice said it half in jest, but Jake didn't laugh.

He looked deadly serious. "If I have the privilege to, I would guard you with my life."

It was a heavy statement to hear.

And unexpected.

Surprisingly unexpected.

CHAPTER THIRTY-THREE

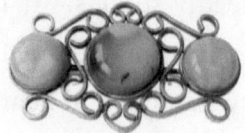

The meeting with Benjamin was postponed to give Beatrice and Jake time to peel back the layers on the postcard after the x-ray showed a hidden layer sandwiched between the front and back.

Someone had meticulously sliced apart an original postcard, added an extra layer, and then glued everything back together again.

The middle layer was transparent, with circuits drawn in thin gold. For all practical purposes it looked like a circuit board.

"A message in a bottle," Beatrice declared as she held the exhibit for all to see. She had put it in a plastic bag so that her fingerprints didn't get on the circuit board.

"Gimme." Kenichi remained seated, surrounded by his laptops and monitors at one side of the conference room.

Beatrice walked around Jake and the conference room chairs to get to Kenichi.

He studied it. "I need more tools, and they're in our big lab in Charleston. We don't have the equipment on board."

A wall monitor showed that they were one hour outside of Atlanta. They could reroute the flight to Charleston. "How long do you think you'll need?"

Kenichi shrugged. "Never seen this before. Hours. Days. I don't know."

"Do we have days?" Beatrice wondered.

"We had years. What are a few more days?" Kenichi laughed.

The issue was more than going to the lab. Beatrice was concerned about taking Jake too close to home. What if he discovered where the Glynn Estate was? Benjamin would never forgive her for leading him to their hideaway.

Then again, they were only going to the laboratory right outside Charleston, next to a small museum that welcomed no outside visitors. That had been their front office for years. It was no secret.

Beatrice turned to Jake. "You okay with this?"

"I'd like to see your lab. What do you do there?"

"Research. Analysis. Basically, the nitty gritty details of treasure hunting." She searched his eyes for any clue to what he was thinking.

He merely nodded. "I don't think I've ever been to Charleston."

"However, you do know where our lab is."

"Of course. I know some things about you all that you might not think I know."

Beatrice cocked her head to one side and put a hand on her waist. "Yeah? Like what?"

"Like...things."

Beatrice nodded. "Okay. Someday you'll tell me?"

"Over dinner, I will."

"Did you just ask me out?" Right there, in front of Kenichi, who would probably report back to Benjamin?

"We already had lunch," Jake said. "Dinner seems to be a natural progression."

"Is it?" Beatrice called the pilot and told them they had to go to Charleston instead of straight to Paris.

As she talked, she walked out of the conference room without looking back at Jake.

∼

The Charleston pit stop turned into two days of waiting for new equipment to arrive so that Kenichi could read what was on the circuit board.

Since Beatrice didn't invite Jake to her family home, he ended up at a hotel in downtown Charleston where he found himself doing nothing but resting and eating. Helen Hu had paid for the small but comfortable room with a balcony over-looking some tourist-infested market street with its outdoor cafés and horse-drawn carriages.

On the second morning of his rest and relax-ation, Jake checked in on Earl, who was chilling out in a beach house on Tybee Island.

"I think yours is a better deal," Jake said on FaceTime.

On the screen, Earl was reclining on a deck lounger, sunglasses over his eyes. Jake could hear the ocean behind the phone and every now and then, seabirds.

As for Jake, he was sitting on his bed, his back propped by a couple of pillows. Near the bed, the doors and windows opened to the blue morning sky over Charleston. He could hear the clip-clop of horses and smell them coming up the road.

"I earned it, my friend." Earl pointed to his stomach. "I almost died."

"You didn't almost die."

"Well, I still earned it."

"Is Helen giving you some paperwork to keep you busy?" Jake asked.

"Paperwork? Are you kidding me? No." Earl laughed. "What about you?"

"I'm supposed to stick close to my new friends, and try not to get shot."

"Good assignment. Tell me what she's like."

"She who?"

"Beatrice Glynn."

Ah. Where to begin? "There are still things I don't know about her."

"She at the same hotel?"

"No, actually. She didn't say, but I'm assuming she goes home to where her brother lives. I don't know where that place is."

"I can dig around," Earl offered.

"You're on sick leave."

"So? It beats paperwork."

"All right. Keep it on the down-low."

"Sure thing. So she lives somewhere near Charleston. The others? That Ken dude and the Ninja woman?"

Jake shook his head. "I didn't ask. I'm assuming

they have their own places they go home to whenever they're in town. This is their base of operation."

"They have a museum or something?"

"Well, not exactly. It's an office with a lab attached to it. They scan and x-ray artifacts, plus whatever else they do there. She gave me a brief tour, but it's a lot to take in."

"A lot? You're saying it's a big lab."

"It's more like a warehouse that they turned into a lab. There's a storage area and she showed me some old music boxes—like from the nineteenth century—that they're trying to restore. Parts and pieces everywhere."

"Music boxes. Does she collect them?"

"She likes them, yes." Jake adjusted a pillow behind his head. "That's something new about her that I didn't know. She says her brother collects puzzle boxes and she collects music boxes."

"She didn't show you any that work?"

"Nope. They're probably at her house somewhere." Jake was curious about where she lived, but he knew he wasn't ready to go that far yet.

For now, he was getting to know Beatrice, and they were at a good pace in his effort to draw her to him.

"While I have you on the phone, Helen has a

secret project coming up in a few weeks," Earl said. "I might not be well enough to resume work, but would you be interested?"

Jake knew right away that the answer was no. "I don't know, Earl. I'm in transition, but my goal is to return to the bureau."

"A career agent. You think they'd take you back?"

"If God wants me back there, I'll be back. If not, Helen has offered me a permanent position. We could potentially be colleagues, after all."

"We have great benefits." Earl panned his phone around so that Jake could see the panoramic view of the sand and surf.

"Wow."

"I know, right. All paid for."

"You had to get shot to earn that view."

Earl nodded. "Perks of working for Helen, is all I can say."

"Speaking of houses and cottages, did you ever find out who died in that lake cabin I told you about?" Jake asked. "The one outside Eureka?"

"Yeah. Glad you asked. I almost forgot. Some woman who had lived there by herself for many years. She just up and died one day, and that was that. I'm not sure what the cause of death was, but the cabin was locked from the inside, and there were no signs of break-ins. According to my contacts."

"How sad." Jake determined that he did not want to die alone, if at all possible.

"Well, I'm putting in an offer for this cottage right here," Earl declared.

"Must cost some serious money to buy that view."

"Yeah." Earl pointed to the camera. "I couldn't do this if I were still back at the CIA, you know?"

Jake agreed with him, but he also knew it was a matter of perspective. "Well, serving the country is a different mindset. I'm all over the place all the time. If I bought a beach house, I probably wouldn't see it most of the year."

"True."

"Someday, when I don't travel as much, I'd love to settle down in a house like that."

"Settle down? Did I hear you right?" Earl laughed.

"I meant, stay put in one city." It was too late to correct what he had said. "Isn't it obvious that I can't do this forever?"

"Maybe you got fired because it's God's way of telling you to move on already."

"I don't know." Jake wondered whether he

would have been able to get that close to Beatrice if he were still in the FBI.

Maybe not that close. He would have crossed the line with his feelings for her.

His strong, unshakable feelings for her.

He missed her every day he did not see her. Like today. And it was only morning.

Is this real, Lord? Am I in love?

After lunch, Jake was scheduled to head back to the lab, but Beatrice might not be there. Kenichi had said she was supposed to have a long budget meeting with Benjamin. When Jake found out that he wouldn't see her all day, he felt bereft.

Bereft?

Yes, bereft.

That said everything.

CHAPTER THIRTY-FOUR

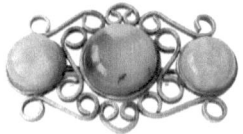

O n their third day in Charleston, there was good and bad news.

The golden key search yielded no known matching door anywhere in Europe and the United Kingdom. Beatrice ran more searches on old doors in North America, but the probability of a specific medieval door showing up in the USA was nil—not the one guarding the particular treasures they sought.

All attention turned to the postcard, not in its original form. The circuit board was supposed to be Kenichi's department, so all eyes were on him.

Not all eyes.

Beatrice kept glancing back at the door to the

lab. Where on earth was Jake? Did he want to be in on this or not?

She started to lose track of what Kenichi said. He was in a conversation with Benjamin, who had joined their meeting on audio only.

Raynelle had opted to sit out of this meeting when she discovered that Benjamin was attending. While Beatrice wished that those two would get along, she also knew that she couldn't make them like each other. They were adults.

They were all a team, though. If not for Beatrice, Raynelle would have quit on account of Benjamin.

The door finally opened.

"Sorry I'm late." Jake held three small paper sacks in his hands. He handed one to Beatrice. "Something for you."

"What is it?" Beatrice unrolled the top and peeked inside. "Pralines?"

"Pecan brittles. My Uber driver told me about this shop filled with local goodies. I thought I'd get you some and hope you're not allergic to pecans." He walked slowly to Kenichi and gave him one of the other sacks. "For you."

"Thank you." Kenichi put it next to his laptop by the circuit board. "Actually, we're not supposed to eat in here. The break room is downstairs."

"Oh, I'm sorry. I already had a whole bag on the way here." Jake chuckled. "It was so delicious that I had the Uber driver take me back there so I could get you all your own brittles."

"And thus end up being late to an all-important meeting," Kenichi said.

"Which looks like it's happening a mile a minute," Jake shot back. "Where's Raynelle? I got her some brittles too."

"She's out jogging." No, Beatrice was not jealous at Jake's generosity. If Raynelle didn't want all that sugar, Beatrice would be happy to eat them for her.

"Okay." Jake put the bag on the table next to Beatrice. "What did I miss?"

"The old key is probably a red herring," Beatrice said. "Ken's still figuring out the circuit board— and obviously frustrated. My brother's searching for the two-amber brooch."

"Your brother? Will he attend this meeting?" Jake asked.

"He's here," Beatrice said. "Ben?"

"Yes?" Benjamin's voice came through the speakerphone.

Beatrice knew that Benjamin could see them because of well-placed cameras in the meeting room, but they could not see him.

"Ben, meet Jake. Jake, the best brother in the world, my Ben."

"Hi, Ben." Jake even waved his hand. "Sorry I didn't get you some brittles too."

On audio, Benjamin grunted half a greeting of some sort.

Sometimes Beatrice wondered why it pained Benjamin to say full words. There were times when he'd grunt out a "Y" instead of saying a full "yes." How hard would it be to say a one-syllable word?

"Ben, how much longer would it take to extrapolate the location of the amber panels with just two brooches?" Beatrice asked.

"Hard to say. You know that the brooches may not lead to the rest of the Amber Room at all."

Beatrice nodded. "Yeah. It could be a dead end."

Kenichi threw up his hands. "I have nothing here."

"If Dad left the circuit board for us to find, then he would expect us to figure it out," Beatrice said.

"How did he know we'd be at the cabin?" Jake asked.

"Let's back up a bit," Benjamin said. "We're assuming he's still alive. For all we know, Philomena might have left the leather pouch under the table."

"True," Beatrice said. "Anyone could have found the pouch. Molyneux's people were all over the place before they took us there. What if they planted the pouch to throw us off course?"

"It's not a tracker," Kenichi said of the circuit board. "That, we know."

"Well, you two have been working on these for three days," Beatrice said. "Why don't you swap? Let Kenichi take a crack at the brooch box—while he's still waiting for a signal on the fake one—and you see what you can do with the circuit board."

"Good idea." Kenichi stretched his arms. "Make Ben come down to the lab."

"I'll send a courier to bring the board to me," Benjamin said. "I have a lab here."

No one could make Benjamin leave the house.

"I'll bring it," Beatrice said.

"Come alone."

Beatrice rolled her eyes. Did Benjamin think she was going to bring Jake?

"I have a better idea. Why don't I go?" Kenichi said. "I'll help him set this up. Then I'll bring back the brooches."

"The brooches are not in the safe?" Jake asked.

Beatrice studied his face. Was he expecting to be informed before the brooches were moved?

Jake seemed to be waiting for an explanation.

Beatrice reached for his hand. "I'm sorry. We were so busy yesterday it slipped my mind. I didn't want to call you or text you while you were napping and resting. And then we got busy and I forgot all about it. Forgive me?"

"Always," he whispered. He still held her hand.

Always? Did he mean that? Beatrice wondered if he could truly forgive her no matter what she did.

On audio, Benjamin cleared his throat. "Something going on between you two?"

Beatrice blushed.

A lot more could be going on between us two.

CHAPTER THIRTY-FIVE

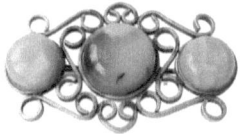

With the brooches safely returned to within his reach, Jake felt better about it. He had forgiven Beatrice for not letting him know that the brooches had left the lab safe because she seemed to have simply forgotten.

Still, he had stayed at the Glynn Research offices after lunch and into the late afternoon, although he should be resting his thigh. He had to keep an eye on things. Other than that, he felt a bit useless.

"We seem to have more questions but fewer answers." Beatrice stared at the two brooches on the table. "We are missing a third brooch, and we don't have the box—or tray, more likely—that the brooches originally came in."

"And we are nowhere near finding what remains of the Amber Room," Kenichi said. "I think it's time for dinner."

With that declaration, Jake was happy to take a short break. Beatrice looked worn out. It wasn't just because her bare face was without any makeup. She genuinely looked exhausted.

"Have you had a break in three days?" Jake brushed a strand of hair from her face.

"Break?" Kenichi laughed. "She hasn't slept in three days."

Jake's jaw dropped. No wonder she had forgotten things. "Why?"

"Why? Because she worked, is all. What have you been doing the last three days?"

As Kenichi spoke, Beatrice padded out of the lab. Outside the lab, staffers walked to and fro from the other labs up and down the hallway.

Jake followed her, counting the number of people around them. "Anything I can do for you?"

She waved him off. "I have a bad headache right now."

Kenichi came out of the lab. "I'm ordering takeout from the Chinese place. The usual?"

"Yeah." Beatrice kicked off her shoes and

climbed onto a sofa in a corner sitting area. "Just put mine in the fridge."

Jake sat across from the coffee table, empty except for someone's tablet that had been left there.

"What would you like?" Kenichi limped on his crutches toward Jake. "Chinese takeout but they also have sushi."

"Do they have shrimp and walnut?" Jake wondered how Kenichi was going to drive with a broken leg.

"They all do."

"That's what I want then. Plus two egg rolls. No soup. And brown rice instead of white." He fished for his wallet. "Why don't I pay for everyone?"

"No need. We're on company time."

"Are they delivering?"

"Yeah, I don't have time to go pick up. Plus I can't drive for a while."

"Is it safe to have it delivered?"

Kenichi wagged a finger at him. "You're even more paranoid than I am."

"I don't want people coming here knocking on doors with those two brooches lying around."

"Speaking of which..." Kenichi turned to Beatrice, who was dozing off. "Bee, you need to take the brooches and put them back in the safe."

Beatrice groaned.

"I thought we were studying them," Jake said.

"I've been bashing my head against an amber wall. I need a break." Kenichi hobbled back to the lab, and emerged with the two brooches, which he carried in his shirt pocket. He put the brooches on the coffee table in front of Beatrice.

"Make sure she puts them in the safe." Kenichi limped away.

The brooches looked ordinary and older than the rustic coffee table. For all they knew, the jewelry might not be worth anything at all.

Perhaps it had been a ruse.

"How do we know they're even authentic?" Jake asked no one.

"My brother analyzed them." Beatrice's eyes opened. "Nineteenth century."

"Not World War II era?"

"No. Sometime during or after World War II, someone took the brooches and turned them into what we think is a map—or at least a locator."

"Your father?"

"I doubt it. He was born after the war." She sat up slowly and put on her shoes. She picked up the brooches. "Would you like to see the safe?"

Jake nodded. Wouldn't hurt.

"Thank you for trusting us." Beatrice led him down a stark hallway.

At the end of the hallway, a nondescript door opened to a cluttered office. It was small and cramped. On the walls were digital maps with pins everywhere, one map per continent, except Antarctica.

"All the places you've been?" Jake asked, leaving the door behind him ajar to give them both some privacy and so that nobody could say they were *too alone* in the room by themselves—if there was such a thing as being *too alone* together.

"All the places stolen World War II artwork might have been stashed." Beatrice had unlocked the safe while Jake was distracted by the maps.

"It's a noble cause." Jake wasn't happy with himself for not paying attention to what Beatrice was doing.

"Someone has to deal with it." Beatrice placed the two brooches in the safe.

"Why?"

"Why not?" Beatrice locked the safe. "Before Dad got sidetracked hunting for the Amber Room, he helped his many Jewish friends look for lost family heirlooms."

"So you're continuing his legacy."

"The good side." Beatrice's voice was quiet, perhaps tinged with shame.

Jake wondered what he could say. "We're not our parents. The skeletons in their closets are theirs, not ours."

Beatrice nodded. "That's one way to look at it."

"Their penances are not ours," Jake emphasized.

Beatrice led the way toward the office door. "Easy for you to say because your parents are normal. And biological."

Jake chuckled. "Imagine if your biological parents were nefarious and irreformable criminals of the war crimes kind."

Beatrice stopped. Turned toward Jake. "Why are you doing this?"

"Doing what?" Jake was reaching for her hand.

"Trying to make me feel better? Some things will always hurt, you know."

She had a point there, but Jake wanted to keep trying. "I don't mean to suggest that you look for your biological parents to see what kind of people they are."

"Oh, they could be worse than Dad...and Mom." Her voice tapered off, as if calling Molyneux "Mom" was to commit an unpardonable sin.

"Just to know, though? Maybe to avoid genetic illnesses." Jake heard something from outside the door, but he ignored it. It could be unfamiliar sounds to him because he had never been in this building before.

Beatrice tilted her head. "Are you trying to distract me from my current quest?"

She didn't seem to have noticed the sound of potential scuffling out there. Maybe it was an echo. Maybe Jake was hearing things.

"I was just saying." Jake shook his head. Yep, he was hearing things. "Maybe you wouldn't feel bad about your adoptive family if you also knew about your biological heritage."

"I'll think about it later."

Jake let the matter drop.

They were about to leave the office when Jake heard more scuffles. A thud on the cement floor out there. Then another.

They were all distant, as if coming from television speakers in another room.

Jake tried to remember the layout of the laboratory. There was a front office somewhere. Then double doors with key cards to the cavernous lab space.

This office seemed to be at the far back end of the building.

A muffled shout put Jake on high alert.

Instantly his arm was out in front of Beatrice, preventing her from touching the door. He closed it. Locked it.

"Stand back," he whispered.

Beatrice's phone flashed red. "Lockdown."

Jake nodded, wishing he had more than a Sig Sauer with him.

Beatrice sat down at the desk and logged in to her desktop computer. She pointed to the screen. "Intruders. Why didn't the alarm go off?"

Jake went around the table to find five or six security screens showing armored people in oxygen masks sweeping through the entire building.

"Where's my security?" Beatrice mumbled, clicking buttons.

The cameras outside the building showed a carnage of staff members on the floor, passed out or dead. The computer showed a high level of carbon dioxide in the front office.

"Did they pump carbon dioxide into the building?" Jake asked.

"We can still breathe, so I'm guessing they did it just enough to get through the security."

Beatrice's phone flashed again. She picked it up. "Ben, we're under attack."

Jake was close enough to hear Benjamin say, "I know. Ansel is on his way."

Whoever Ansel was.

"Ansel is our chief of security. He works from the house." Beatrice pulled open a desk drawer. Inside was a small Glock.

Jake thought that was not nearly enough.

"Where's Ray?" Beatrice was back at her desktop, viewing the various security points. "Okay, I found them. Ray's in the break room. Ken is... There. He's in the bathroom downstairs."

Beatrice texted Ken and spoke as she did so. "Stay there. Ansel is on his way."

Jake's mind was elsewhere. Would the door hold? "Is that a fire door?"

Beatrice nodded. She clicked on something, and a far wall where there was no map slid open, revealing a secret closet—

And a cache of weapons.

"What in the world?" Jake asked, walking toward it.

Beatrice was right behind him. "We need oxygen masks. If you want something bigger than your Sig, take your pick."

Assault weapons, semi-automatic, several Israeli products...

"Take my pick?" Jake's jaw dropped. "You know how to use all these?"

"You can blame my brother. He thinks of everything." She pointed. "See there. Hazmat suits. Over here, vials of antiviral medicine. I told him he was nuts, but now I'm glad we have spare oxygen tanks, aren't you?"

Jake nodded.

"We have to get out of this alive, or Molyneux wins."

"We're assuming it's her people out there."

"I assume nothing, but I'm wondering how she knows we're here," Beatrice said. "We should have scanned ourselves for trackers."

"Or a mole," Jake suggested.

"That would be bad. We're a small team here. Who could it be?"

"Have we established that she wouldn't want you dead?" Jake prayed and hoped it was the case. It could buy them time.

"I used to think that, but she's insane." She handed Jake a mask.

It was heavy. Came with its own oxygen canister stored in a backpack he would have to wear over his shoulders. "How long is this going to last?"

"Only long enough for Ansel to arrive."

"And that is?"

"Fifteen, twenty minutes."

We could be dead by then. "Maybe you should stay in here and wait."

"Me? What about equal opportunity and all that?" Beatrice asked, zipping up her Kevlar vest. She pointed to a helmet.

Jake picked up the helmet. "Maybe we should both stay."

"Ray and Ken need our help." Beatrice pointed to a few Kevlar vests.

Jake fell behind. Beatrice was donning her oxygen mask before Jake put on his Kevlar vest. She was checking the safety of a few weapons before he had found his weapon of choice.

He did not want her in the firefight.

He did not want her to leave the office.

And yet, he respected her right to make decisions for herself.

Why did it affect him so?

Their equipment was heavy, and Jake had a hard time moving. Beatrice seemed to do better, but her head was down.

"You okay?" Jake spoke into the microphone attached to his helmet.

Beatrice nodded. "We forgot to pray."

"We can pray now."

Their foreheads mask to mask, Jake said a quick

prayer for protection and safety. When he looked up, he found Beatrice's eyes staring straight at him.

Brave eyes.

And so beautiful.

"We're going to get out of this," Jake said. "And then I'm going to marry you."

CHAPTER THIRTY-SIX

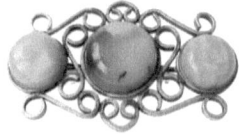

Her gear was so heavy that Beatrice could barely walk across the rug in the office. Her head was down, checking her steps.

The large floor rug with the geometric pattern had been a gift from a grateful but anonymous client. It was handmade in Persia, but it was ultramodern. The patterns ran in grids, like a...

Circuit board.

Wait.

The nodes on the board were large circles, reminding her of the amber cabochons in the brooches.

Maybe...

Shots fired outside the office interrupted her thoughts. She'd have to return to this later.

Her headset crackled. "Ansel, where are you?"

"We're outside. Can you get to where Ken is?"

"He's in the bathroom downstairs."

"Not anymore. He's with Ray and they're in the bunker. Get to the bunker and we'll find you."

"Copy that." Beatrice was about to tell Jake what Ansel had said.

"I heard that too."

"Thank God Ansel canceled his plans of going to Paris to wait for us."

"Yeah." Jake was at the door. "You saw the swarm. We're up against an army."

"There's a back stairwell."

Jake nodded. "Lead the way."

Beatrice wasn't sure if she wanted to be in the lead. She unlocked the door, but Jake got out first, shielding her.

He nodded to her, but Beatrice had no idea what that meant. He pointed this way and that. All she knew was that she had to get them to the stairwell.

Beatrice took the lead and Jake followed her down the hallway.

It was filling with smoke, and Beatrice had a

hard time seeing. She could hear noises coming from the now distant lab—people ransacking and breaking things.

The insurance would pay for all of that, but they had to stay alive to collect.

Beatrice didn't know why that popped into her head. She was sweating now, and her brain was going blank. She had never been in this situation before.

"Stairs," Jake whispered into her earpiece. It was as if he had sensed her hesitation.

She nodded. It was too late now to return to the office to get their night vision goggles.

In the low visibility, Beatrice found the Exit sign above the stairwell. Quickly, they entered it.

They made their way down two flights of stairs. Jake groaned a couple of times, and Beatrice knew his leg was hurting.

Jake went out of the door first before he motioned for Beatrice to come along.

The hallway was empty. No smoke. No people.

"This way." Beatrice pointed to her left. The bunker was one floor down.

They walked as fast as Jake could go toward a door that led to the bunker—

It was locked.

Beatrice took off her gloves and pressed her palm on the biometrics scanner. It rejected her. She knew she had to take off her oxygen mask so the scanner could read her retina.

She checked her wristband that came with the oxygen mask. The oxygen level was normal. She showed the readings to Jake. He nodded.

She took off her mask.

And heard multiple clicking sounds. Surrounding her were weapons pointing at her head, ready to blast her to kingdom come.

Where had those people come from? She hadn't heard them at all. How could they have sneaked up on her?

Slowly, she raised her arms in the air.

J ake woke up on a cot in what looked like a small medical clinic. Busy nurses and doctors walked back and forth, attending to patients in paramilitary uniform.

He tried to get up, but it hurt everywhere. There was something on his neck.

A bandage.

He pressed on it. It was soft and painful.

"Ouch."

Someone in paramilitary uniform hovered over him. "You're awake. Good."

"Where's Beatrice?" Jake asked.

"We all want her back."

"Are you Ansel?"

"Yes, sir."

"What happened?"

"Molyneux's men attacked the lab, put everyone to sleep, and abducted Bee."

Jake recalled being with Beatrice as they headed to the bunker in the basement. They were stopped by armed men. He didn't remember anything else.

"How did you stay awake?" Jake asked.

"Years of training, son. Years of training. And a good gas mask with a perfect seal." He chuckled.

"Glad you got us help. Where are we?"

"Normally you'd be in the local hospital," Ansel said. "However, Benjamin recognized you, so we brought you here."

"The Glynn Mansion in the Glynn Estate."

Ansel neither confirmed or denied it. He looked Jake over. "They changed the bandages on your thighs. Can you walk? We have a meeting to attend."

Slowly, Jake sat up. He felt pain here and there. "I could use some Tylenol."

Ansel motioned to a nurse. "You got something for him?"

She nodded.

A few minutes later, Jake walked with Ansel down a very long hallway and up a flight of stairs— which took Jake forever to climb because of his injuries.

"Are we mounting a rescue mission?" Jake asked as he was ushered into a large meeting room that looked like it had once been a ballroom back in the mansion's glorious days.

Beneath the vaulted ceiling with old-world chandeliers, there was a long and ornately carved table that reminded Jake of something similar that he had seen in a medieval castle somewhere.

At the far end of the table, a man who was about Jake's age paced back and forth. Taller than Jake by at least four or five inches, he towered over the table. He had the same color hair as Beatrice. Could that be Benjamin Glynn, the recluse?

"Ben, this is Jake Kessler," Ansel said.

"We met virtually in some of Bee's meetings. Did you bring me any pralines?" Benjamin's voice echoed in the cavernous room.

"I didn't get a chance. Next time?"

There was no "Nice to meet you, finally!" from Benjamin. He was all business. When he sat down, everyone else did—everyone else being Jake and Ansel.

Truth be told, Jake did not want to attend yet another meeting.

He wanted to find Beatrice.

Benjamin drank some water from a covered glass in front of him. Slowly.

It was so deliberate that Jake almost jumped up and walked out.

I'm not myself right now

He closed his eyes and prayed for calm and wisdom. Slowly, he also reached for the glass of water in front of him. It tasted like spring water. Crystal clear and odorless.

"It's good, isn't it?" Benjamin said.

"Yeah. Wow." Jake didn't want to make small talk right now, but if Beatrice were there, he would've asked her to tell him about the source of the spring water and so forth.

"Ansel, what do we know?" Benjamin turned his attention away from Jake.

Just as well. Jake wanted to sit there and mope about failing to protect Beatrice. It didn't matter that they had knocked him out with a blow to his neck. He should have been more prepared.

Prepared how?

He didn't know. All he knew was that he had failed Beatrice.

Jake already knew half of what Ansel said. Yeah, yeah. The intruders knew where the lab was. In fact, it wasn't hidden from anyone.

"I should have moved you all to the house," Benjamin said. "Bee insisted that the lab was a fine place to work."

"I should have beefed up security," Ansel said. "I'm sorry."

"She's not dead," Benjamin said. "If Molyneux has her, she'd want Bee alive for what she can do for them."

"Like what?" Jake couldn't think of anything.

"My sister has been searching for the Amber Room for over ten years. Molyneux could use her expertise."

"What if that's not why they abducted her?" Jake wasn't trying to throw a stone into a spinning wheel, but he knew he offered a perspective that the Glynn family might not have considered.

"You think she's doing this to draw the rest of us out?" Benjamin chuckled. "Molyneux doesn't care about me."

"If your father is still alive…"

Benjamin seemed to consider it. "It's true that

Molyneux has tried to kill him twice, but if he still hasn't died..."

"Someone left the postcard and key in the California cabin," Jake reminded everyone. "Someone gave Philomena the two brooches to sell to me."

"We have many unresolved mysteries." Benjamin got up from his chair to get more water from a trolley by the wall. Against the wall was a tall mirror. Through the mirror, he seemed to be looking directly at Jake.

"How is the circuit board coming along?" Jake asked. "What is it? What does it say? What does it do?"

"I have no answer for you. It seems like a dead end. Would you like more water?"

"Yes, please." Jake asked him to leave the jug of water on the table. "I'm gathering that if we put together what we have so far, they would lead us to Molyneux, and there is where we'll find Beatrice."

"That's obvious."

"Is it? The postcard is a dead end. The golden key, likewise. We have one brooch short of a complete set. We don't have the original brooch box. The fake brooch box is flying out there somewhere in the world."

Benjamin grinned. "If Bee were here, she'd tell you to stop being so negative."

JAN THOMPSON

"I'm not negative. I was merely stating the facts."

"She tells me I'm negative all the time. Maybe this was a ruse to get me out of the house." Benjamin sat down in his chair again. "Since I can't leave the house, you have to go in my place."

"Me?" Jake realized now that it was the reason Benjamin had invited him over.

"I'm assuming you do want to rescue Bee."

"But we don't know where she is."

"We will soon know. Ken is working on it. He's built quite a friendship with those hackers from Binary Systems. Plus, Ken has his own network of specialists. The whole world is looking for my sister."

His words sounded cold, but Jake could feel the compassion. Benjamin truly loved his sister. He would leave the house for her if he could.

Jake leaned forward, elbows on the conference table. "I'll go if you go too."

Sitting on the other side of the table, Ansel looked up, concern on his face—like the concern of an older man for his ward. Ansel was about Jake's dad's age. Ansel could be in his sixties. Probably retired military. Here for one purpose only: to protect the Glynn family.

"Thank you for the invitation, but I can't." Benjamin's eyes were steel gray.

"I learned that if I don't go forward, I may regret it the rest of my life," Jake said. "I have many stories of regret if you want to hear them."

"Spare me."

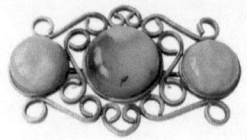

CHAPTER THIRTY-SEVEN

Beatrice had no idea if she was still in the United States or outside. Abducted in Charleston, where could she have been taken in a matter of hours?

Practically anywhere in the whole wide world.

She wished she had left a trail of some sort for Benjamin and Jake to find her.

Jake.

Oh, Jake.

Beatrice prayed that Jake would recover from that blow to his head back at the lab. Then, as the weapons were pointed at their heads, Beatrice had felt a prick in her neck just as she saw Jake collapse on the floor. The rest of her memory faded to black, and she had woken up here, in some vehicle.

It was dark all around her, but from the way the vehicle moved, Beatrice guessed she was inside a van of some sort—not dissimilar to the vans she, Kenichi, and Raynelle drove around in California. This one smelled of grease and gunpowder, a strange combination to her nostrils.

If they took her to Molyneux, to where the fake brooch box was, she could stay close to the box. Perhaps Kenichi would soon find a way to track down the box.

Regardless, her only hope was in God and Him alone.

After a long drive in the back of the vehicle, she felt sleepy. She was used to sleeping in the backs of vans, so it wasn't too torturous for her—except she was tied up and had another piece of tape over her mouth.

She wasn't sure what would happen to her next, so whatever she could do now had to be done. She counted two things: pray and sleep.

When she finally awoke, she could hear voices outside the van. Spanish words everywhere. Since she didn't understand the language, she couldn't figure out what was happening outside the van.

Finally, the door opened.

She was in a garage of some sort. No one spoke English around her.

They made her walk to another van. This one had a Mexican tag on it.

Are we in Mexico?

How long had they driven her? As far as her recollections went, driving from Charleston to the border of Mexico would take at least twenty-one hours.

Had she slept all that time?

Or had she been drugged?

Strong arms pushed her into the back of the Mexican van. She felt a sharp sting on her arm. A syringe?

Before she could think about it, she felt another lull...

And woke up in a canopy bed surrounded by the sounds of birds outside the diamond-shaped leadlight windows. The glass looked old and salvaged, but the cames seemed to be authentic lead.

Where am I?

She lifted the comforter off her, and found herself in a pair of pajamas. She did not recall changing clothes.

She stayed still for a moment, trying to collect her thoughts.

I'm alive.

The door opened. A woman walked in carrying what looked like her clothes.

"Washed and ironed for you, madam." She placed them on an armchair next to the bed. "Molly asks that you get ready and join her for tea."

"Tea?"

"She said you asked to be invited to tea, and here you are."

When she last talked to Molyneux back in California, she hadn't expected to follow through on tea time with the certifiably insane.

"Where are we, exactly?" Beatrice still didn't move.

"You're in Poland, madam."

"Poland? As in Europe?"

"Is there another?"

"I just want to make sure," Beatrice said. "Why am I in Poland?"

"This is where you'll have tea with Molly."

Slowly, Beatrice got out of bed. Her bare feet dangled over the mattress. "Help me."

"You have fifteen minutes to get ready or the tea will be lukewarm by the time you show up."

"Help me," Beatrice tried again.

"Help you to do what? To change your clothes? Comb your hair?" Her voice was calm.

"Help me get out of here." Beatrice slid off the bed and landed on her feet.

Immediately, the woman pulled out a small pistol.

Beatrice tried not to freak out. "I'm going to brush my teeth, take a shower, and put on some clean clothes. Is that okay?"

"Fifteen minutes." The woman backed away slowly to the door. She left without another word.

It took her longer than fifteen minutes to shampoo her hair three times to get the smell of grease off. Then she took her time drying her hair with a small hair dryer they had provided.

By the time Beatrice came out of the bathroom in a towel, Miss Pistol was sitting in an armchair waiting for her.

"Please leave. I need to change," Beatrice snapped.

"You're late."

"It's better to be clean than early. Tell Molly that." She waited for Miss Pistol to leave.

Beatrice took her time changing into her clothes. There was no lotion anywhere in the room. She reminded herself to ask for lotion and an extra towel. She'd rather air-dry her hair if possible.

She turned the knob, but the door was locked.

The knob was another thing. Along with the modern bathroom, they told Beatrice that this building had not been restored to its original state. Not that it mattered to her.

She just wanted to go home.

She knocked on the door.

Miss Pistol opened it from the other side.

The hallway and walls were all made of stone. They were quite impressive.

"Is this where Molly has been staying all this time we couldn't find her?" Beatrice asked as she was escorted by Miss Pistol and two armed guards down the hallway to tea with the queen of death.

"This is a rental," Miss Pistol said.

"Thank you for the information."

Miss Pistol pursed her lips. Perhaps she had spoken too much.

A rental castle. Interesting.

Beatrice wondered if it had modern conveniences like a cell tower nearby. She would need a phone to call home or for help. Did 911 work in this part of the world? She had never been to Poland in her life. Most of her searches for World War II artifacts were in Germany and France, though every now and then she expanded her location.

Poland had been decimated in World War II, with the country losing its name and identity. Destroyed beyond recognition.

Perhaps that was the irony of it. With few people looking this way, who was to say that the Amber Room looters had not decided to hide the remaining panels in plain sight?

Then again, many believed the Amber Room had been destroyed in Königsberg during the war. If any panels or pieces of it remained, they would be highly sought after on the black market. Perhaps they might never be found or seen again.

However, right now there was a more pressing matter.

Beatrice wanted to be found alive. Would Benjamin and Jake know that she was here?

Ten minutes later, Beatrice realized it didn't matter. Molyneux was never in the castle. Tea time wasn't happening.

Miss Pistol had lied by omission. Never once did she deny what Beatrice had asked or assumed.

CHAPTER THIRTY-EIGHT

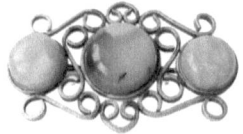

Molyneux was shorter than Beatrice remembered, but her eyes were more intense than Beatrice had seen over the live chat the week before. Her mannerism was aggressive and combative, and frankly, she scared Beatrice every time she opened her mouth.

But she wanted tea.

Did Beatrice dare to say she had changed her mind and preferred coffee these days?

Did she want to die?

Never in her life had Beatrice expected to die in an old unused church somewhere in Poland, but here she was.

Standing there at the old wooden door leading

to the small room where a work table filled up half the space, Beatrice waited for Molyneux to make the next move.

It felt like chess.

Except that no matter what Beatrice did, the guards around her wouldn't let her get away with anything.

She felt like a pawn.

Then again, a pawn could take the queen.

Molyneux turned away from her and looked at a painting hung on the wall. It probably didn't come with the place because it showed a wedding scene with the couple kneeling at an altar, facing away from the audience.

"You'd think that if we made our wedding vows before Almighty God, that he would at least keep it." Molyneux's voice was British with a faint accent.

It sounded less intimidating when Molyneux spoke calmly instead of yelling all the time.

Beatrice tried to recall the first five years of her life, but her mind drew a blank. All she could remember was that, back when she had been sweet Imogen Wright, Molyneux was gone a lot. Dad had been left to raise the two kids alone.

One could say that being lonely might have driven Dad to adultery, perhaps?

"We were a beautiful couple," Molyneux added. "Thirty-five years ago."

Beatrice had nothing to say. She was no counselor. And Molyneux needed help. She had been divorced for twenty-five years—just before she tried to kill Dad for the first time—and she still talked about her wedding day today.

Molyneux turned back toward Beatrice and smiled. "I have him back now, though, for one final time."

Perfect teeth and all. She could have been beautiful, Beatrice thought. Instead, that woman had turned into one of the ugliest terrorists the world had ever known.

Beatrice wondered how many people Molyneux had killed.

And yet, was salvation possible for such an evil person?

Or was she beyond saving?

Wait. Beatrice's eyebrows rose. "What did you just say?"

"It's the way the world goes, sometimes." Molyneux walked toward Beatrice. "I tried to kill him twice. Each time he'd sent a decoy."

"A decoy?" Beatrice's jaw dropped. "Is Dad..."

"He will be soon." Molyneux motioned to her guards. "For now, he's still useful to me."

"Am I useful to you?" Beatrice wished she hadn't asked.

"It depends if you're your mother's daughter or your father's." Molyneux touched Beatrice's chin and lifted it slightly. "You have my eyes, but I didn't give birth to you."

Beatrice didn't know the answer either.

"Don't try to find your birth mother," Molyneux continued.

Beatrice's heart raced.

"She is dead."

Beatrice could hear her own heartbeat thumping in her chest.

"Your father knows who she is."

"I thought both of you adopted me together?" Beatrice asked.

"We did, but he found you first."

Interesting. Potentially, Dad could tell Beatrice who her biological mother was. Beatrice recalled Jake asking whether she'd ever be interested in looking up her own genetics.

Speaking of Jake, Beatrice prayed that he and Benjamin would try to find her. She felt that she was about to regret the plan she had set in motion that had somehow turned awry. Now she had to find the Trojan horse brooch box in the hope that Kenichi could locate it and come get her.

Molyneux walked past her, and the whole entourage followed. "We'll talk about family later. Right now, I need you to open the door."

"Open what door?"

CHAPTER THIRTY-NINE

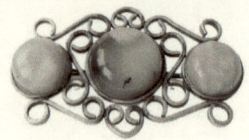

Beatrice did not want to go down the stone stairs. Something smelled horrible and it wasn't the guards on both sides of her.

"Move!" Molyneux yelled into her ears.

"No!" She stood her ground at the top of the stairs, hugging the stone wall to one side.

She could see shadows as the flashlight danced down the stairs. At the bottom of the short flight of stairs, she saw stacks of skulls.

"What is this place?" Beatrice barely got the words out.

"They're all dead. They won't bite." Molyneux motioned for her guards to take Beatrice down.

They couldn't carry her because the ceiling was too low. Two guards held each of her arms. They dragged her and gave her no room to fight. Her hiking boots thumped-thumped all the way down the stone treads.

At the bottom of the stairs, they dropped her to the ground, right in front of a wall of skulls.

Beatrice screamed.

"Tsk. Tsk," a man's voice said. "We agreed to leave the kids out of this, Imogen."

Dad?

The flashlight wasn't bright, but the man came out of the shadows, extending a hand toward Beatrice.

His cheeks were chubby and his eyes were kind. He even had white hair. All he needed was a red suit for Beatrice to think it was Christmas.

He helped her get up. On her feet, she was a foot shorter than the elderly man, who seemed to be in his seventies.

"What would you like to be called? Amber? Amberlyn? Beatrice?" he asked.

Beatrice was too stunned to speak.

She looked for familiarity, but she felt very distant from this man in front of her. It was like when she had looked at those photos on the mantel in his cabin before it burned down. There were memories there, but she felt no sorrow.

It was a good thing she also felt no anger.

"Nothing to say to your own father?" he asked.

Beatrice opened her mouth, but no words came out.

She swallowed.

Closed her eyes to release a small tear. She didn't know what that tear was for.

"Y-you were dead," she finally said.

"Dead to the world." He laughed.

"Why did you ghost us?" So many lost years.

"To keep you and your brother alive." He pointed to Molyneux. "She was looking for you two. If I distracted her, you could go live your own lives."

Molyneux shrugged. "Little did you know that both of them would be looking for me instead. Oh, the irony."

Dad laughed.

Dad? I called him Dad.

Beatrice stared again. She couldn't have imagined this moment in her life. She had been so focused on Molyneux, all the while expecting Dad to be dead, that she could not fathom seeing him alive now.

And working with Molyneux.

She frowned.

"You frown like your brother," Dad said.

"Even though they're not biologically related," Molyneux said.

Is that still true though?

Beatrice didn't want to endanger her brother. Oh, the dilemma. She knew that Benjamin could track her down, but wouldn't that put him in danger?

Kenichi and Raynelle would help, but to what extent? They were both recovering from injuries. There was no telling if they had been more injured at the lab a few days prior.

Then there was Jake.

Would Jake be able to track her down? Would he do whatever it would take?

Beatrice missed him already, but right now she had to survive this to send an SOS.

"What are we doing down here?" She braved herself to ask.

"Did you bring the key?" Dad asked.

"What key?" Beatrice had dismissed the golden key as a red herring. Now what? "The golden key?"

Dad laughed. "No. The brooch box."

"The what?"

Philomena had only tried to pawn off the brooches.

"It's missing a two-amber brooch," Beatrice said.

"I have that brooch. The other two brooches and the box, I have not," Molyneux said.

"Are you sure?" Beatrice asked. "As far as I know, your people robbed it from me when I came out of the bank in San Francisco. Remember?"

"Her people." Dad turned to Molyneux. "You didn't."

"So you have the box, don't you?" Beatrice asked, praying they did.

Everyone waited for Molyneux to answer.

"If you do have the box, then why do we even need Beatrice here?" Dad's voice was deeper now.

"We don't need it anyway," Molyneux said. "I say we blow it all up and start digging."

Dad laughed.

It was similar to Benjamin's laugh.

How could that be possible?

"Do you or do you not have the box?" Dad asked again.

"Yes, but there was nothing there."

"The box is the key. The brooches are the buttons." Dad made a big noisy sigh. "Tell me you still have them."

Molyneux nodded.

"Where?"

"Nearby."

Beatrice's heart soared. There was hope for a rescue yet.

That was, unless Molyneux figured out that the box was fake—before help arrived.

CHAPTER FORTY

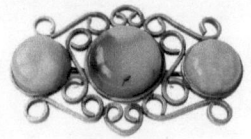

Covering the sides of her eyes with her palms, almost like blinders on a horse, so that she avoided seeing more skulls, Beatrice followed Dad—or someone who looked like photographs of him—through the tunnel into a carved-out cavern.

It looked like a staging area to prepare bodies for burial.

Beatrice did not want to be there at all. She prayed for deliverance.

Even though Molyneux had gone to retrieve the brooch box that she believed to be real, Beatrice was not alone with Dad. Several guards stood watch around them. They didn't speak much

English, but Beatrice was confident they could understand anything she said to Dad.

Well, what would she say to Dad?

Let's escape together?

It seemed apparent to Beatrice that Dad was working for Molyneux. No one worked *with* her, so they must all work *for* her.

"Why would you work for her?" Beatrice blurted.

Dad sat down at the table and began poring over maps. "Somewhere in these catacombs, there is a door. That door can only be opened with a special key. Are you going to ask me what's behind the door?"

"I don't know. And I don't care at this point. I just want to go home."

"Where's your sense of adventure?" Dad waved for her to sit down in an empty chair next to him. "All these years, you've developed a system. I've watched your excitement finding lost treasures—"

"You what?" Beatrice sat down.

"Think about it. How did the Glynns pay cash for the Gulfstream and the mansion?"

"They were venture capitalists."

Dad shook his head. "I sent them money."

"What?"

"They will never tell you because I made them promise."

Beatrice didn't want to believe him. "What did you pay for?"

"Other than the jet and house, I made sure you graduated out of university without student loans."

"That's considerate of you." Beatrice didn't buy it.

"You might never know and they would never tell."

"Why are you telling me all this now?" Beatrice asked.

"Because after this, we may never see each other again." His voice was solemn. As if this was his last stand.

"You're ghosting us again? So what's new?"

"You're angry."

"Why shouldn't I be?" Beatrice folded her arms across her chest. "Twenty-five years. We thought you were dead for twenty-five long years."

"You were fine with your new adoptive parents. They took good care of you and raised you better than I could ever have done."

"Where did you go?" Beatrice sat back in the chair to distance herself from Dad.

"Well, Philomena and I..."

Beatrice made a face. "Your mistress."

"Your mother, Amber. Your mother."

"Wh-what?" Okay, this was too much for her. She wanted to throw up right then.

Beatrice closed her eyes and prayed for calm. She told herself she hadn't just heard what she heard.

When she opened her eyes, Dad was smiling.

"Who is my dad?" Beatrice asked.

"I am."

"No..."

"I thought you'd be happy to know you're not an orphan."

"But you're a crook, a thief, a criminal!"

"Well, even criminals can have babies." He shrugged.

Beatrice slid off her chair and stepped away. She drew a deep breath but only choked on the dust. "Is there oxygen here?"

"Recycled. You should be used to it since you fly a lot."

"Let me get this straight, Ben and I are your real kids." Beatrice's palm was on her head.

"No. Just you."

"What?" Beatrice's eyes started to sting. "A-am I your real daughter?"

"It's not that bad, is it?" Dad knitted his

eyebrows together the way Benjamin sometimes did.

"Your mannerisms are like Ben's—or the other way around," Beatrice said. "How could he not be your biological son?"

"Because Imogen and I adopted him when we found out we couldn't have kids," Dad said.

"Five years later, you adopted me together. Did Molyneux know who my mother was?" She did not want to call her by her old name.

"She didn't know—at that time anyway." Dad's shoulders sagged. "She was gone a lot. We had been doing different things for years. Along the way, I met Philomena, a fellow treasure hunter. We were both looking for the remnants of the Amber Room. We hit it off. Next thing we knew, she was pregnant. I wanted the baby because it meant I wasn't impotent."

Beatrice sat down. This was the story of her origins, as bizarre as it might be.

"She had you, gave you up for adoption. I persuaded Imogen that Eugene—your Ben—would be lonely without a sibling. We adopted you. Then I hired Philomena to be your nanny."

Beatrice felt numb. That was all. She did not feel anything else. She had only known her birth mother as her pretend nanny. How could any mother do that to her own children?

Beatrice assumed that all the time, Molyneux hadn't realized her then-husband had hired the biological mother to be the nanny of her own baby.

"Remember your Bible story? Baby Moses floating down the river, the Pharaoh's daughter adopting him, and hiring the baby's real mother to nurse him?"

Beatrice buried her face in her palms. "When did Molyneux find out?"

"You were four years old. She found Philomena and me in bed. She hit the roof. She and Philomena had a big argument and the story came out."

"And you divorced."

"The end."

"Except here you are, working for your ex-wife against your own daughter."

Dad blinked. Something he wasn't saying?

Slowly, he answered her. "Business is business."

Beatrice felt he wasn't telling the truth. Was he here to take down Molyneux in an undercover assignment or was he one of the unreformed criminals?

If it was the former, it might explain why he

had asked for the brooch box. How did he know about the fake box?

"After your divorce, you took us to the States." Beatrice wanted the rest of her family story. She had no idea how much time they had left.

As soon as Molyneux found out the box was fake, it would be over for them.

"I would've stayed in England, even though I still had my American passport. Imogen became Molyneux and put a price on our heads. I had to keep you and your brother safe."

"Somehow you got us into WITSEC with new names."

"Unfortunately, Philomena couldn't come with us. I should have married her." Dad wiped his eyes with the back of his hand. "We worked on it for a few months to get her into the States via the southern border. I picked her up in the deserts of Texas. And we vanished."

"You left us."

"I put you in good hands. The Glynns needed money for their investments. I needed two loving parents."

"Why not take us with you and Philomena?"

"On the run? I didn't think it would work. Eugene was ten and you were five, and both in school."

"You could have homeschooled us."

"No. We were living in an RV traveling from state to state. We were off the grid and under the radar."

"For twenty-five years."

"Twenty. We ended up in California, loved it, and bought a cabin with cash."

"Then you ghosted Philomena?" Beatrice asked. For once, she felt sorry for that woman—whom Dad said was her biological mother.

"After her cancer scare, she wanted to visit her nieces and nephews. We made her a fake passport, but she was antsy to say goodbye to everyone. Of course, she didn't die. The cancer went away, and we went back to our cabin in the woods."

"However, your travels put you on Molyneux's radar."

"Not to mention all the different government agencies around the world."

"So you fled town to protect Philomena?" Beatrice didn't feel a thing as she said her name. She did not feel anything at all about who her real mother was.

She would need proof, and now wasn't the time.

"I gave her strict instructions to stay inside the

cabin. I spent the next three years looking for Molyneux."

"What did you think happened to Philomena while you were gone?" Beatrice asked. Perhaps he had been stuck in this cave for too long.

"She should've been fine. I left her plenty of money and supplies. Told her to stay in the cabin until I got home."

"Philomena went to Cannes six months ago to sell jewelry to the FBI." Beatrice could see the shock register on Dad's face. "A couple of weeks ago, she showed up in San Francisco with two brooches to sell. Who did she sell the third brooch to?"

"Brooches? As in the key?" Dad groaned. "I hid it."

"In the cabin you shared with her. She found them and tried to sell them."

"That can't be her. She would never sell my stuff." Dad shook his head. "It had to be an impostor."

"She died of poisoning in a café that night. There were no records of her on file anywhere. They called her an undocumented immigrant."

Beatrice waited to see how Dad would react. His reaction was slow. There was no shock on his face. Only resignation.

Finally, he nodded. "I told her not to leave the cabin. Told her I'd be back. It just took time, that's all."

"Three years. How was she going to support herself, being an illegal resident of the country?"

"I left her enough to live by."

"Sometimes we need more than money and things."

"Don't judge me, Amber." His hung his head.

"Beatrice."

"Whatever. Don't judge your old man." Tears fell from his eyes.

Beatrice wanted to hug him, but she did not.

"Part of me did not expect Imogen to get to Philomena," Dad said.

"Why not? She's killing everyone."

"Because they're cousins."

"Are you kidding me? Cousins?" Ah, that would explain why Jake had thought Beatrice looked like Molyneux. "Yikes. That means Molyneux is my flesh-and-blood aunt?"

"There's always a black sheep in the family."

"So you dated two cousins?" Incredible.

"Not at the same time."

"Does that make it better?"

"I didn't know at the time. Both of them hid the fact from me. I had no idea they were rivals in everything, and they each wanted what the other had."

"And you were the pawn in the middle of two queens," Beatrice said.

"Still, I thought Imogen would spare her own cousin. That she would be safe in the cabin." Dad shrugged. "You were never supposed to go there."

"Well, we did. Did you leave me a pouch with a postcard and a key in it?"

"Wasn't me."

His answer was too quick. Beatrice realized Molyneux was probably listening to their conversation. She decided to ask him later if they had another opportunity.

"You can't keep running." Beatrice felt sorry for him.

He lifted his face. "I'm not running anymore."

"You can't run even if you want to." Beatrice waved her hands. "Look at where we are. This is a literal dead end. A tomb."

"We'll take care of this once and for all," Dad announced.

"Is that even possible?"

"We'll take care of it." Dad began to weep softly. "We'll take care of it, Philomena."

CHAPTER FORTY-ONE

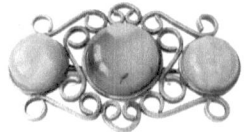

J ake stirred when turbulence hit the Gulfstream. He climbed out of his small bed and splashed warm water on his face. He brushed his teeth while still groggy from the interrupted sleep.

He ambled out of his private cabin, and made his way to the main sitting area.

Benjamin was already awake, sitting upright in his leather seat, his seat belt strapped. He pointed to the empty seat across from him.

"I still cannot believe a total stranger persuaded me to leave my house," Benjamin said.

"I can't take all the credit." Jake sat down. "We have to find your sister. All hands on deck."

"I'm not a coward." Benjamin drew a deep breath.

"No one says you are."

"I don't have a fear of flying."

Jake nodded. "I can see that."

"I'd rather stay home."

"We've established that."

"But someone has to go rescue my sister."

"You'd be worried sick if you stayed home," Jake said.

"Probably. She's my only family." Benjamin ordered another sandwich.

The flight attendant was cordial, but Benjamin gave her no time of day. He was stoic, yes, but to Jake, he behaved like a grumpy old man.

"Besides, Beatrice needs a chaperone, from the likes of you." Benjamin pointed with his sandwich.

"Better me than the likes of Molyneux," Jake riposted.

Benjamin stared at him for a moment, and then laughed. "Careful. I might start liking you over Bee's other boyfriends."

"What other boyfriends?" Jake decided to be cool about it, but inside he was all jumping jacks.

"Exes."

"Ah, okay." *Whew.* "Say, that looks like some sandwich. Roast beef?"

"Triple layer of cheese with horseradish. You want one, they can make it for you." He motioned for the flight attendant to take Jake's order.

When he was done, Jake checked his phone for the right time zone. "When do we land in Paris?"

"We're not going to Paris." Benjamin swiped his tablet. "While you were sleeping, the fake brooch box sent a signal. Kenichi tracked it to Kraków."

"Kraków, Poland?"

"We arrive in five hours."

"Five." That meant Jake had slept for almost ten hours. He must have been exhausted.

"Ansel is preparing his team."

"Will they let him bring his weapons into town?"

"Who says we're bringing our own weapons?" Benjamin smiled. "We have contacts on the ground —private militia. Costs me a fortune, but this is my sister we're talking about. I pray she is still alive."

"She has to be. I don't think Molyneux wants her dead yet."

"Why do you say that?" Benjamin crossed his legs.

"They made plans for tea."

"Seriously? I'd be surprised if a tea party prevents a murderer from murdering."

"I think Molyneux likes Beatrice and wishes she were her real daughter."

Benjamin frowned. "I want to see Molyneux up close, see what kind of a person would steal Dad's heart and then kill him."

"She's complex," Jake said. "The last time I saw her, I was surprised at how ordinary she looked. Even as she was torturing me, she looked like the woman next door who walks her dog and talks to strangers."

"Huh. As she was torturing you?" Benjamin drew a deep breath. "How can you even talk about it objectively?"

"By the grace of God, I survived. Your sister called for help."

"Sounds like something she'd do."

"However, when I was inside Molyneux's organization, she had hollow eyes, looking over her shoulders all the time. Drugged out or something."

"Sin will find you out."

Jake was surprised at the verse that Benjamin just cited. "Numbers 32:23."

But if you do not do so, then take note, you have sinned against the Lord; and be sure your sin will find you out.

"God is my guide."

"Same here." Jake thanked the flight attendant for the roast beef sandwich.

"Let's pray that God will protect my sister and that we will all return alive."

"How about we pray now?" Jake asked. "I need to thank God for my food."

"Go ahead."

And so, Jake did. Except he got carried away praying for Beatrice. He choked up a little when a fleeting thought raced through his mind, the thought that his suspicion might be wrong, that Molyneux would not spare her adopted daughter, and that he might never see Beatrice again.

Jake wondered if he could carry on if that happened.

And that was the moment he knew he had fallen deeply in love.

"Please, Lord, let Beatrice be alive and well," Jake whispered with his eyes shut. "Let her know that we're coming to get her. In Jesus' name I pray. Amen."

"Amen." Benjamin looked up. "She knows we're coming."

"How?"

"We've discussed potential scenarios over the years," Benjamin explained. "And the last thing she did—the Trojan horse brooch box—might be a lifesaver."

"Wow. Romans 8:28."

And we know that all things work together for good to those who love God, to those who are the called according to His purpose.

"You know your Scripture," Benjamin said.

"Does that mean you'll treat me like family?" It was worth a shot. Jake waited.

"Nope." Benjamin frowned again. "Like I was saying, the fake brooch box might have arrived in Molyneux's web, and finding it might take us to Bee."

"You're thinking that the brooch box and Beatrice might be at the same location."

"We know from Molyneux's activities the last couple of weeks that she's firing all cylinders to get to the Amber Room—or what's left of it. That means she's closing in or she has leads. Either way it also says that she's running out of money. When was the last time you heard of a terrorist attack attributable to her?"

"Not in at least six months."

"Exactly. Ever since many of her income streams dried up due to governments clamping down on her activities, she has been increasingly desperate."

"You've been following the news."

"I have to. Molyneux is a menace to all of us."

Jake nodded. However, the problem remained. "What if you're wrong about where the brooch box is?"

"Then Beatrice is in grave danger. Or dead."

CHAPTER FORTY-TWO

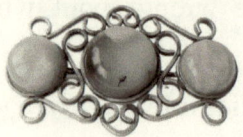

"Behold, the door." Molyneux stood in front of an old steel door so unusually located in the catacombs that Beatrice suspected it had been transported here from somewhere else.

When was the last time she had seen a steel door installed two floors beneath an old unused church in the middle of nowhere?

Not once.

Beatrice wanted to ask about the history of the door, but she felt constricted. The vest tied around her chest was ridiculously heavy and loaded down with enough C-4 explosives to take out half the church above. She wanted to sit down on the floor, but she was afraid of setting something off.

Molyneux seemed unperturbed by her discomfort. She kept talking, kept swinging that remote control in her hand.

What if she dropped it?

Beatrice started to sweat, but it was nothing like Dad. Kneeling at the door, trying to get it to open, his hands started to shake. He was sweating bullets. His hair was all matted.

Only twelve hours before, Dad had seemed normal. Now he looked pale and ill.

"Dad needs a break," Beatrice finally said.

"He gets one when he gets the door opened."

"Obviously you need a key."

Dad panted. "Or we can blow it up."

"You know the church will cave in and whatever is behind that door will be gone." Molyneux wasn't smiling. "If you want to go that route and kill us all, go ahead."

"It's an idea." Dad paused to catch his breath. "This vest is heavy, Imogen. Must you?"

"You were taking too long," Molyneux said. "Chatting with your daughter when you two should be working."

Beatrice believed she had heard their conversation at the far end of the catacombs. Then again, Molyneux already knew almost all the things that Dad had said.

In fact, Beatrice suspected that Molyneux was

responsible for Philomena's death. If Dad found out, would he do something irrational or drastic?

Dad turned to Beatrice. "Want to give it a go?"

"Me? I'd rather not." Beatrice wanted to stretch time. That could give Benjamin an opportunity to send Ansel to Poland—wherever they were. Flight from Charleston to Poland would take at least ten or twelve hours, she figured.

So, yeah, the longer they waited, the greater the chance they'd be rescued.

Dad sat down.

Molyneux pointed to the door. "Now."

Beatrice didn't move.

Once again, the guards came and hauled her over.

She glanced at Dad. He had a twinkle in his eye. Did he approve something?

Beatrice looked at the brooch box on the floor. It was the same box that Kenichi had worked for six months to prepare. The one they had paid a lot of money to the now-deceased jeweler to reproduce.

The all-important fake box.

A Trojan horse.

However, they were underground. There was no way the signal would work from here.

Beatrice prayed that the signal had worked upstairs when Molyneux's people transported the box from wherever it came from to this unused church.

On the floor, Dad had placed a large piece of paper—a butcher's paper—with lines crisscrossing it. At various intersections, he had placed the amber cabochons he had extracted from the two fake brooches and one real brooch. Surrounding the paper were assorted permanent markers and a mix of natural and manufactured amber pieces.

Beatrice sat down on the floor.

She had no idea how they were going to make this work. The only thing she could do was pray to God for wit to stall Molyneux until help arrived.

At the back of her mind, she wished that Dad was working undercover for some government entity with enough firepower to take out Molyneux. What if Dad were working for the Catherine Palace that currently housed a reproduced version of the Amber Room? Or the Russian Consulate?

Now would be the time to come and help us!

As Beatrice stared at the diagram Dad had drawn, she recalled seeing a familiar pattern at her Charleston laboratory office. The floor rug. A gift from a client.

Who could the client be? Had it been Dad?

"I've seen this pattern before," Beatrice said.

Dad raised an eyebrow. He waited.

"Even if I have, I still don't know what to do with it."

"It flows," Dad said. "Like a circuit board."

Circuit board.

The fact that Dad even mentioned it made Beatrice suspect that he was the one who had taped the old leather pouch to the table in his California cabin in the woods.

Or did he?

"What do you know about the circuit board?" Beatrice asked.

"I've seen it before. Sometimes Philomena made jewelry out of old boards."

Ah. Philomena must have played a bigger role than Beatrice expected.

The bad news was that Beatrice had handed the circuit board to Kenichi and Benjamin. She hadn't paid enough attention to the board, and even if she had, she did not possess a photographic memory.

All she remembered was the pattern on the rug inside the lab office because she had walked over it for years.

She closed her eyes.

She couldn't see the rug now.

She closed her eyes tighter. Placed her fingers on her forehead as if that could help her remember.

"You have a headache, girl?" Molyneux asked.

"No. I'm just thinking. Shhh." Beatrice felt brave.

Slowly, bits and pieces of the pattern on the rug appeared. She picked up a red marker from the pile of markers on the floor, and attempted to complete the pattern on the butcher paper taped to the floor with masking tape.

She hoped that whoever Benjamin sent would bring the circuit board and golden key. They might be useful.

It was odd that Dad would leave such an important piece of clue in the cabin, but fortuitous that Beatrice had picked it up when she did before the cabin burned down.

If Dad had left it, he would have known to get it before he came here.

Unless he didn't know about the stash.

Could Philomena have left the pouch for her? Or for anyone?

Twelve hours prior, Dad had mentioned that Philomena was a "fellow treasure hunter."

Could Philomena have found the lost Amber Room, but didn't tell anyone, not even Dad?

"Hurry up!" Molyneux barked into Beatrice's ears.

"If you push me, I'm going to blank out, and then we will get nowhere," Beatrice said.

"You're weaker than your birth mother!"

"She's dead, so I'm doing better than she is, am I not?" What Beatrice said threw off Molyneux.

"You're more like I am than Philomena," Molyneux said. "How can it be?"

"You raised me until I was five years old, remember? You adopted me and cared for me as a mother would."

Molyneux went silent. Her eyes softened. Perhaps she thought she had a daughter after all.

It wasn't Beatrice's intention to reestablish a mother-daughter relationship. She just wanted to make sure Molyneux didn't set off the C-4 in her vest and that of her dad's.

"Right now, we still have a puzzle to solve," Beatrice said. "If we mess up here, we could all die in a cave-in. Maybe you should go upstairs and wait."

"No," Dad snapped. "Imogen stays here with us. If we die, she dies with us."

Molyneux laughed. "Look at you two. You just found each other twelve hours ago and already you're bickering."

Beatrice took a deep breath. She coughed. The air in this end of the tunnel wasn't that great. She wondered how much oxygen they had. "How's the oxygen level in here?"

"It's fine. Shut up and open the door."

Dad drank some water. He offered the bottle to Beatrice. She quickly shook her head. Biological father or not, she wasn't going to drink from the same water bottle.

"Isn't it ironic, Imogen?" Dad wiped sweat off his head. "You want us to open the door carefully, but you made us wear vests with explosives all around. If we explode, the whole church explodes with us."

"We already established that." Molyneux paced the floor. She motioned to one of her guards surrounding them. In minutes, a director's chair appeared and she sat on it.

"Dad, help me figure this out." Beatrice reached for the brooches. "I think if we put the cabochons on the right intersections in succession, the door would open."

She looked up. The steel door had an array of indentations in a grid. She looked down at her brooches. Maybe the cabochons fit into those indentations.

She started with the two-amber brooch because

she knew it was real. She could not pry the amber off the brooch.

"What are you doing?" Molyneux looked alarmed.

"Testing something." Beatrice knew that if she succeeded, then she would immediately fail with the other two brooches since they were fake amber.

She wondered if the indentations checked the weight of the amber pieces. If they did, she was a goner. Molyneux would immediately know that the brooch box she had stolen from Beatrice at the San Francisco bank the other day was all a set-up.

God, help us get out of here ASAP.

"Your father and I were quite a team," Molyneux said. "We would probably have found the Amber Room a long time ago if he had been able to control his urges."

"You were gone a lot," Dad said.

"Still, no excuses. A marriage is a bond of life-long trust." Molyneux turned to Beatrice. "Remember that when you get married."

Beatrice nodded. Taking advice from a mass murderer?

"He cheated on me so many times I lost count," Molyneux said. "I never expected he would go for your nanny, but now I know she wasn't a real nanny after all. It was only a ruse—for which I paid fifty percent!"

Beatrice didn't want to get into her parents' issues, but here they were. "He lived for another twenty years after you tried to kill him the first time."

Molyneux shrugged. "Longevity runs on his side of the family."

"How did you find him again a second time?" Beatrice asked.

"Yeah. Tell her how I ended up here," Dad said. "You never told me."

"One name: Philomena. Your greatest love was also your greatest downfall."

Beatrice wondered what could have happened had Philomena still been alive. "She sold her family treasures to make ends meet after Dad ghosted her, and you tracked her to Cannes and California."

"Your boyfriend was in the way." Molyneux snarled. "If I see him again, he's dead. You can find someone else."

There is no one else.

Beatrice was surprised at her own thought.

Very surprised indeed.

CHAPTER FORTY-THREE

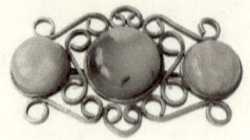

Leaves rustled in the night but there was no breeze. Crouched behind a mausoleum, Benjamin and Jake drew their weapons.

A shadow moved.

Ansel?

Jake thought the security chief had gone round the old church to secure the perimeter on the other side, around the large narthex entrance.

Jake adjusted his night vision goggles to see better as several shadows came closer. He held his breath.

Benjamin didn't move either.

Then they heard whispers. Men and women. Russian.

Someone large and heavily armed approached the two men, weapons down.

"FSB. We're here to assist." In English now.

"To take home the Amber Room or parts of it?" Benjamin asked.

"Whatever you find belongs to Russia."

"Of course. May I see some identification?"

The man complied.

Jake wasn't sure how Benjamin could read the ID in such low light with only the glow of his wristwatch. Besides, it was probably in Russian.

Benjamin took a photograph of the identification card.

The Russians wanted an assessment of the situation. Jake hesitated to say anything. They didn't know for sure what was going on inside the church.

All doors were heavily guarded.

Jake noticed that Benjamin did not mention Ansel or his team.

"Is Molyneux inside?" FSB asked.

"Presumably." Benjamin didn't say more.

"Then we take her home in a body bag. She is wanted in Russia."

Jake remembered that Beatrice wanted Molyneux alive so that she would have more opportunities for repentance. Truth be told, some people had gone too far to repent. While he hoped that

Molyneux had more chances yet, he also knew that only God could read the human heart.

As a former FBI agent, Jake no longer had jurisdiction here. He had come as a civilian working for Hu Knows, Inc. If he still had his badge, he could claim that Molyneux was his to take home to the USA or to hand over to the International Criminal Court in The Hague.

From the corner of Jake's eye, he spotted more people fanning out. "Ben, better let Ansel know."

Benjamin nodded. He texted Ansel.

Ansel replied that he had already met his FSB counterparts. It helped that Ansel spoke multiple languages, including Russian.

When Jake saw the weapons moving all around him, he was more than worried.

Beatrice was inside.

But inside where?

Jake prayed silently that God would let Beatrice know they were coming to rescue her. He wasn't sure if such a prayer would be answered, but God could do anything. It said so in Luke 1:37.

For with God nothing will be impossible.

Jake whispered the verse into the wind. Then

he felt little drops of water on his exposed forehead, and more water on his night vision goggles.

Then the rain poured.

Great.

J ake could barely hear Benjamin in the pouring rain. They were the last people behind the mausoleum.

Benjamin checked the map on his water-proof phone strapped to his wrist. He tilted it so Jake could see the map of the thirteenth-century church.

"Not too many heat pockets on the main floor," Benjamin said.

"I think they're in the basement."

"In the undercroft," Benjamin said.

"Or further down. The crypt. Somewhere an old golden key could be used."

"Does this place have catacombs?" Benjamin swiped his phone. Shook his head. Then he pointed to what looked like the transept of the church.

Jake nodded.

They made a dash in the rain. Hampered by the wet soil and grass, Jake dragged a bit with his bad leg. It wasn't too bad, but it had only been days. He could use a few more weeks of healing.

Ansel's men stood watch at the transept nearest them. They let Jake and Benjamin inside. At least a dozen of Ansel's men followed them in.

"Look out for friendly fire," Jake told Benjamin through their headsets. He saw a door, just like what Benjamin's phone was showing. "That way."

Crossing silently across the dusty mosaic floor under arches and pillars, Jake and Benjamin headed toward the heat source. The signal from the fake brooch box was stronger now, more than ever.

Jake was confident they were getting to the box.

Whether that also led to Beatrice was another matter.

As they turned a corner, Jake heard voices, male and female. He listened, and recognized Molyneux's voice from his three years of having been undercover at her organization. He could pick out the girl-next-door voice anywhere.

Apparently, Benjamin heard their voices too.

Jake wondered if Benjamin also knew what Molyneux sounded like.

They slowed down. There was light coming out of the hallway.

When they reached the end of the hallway,

Jake realized the voices had echoed out from one floor below. The crypt?

However, the crypt was empty. There was a small chapel there with stone benches in front of the altar. No one was there.

How deep is this small church? Perhaps the builders had envisioned a cathedral but never got there?

The voices kept coming.

Jake followed the voices. He could also hear the rain pelt the church roof outside.

As he neared the stone stairwell, he heard two women talking.

"I don't have children of my own, Amber." It was Molyneux's voice again.

"My name is Beatrice."

Beatrice!

She's alive. Thank God!

"I named you Amber after the Amber Room," Molyneux said. "Your dad wanted to call you Beatrice. I guess he had his chance when you all entered WITSEC."

"Let us go," Beatrice pleaded.

"After you open the door."

Jake touched his cargo pants pocket. He had both brooches in there. Benjamin had taken them out of the lab safe. Somehow, he trusted Jake enough to let him carry them. Technically they had been handed over to the FBI, although Jake had no badge when Benjamin put him in charge of the brooches.

Why did he do that?

Was that a test to see how much Jake could be trusted...with his sister?

At the top of the stairs, Benjamin hesitated.

Jake stepped forward. He had combat experience from his Army days, and also extensive training in the FBI.

Quietly, the team went downstairs, toward the voices, and straight into the vortex of no return.

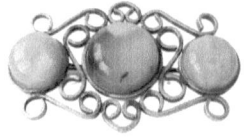

CHAPTER FORTY-FOUR

"Say goodbye." Molyneux left her director's chair.

"No, please," Beatrice pleaded. "We'll try again. Maybe the cabochons needed to be rearranged."

"You've tried it many times in the last two hours."

"We need a laptop to calculate the permutations." Even as Beatrice said those words, she knew they didn't need another computer.

What they needed were the two original brooches back at the lab safe in Charleston. The four fake amber cabochons they had didn't have the right weight to open the steel door.

And yes, they needed the circuit board.

The pattern was there all along.

Since Dad couldn't figure it out, Beatrice was even more convinced now that the one person with the answer had been Philomena. And she was dead.

Perhaps she taped the circuit board to the table so that someone would find it.

Perhaps she had carried that secret with her for so many years.

The golden key made sense now, even though Beatrice couldn't see where it might be used.

"I want to try again," Dad said.

"Let me try again, and please let him go," Beatrice clasped her hands together. "He's seventy-seven years old. He doesn't have long to live. His girlfriend is dead. He missed out on twenty-five years of our lives. Have pity on him."

"What about me?" Molyneux said. "I lost my marriage. Lost my lover. Lost my two children. Who pities me?"

She didn't retreat far from the door.

A whole army, dressed in black from head to toe, leveled their weapons directly at Molyneux and her people.

"Hello again," a male voice said.

Slowly, Beatrice stood up. "Jake?"

The man removed his night vision goggles. The room was bright enough without them.

Sure enough, it was Jake.

"Are you okay—oh no!" Jake yelled.

He must have seen her vest.

The man next to him took off his goggles as well.

"Ben!" Beatrice remained where she was. She was so happy that Benjamin had left the house—but a fire was not what she wanted him to walk into.

"Couldn't let my baby sister have all the fun," Benjamin said.

"Eugene?" Molyneux asked.

"Stop right there," Benjamin pointed his weapon at her. "Stop, I say."

"Eugene, don't you recognize me?" Molyneux said. "I'm your mother."

"I don't think so." Benjamin stepped forward. "You were never my mother."

Molyneux was as fast as lightning as she lifted her arm. Her free hand pointed to the detonator. "Do you know what this is?"

"No!" Beatrice shrieked.

"Calm down," Dad said. He was on the floor with his legs stretched out. He wasn't getting up.

"Dad's got the same vest as I do," Beatrice said. "Molyneux has both detonators."

"Dad?" Benjamin stayed where he was. "You're alive?"

"She tried to kill me at least three times, at the last count." Dad started to cough. "Good to see you, son."

Beatrice wondered if the dust in the room was getting to him. "We have to get out of here."

"No one gets out." Molyneux kept her arm lifted, finger on the button.

Everyone froze.

"The whole church building will cave in," Molyneux said. "We'll be buried together with the crates behind the steel door—"

Beatrice's jaw dropped when she saw someone from the crowd of armed soldiers throw a dagger. It spun its way toward Molyneux's arm, piercing through her hand. She dropped the remote control.

Beatrice saw it fall and she ran toward it—and caught the remote in one hand.

She didn't know how she did it.

Loud voices came through the tunnel. Russian spoken very quickly. Their weapons in front of them, the second team of people dressed in black Kevlar and combat boots marched toward Molyneux, execution style.

Beatrice stepped in front of Molyneux, who held her wounded hand in the other. Beatrice spread her arms. "No! Stop!"

She could hear Jake's voice, asking the Russians to hold their fire. Ansel translated Jake's English words into Russian.

The Russian forces waited, submachine guns in hand.

"Enough killings," Beatrice said. "Let her get a fair trial."

"Step away from her," one of the Russians said in English.

"No. She's my mother—adoptive, but a mother, nonetheless. Someone please call the police. Let the police arrest her."

For some reason, the Russians didn't protest. Their leader nodded. "Let her go to trial for war crimes."

Ansel stepped forward to tie up Molyneux until the police came. He attended to her wounds and stopped the bleeding on her hand.

The Russians turned their attention to Molyneux's guards, rounding them up and disarming them of their weapons, while Jake was all over Beatrice.

"We'll get you out of this." His voice was tense. "I need some tools!"

Benjamin came over, flashlight in hand.

With the help of Ansel and the Russian commander, Jake and Benjamin removed the vests from Beatrice and Dad.

The Russian commander sent someone to take the vests out of the church.

Nearby, Molyneux sat on the floor, watching everything. She was heavily guarded by Russian forces.

By the time Beatrice looked up, the cave was not as crowded as before. Molyneux's guards were gone. She assumed they had been taken upstairs.

She heard a new set of footsteps.

The Polish police had arrived. They talked to Ansel and the Russian commander.

Jake went around Beatrice to Molyneux. "I didn't throw the dagger."

"I know. You wouldn't have been able to do it." Molyneux grinned. "Besides, it was Russian-made. How fitting, isn't it?"

Jake had nothing to say.

"Take care of my daughter," Molyneux said.

"I will."

"I know you will because you love her."

Beatrice heard every word. She waited for Jake to deny it. He did not.

Something in Beatrice's heart fluttered. She hoped it wasn't heart palpitations due to the stress of carrying a vest loaded with explosives.

CHAPTER FORTY-FIVE

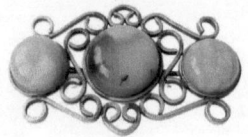

After the vests were removed from Beatrice and her dad, Jake felt a great relief. He silently thanked God and reminded himself to pray with Beatrice later.

"Did you bring the brooches and the circuit board?" Beatrice asked.

Jake handed her the brooches. Their hands touched again. Beatrice gave him a quick hug, and then removed the amber cabochons from the brooches.

Benjamin handed the circuit board to his father. Their eyes were red.

Jake felt sorry for them. Many years had passed them by. Father and son met again, but there was nothing left to say. The damages had been done.

The grief had been wept away. What more was left?

"Why are you still alive?" Benjamin barely got the words out.

"You're not happy to see me?" Chisolm asked. "Your sister was relieved I made it this far."

"After all these years."

"That's what she said too." Chisolm pointed to Beatrice.

"You're not my real father, are you?" Benjamin asked in a whisper.

"What is a real father?" Chisolm retorted.

Jake heard a sniffle, and turned his attention to Beatrice, who was blinking away tears. Silently, he prayed for the Wright family, now that everything in their lives had gone wrong.

Jake stayed by Beatrice's side as she and her brother and dad figured out how to unlock the steel door. It seemed to be holding up the ceiling above it —and thereby the undercroft, the crypt, and the church itself.

Handcuffed and now in the custody of the Polish police, Molyneux asked to stay for a few moments.

"I waited thirty years or more for this," Molyneux told them.

The Polish police ended up waiting with the

Russians, who had been joined by a representative from the Consulate in Poland. All of them wanted to see what was behind the door.

"The circuit board was embedded inside a postcard, you say?" Chisolm Wright, aka Thomas Peterson, said.

Beatrice nodded.

"Isn't the circuit board a modern invention, though?" Jake asked.

"Paul Eisler invented the printed circuit board in 1936, seven years before the Amber Room disappeared," Beatrice said.

"No kidding."

"Philomena knew about this place." Chisolm shook his head. "Yet she never said a word. All those years and not a single time did she talk about this place."

"Why is that?" Jake asked.

Chisolm shrugged. "Maybe she felt that history was best left alone."

"If so, why did she try to sell the brooches to the FBI?"

"People do things we don't understand. Now I realize that I didn't know her at all."

Jake wondered. How long had Philomena known about this vault? Why hadn't she told anyone? It could've been her insurance.

Instead, the very person whom Molyneux killed was the one who could have led her to the Amber Room.

That was, if there really was anything left of it.

From the size of the door and the church above, Jake figured that only small parts of the Amber Room were behind that door—if any at all. Many historians believed that the original Amber Room no longer existed.

After a couple more hours of rearranging the stones to fit certain permutations, one of them worked.

"Take a photo of the pattern, Ben." Beatrice wiped her forehead.

Her face was red and her blouse was soaked through. Rivulets of sweat flowed down her forehead and cheeks.

Jake had ordered fans to be brought in, but it took a while for them to arrive.

Click!

Everyone froze.

Beatrice nodded to her dad. Benjamin helped the white-haired man to stand up. His hands shook as he pulled the door handle.

As soon as the door opened, a whoosh of dust came out, and the fans blew it all around the room.

Everyone coughed and covered their noses and eyes.

Jake heard a soft trickle of what sounded like water.

The floor in the room was wet.

There, among statues, sculptures, gargoyles, and work tools from the nineteenth century, were crates. Five, six, seven or more of them.

In shackles and handcuffs, Molyneux and her handler shuffled to see, but she didn't get first dibs. Representatives from the Russian Consulate, holding their phones while live-streaming the event to the Catherine Palace curators in Russia, were the first to enter the space.

Jake knew there was a reward for finding the Amber Room, and it seemed that this discovery would go a long way toward helping Chisolm stay out of long-term prison. A thief he might be, but he was no murderer like Molyneux.

"Open a crate already," Chisolm said, waiting at the door.

"This could have been ours," Molyneux said to him.

"It belongs to the Russian people," Chisolm replied.

"And that might be why Philomena never told you about it."

Chisolm didn't say a word to her.

Jake found himself standing next to Beatrice. She had tears in her eyes. Jake leaned toward her and whispered in her ear. "It's going to be okay."

Beatrice reached for his hand. "My birth mother died for this."

"Who?" Jake asked. "I thought you didn't know who your birth mother was."

"Dad told me."

Slowly, the realization hit Jake. "Philomena?"

Molyneux had killed Philomena. And everything Molyneux had done in the last four or five years was for the express purpose of getting to the Amber Room.

It would have made her at least half a billion dollars richer if she had sold pieces of it on the black market.

"A very small part of the Amber Room," Chisolm said. "Open up, people. I waited decades for this."

Using one of Molyneux's crowbars, the Russians opened the first crate.

There were panels and more panels of eighteenth-century art carved into amber. Stacks and stacks of them.

Pieced together, they would form parts of the

Amber Room. Jake didn't know what percentage of the room would be covered.

"Someday we'll go to Russia and see the Amber Room with these real panels in it," Jake said to Beatrice.

She nodded. And squeezed his hand gently.

CHAPTER FORTY-SIX

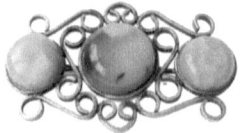

R einstated as an FBI Special Agent, Jake Kessler spent the next six months at a temporary position at the cybersecurity arm of the FBI overseeing hackers and going under-cover to keep an eye on them. He felt like he was on a stage, acting in a play.

It was less dirty work than when he had been in deep undercover at Molyneux's lair. Jake felt relieved to see her on trial for war crimes. However, it wasn't over yet.

Meanwhile, he had a new job to do.

Jake's colleague, long-time FBI Special Agent Stella Evans had vouched for him at the National Cyber Investigative Joint Task Force, getting him a position there. Yet he wasn't interested in his own heroics.

He took the job because the jailed Molyneux refused to cooperate with the authorities about her extensive cyberspace presence. Since the FBI needed the information to shut down her operations, it must be mined in another way.

This was where the NCIJTF came in. Stella's team stood poised to destroy Molyneux's Internet stranglehold. Jake would deliver the black box, so to speak.

After this was over, Jake might choose a career outside the federal government. Maybe he could leave the Bureau altogether and go to work for Helen Hu, or better yet, work with Beatrice Glynn. Right now, neither one had panned out.

Helen had enough people working at Hu Knows, Inc. Jake would end up as a contract investigator, if at all.

As for Beatrice, their adventure ended, and Jake had no reason to hang around Charleston, especially when Beatrice was probably not there.

In fact, he had no idea where Beatrice went. She traveled a lot, and that was a problem for Jake.

He wanted to settle down. He did not want a relationship in which both spouses traveled to everywhere but home.

Perhaps Beatrice was not for him.

Perhaps God had other plans.

Had he considered moving on?

That might be another reason he needed work. He had to get his mind off Beatrice.

After church one Sunday, he packed for a weeklong conference in Zurich. He had been given a choice to attend a conference in San Francisco or Zurich.

He didn't want to go back to California. Too many memories of Beatrice. Every time he thought about it, his heart simply ached.

So Zurich it was.

Unfortunately, his new partner and old friend Stella Evans had been preoccupied with babysitting a bunch of hackers in Atlanta in a classified project. She could not go.

His direct supervisor told him they would send someone else to go with him to the Cyberspace Meets Real Life conference, which a surveillance target of theirs would attend.

The target was the missing link between a Libyan arms dealer and Molyneux's organization.

The cybercriminal known as 819A repeatedly broke into museum computers and manipulated their security systems. After he cracked open the museum back doors, his clients would enter later to steal artifacts worth millions of dollars.

If Jake could record 819A talking to at least two or three prospective clients about what he would do for them and how he made his living, Jake would hit the jackpot.

The FBI Art Crime Team would like to talk to him, as would several countries in Europe whose museums had been broken into in the last several months.

Shortly after Jake packed, he made the fifteen-minute drive to the Baltimore/Washington International Thurgood Marshall Airport, where he boarded his airplane to Zurich. It would take over sixteen hours of flight with two stops, one in Atlanta and the other in Amsterdam, where he would change planes.

On long flights like this, he'd rather not be alone, but there was nothing he could do about it. However, long flights afforded him a chance to catch up on sleep, undisturbed. He wore a travel mask, as had been his routine when flying overseas —so that he didn't catch cold and flu germs from anyone. One time, some kid sitting next to him coughed and sneezed the entire time, and there was nothing Jake could do about it on the overbooked flight, except to ask the flight attention for a travel mask.

In the business class, the seat next to Jake was empty. It was supposed to be Stella's seat. Since it was an aisle seat, Jake moved and sat there instead. He stretched his long legs.

As everyone took their seats, Jake recharged his phone at the USB socket in front of him. He thumbed through the movie offerings. Seeing nothing of interest, he decided he'd take a short nap until they reached Atlanta, and then take a longer nap—something like eight hours—on the connecting flight to Amsterdam. From Schiphol airport to Zurich, he probably should stay awake for the two-hour flight.

He wished he had someone to talk to on the flight. He recalled his conversations with Beatrice in her Gulfstream. He had never gotten along with anyone else better than he had with Beatrice.

Think about work, Jake.

In his head, he ran through the itinerary for the next day. He was supposed to hit the ground running by attending something like five workshops that were useless to him. That would go on for four days and then on the fourth night, he would attend a ball. Since he didn't dance, he'd have to do other things while all the time trying to get close enough to 819A to record his conversations.

He closed his eyes and thought of all the things he could do to kill time when he arrived in Zurich the next day.

Read a book.

Read two books.

Watch the news.

Read more books.

Maybe keeping busy would take his mind off Beatrice. He wondered what she was doing and thought of texting her as he had done occasionally in the last six months since they had put Molyneux away.

He tried to see her face in his mind. Her smile.

Jake could hear her voice. Calm, quiet, unassuming.

He smiled as he recalled the times she had saved his life.

Calling Helen when he was drowning in the fishing vessel at sea outside France.

Pulling him to the ground so he didn't get shot in San Francisco.

Rescuing him and Earl in the redwood forest. He did return the favor by keeping her safe later on.

Rescuing him again in her dad's cabin when Molyneux's men beat him up and tortured him.

And fighting off Molyneux before she could blow them all up to kingdom come.

Being rescued so many times made Jake feel like he had only been a hero once. Of course, he had come through when duty called, but she did more things for him than he had done for her.

The plane left for Atlanta, and he dozed off for the entire flight without eating anything. An hour and forty minutes later, he disembarked and boarded a bigger plane for Amsterdam. All around him, some people wore masks and some didn't.

Jake found his seat, and once again, the aisle seat was empty.

He moved over and buckled in. He tried to go to sleep sitting up. He could hear voices all around him, and prayed that there would be no crying babies on board, because his earplugs were in the overhead bin, and he didn't feel like getting up to retrieve them.

"You're in my seat."

Jake's eyelids sprang open so wide that his eyeballs were going to pop out. Fortunately, he was wearing a mask, so no one could see his jaw drop.

He was hearing things, surely.

He blinked. Looked to his right.

Big brown eyes above a floral mask smiled back at him. He could recognize those eyes anywhere. Her hair was hidden beneath a baseball cap. She wore a simple sweatshirt and a pair of sweatpants.

"Bee...uh... What's your name?" He almost gave away her name in front of all these strangers.

"Sandra. And you are?"

"Matt."

"Well, Matt, you're in my seat." She waved her phone at him.

He thought he was looking at an e-ticket, but the message said, "Hello Jake."

Jake's heart swelled, and he unbuckled his safety belt. He returned to his original seat.

"Thank you." Beatrice sat down. She was carrying a small crossover satchel to match her mask.

"Where are you heading?" Jake swallowed.

"Zurich. You?"

"Same."

"Really?" She chuckled. "What are you doing there?"

"Meeting some friends. I might see someone whom I...love."

She went quiet before she said, "Sounds like a vacation."

"It can be when I see the right people." He was surer of it now, more than ever.

"Does that person know about your love?" she asked.

"I don't know if I'll ever tell...her."

"Oh? Why not?" Beatrice placed a blanket on her lap.

"Because I'm not sure if it'll ever work out. We work in different worlds. We might not get to see each other all year long."

"It's hard to be separated like that."

"For sure."

"Well, nice to chat with you now but don't expect me to talk much throughout the flight," Beatrice said. "I'm planning on sleeping most of the way."

"Same here."

"Good. Glad we established some ground rules —I mean, flight rules." She buckled in and closed her eyes.

Jake had questions for her.

Would she be attending the same conference as he was?

Who had called her? Hired her? Was it Stella who recommended her?

So many questions.

Yet the most important thing right now was

how God had given him his heart's desire. He had wanted to see Beatrice again.

And here she was.

He leaned toward her. "I can't believe you're here."

She placed her hand in his without saying a word.

He held it.

Even if they didn't talk the rest of the flight, he was simply satisfied to sit with her.

Was this what love looked like? To be together without having to say a word?

Whether it was or not, Jake felt content.

He would sleep soundly tonight.

CHAPTER FORTY-SEVEN

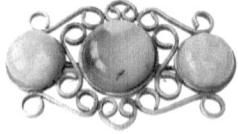

T he Zurich weather in November was cold and colder, but inside the ballroom was anything but cold. The heat was up, especially when Beatrice spotted Jake entering through a set of double doors.

She wasn't supposed to recognize him at all. And yet they had sat in adjacent seats in the airplane on Sunday night, and their hotel rooms were across the hallway from each other's.

Anyone who could put two and two together would realize that this wasn't random.

Tonight, Beatrice had dressed modestly in a shimmery gown that she was afraid of tripping on. As a result, she walked very slowly and carefully along the length of the ballroom, looking for a chair to sit down and watch the couples, hoping nobody would invite her to the dance floor.

Her glasses were thick, but they stayed on her prosthetic nose.

People milled about her, talking. She sat there, listening.

"May I have this dance?"

Beatrice lifted her face. It was Jake, with a poor attempt at a mustache.

"That looks...awful," she said quietly.

"Thick glasses. Another nose," he replied.

"Careful. Walls have ears. You don't want to insult me right now." Stern warning? Too stern?

"I'm astounded you're still here," Jake said. "May I have this dance?"

"I hate to confess I'm not much of a dancer."

"Neither am I."

"Sit with me a while, then." She patted the empty spot on the bench seat.

Jake sat down, but the conversation was cut short.

A tipsy 819A ambled by.

Why would anyone name himself a number? Beatrice wondered what she should call him.

"Excuse me. Sandra, right?" 819A asked.

Beatrice nodded. "Have you considered my offer, Mr. 819A?"

"As a matter of fact, yes." He leaned toward her, the smell of liquor all over his breath. "But first, may I have this d-dance?"

"Of course." Without looking at Jake, Beatrice stood up and went with their quarry.

She tried to enjoy the waltz, but every time they passed by Jake, she could tell that he was not happy to see her dance with someone else—especially someone who had tried to kiss her cheeks numerous times.

She half-expected him to cut in, but was grateful that he did not.

She didn't want to go through this another time. 819A was one of the vilest men she had ever met. This was the only time she had agreed to help Stella.

Because she wanted to get a gift for her brother.

And she thought she would see Jake again.

Although not this pouting Jake.

"I can give you the world," 819A said in the middle of hanging on to her because his footwork was less than synchronous with the live orchestra music.

"Really?"

"Would you come with me to explore the world?"

"Where would be our first stop?" Beatrice asked sweetly.

"Anywhere you want."

"Caribbean?"

"Sure."

"Mediterranean?"

"By all means. You don't ask for much." He tried to kiss her on the lips, but Beatrice was faster than he was and turned the other cheek.

From the corner of her eye, she spotted Jake springing to his feet.

She might be running out of time if Jake came over here and broke up her conversation.

"Are you saying you're more adventurous than I am?" Beatrice asked.

"Yep. I go places you've never dreamed of."

"Oooh. Take me. Take me. Where is one of the most exotic places you have been?"

His eyes lit up. "Have you ever been to Libya?"

"Isn't that in Africa somewhere?"

819A nodded. "In the desert. It's hot and you'll have to take off all your clothes."

Beatrice tried not to react. "Libya is a whole country. Any particular place in mind?"

"Have you ever heard of Benghazi?"

F BI Special Agent Stella Evans waited for Beatrice after the ball that evening, and so did Jake.

"What's taking her so long?" Jake paced the floor.

"She's on her way up in the elevator," Stella said. "I told her I'd be here waiting."

Jake drew a deep breath. He felt more uptight than usual. Maybe it was the memory of seeing 819A putting his hands on Beatrice's shoulders or his incessant kisses on her cheek. Beatrice cleverly averted her lips—something she hadn't done with Jake.

"I've never seen you so antsy." Stella processed something on her laptop.

Jake stopped in front of Stella. "He could've discovered the wire."

"Why would he? It was only a dance. It wasn't like she was going to sleep with him."

Jake bristled.

"I was kidding." Stella chuckled. "It's all spelled out in her contract. What we expected of her and what we wanted her to do to get the information out of 819A."

"Why did she agree to it?"

"She wants to get a special gift for her brother,

and 819A has it," Stella said. "In fact, the moment I saw her searching for that artifact, I knew we could help each other."

"What artifact?" Jake found it curious that Beatrice had agreed to go so far out of her way to get whatever it was she was getting for Benjamin.

"You'll see when she comes in."

"Then she goes home?"

Stella nodded. "First thing in the morning."

Jake felt relieved. "You promise?"

"Yep. She got the information out of him like a charm, and she's done. All in one evening's work."

"Not really," Jake corrected her. "She's been in town for four days."

"And you've been hovering around her like you're her hero or something."

Am I her hero? "I wasn't hovering."

"You were too. You attended every workshop she went to."

That was true. Jake had rearranged his schedule at the conference to be with Beatrice.

"Didn't you have a good time?" Stella asked.

Jake had to admit he did. And he didn't have to pay a dime for it. "Well, I don't think I got much out of the workshops. Most of it went over my head."

Stella laughed as the hotel room door clicked.

Her hand flew to her holster.

Jake stepped back.

Beatrice entered the room and locked the door behind her. In her hand was a small bag.

She looked surprised to see him.

"Are you okay?" Jake asked.

"I need a shower."

"I bet."

"Talk to me afterwards." She grabbed some clothes from the closet and headed for the shower. She took her small bag with her into the bathroom.

As the shower ran, Jake turned his attention to the suddenly quiet Stella.

"This can't be." Her eyes were still on the screen. "I thought they took care of Benghazi."

"What?" Jake was curious now.

"819A said he wanted to take Beatrice to Libya —specifically to Benghazi."

"Because?"

"He said he wanted her to see the desert where his family came from."

"819A is Libyan?"

"Oxford educated, he left Libya as a baby. However, this is just now coming to light."

"Okay." Jake waited.

The bathroom door opened. Beatrice walked

out in a tee shirt and a pair of capris. Her wet hair was wrapped up in a towel.

She must have heard the last bits of their conversation. "Mr. Buchanan was his uncle."

Stella looked stunned. "The now-dead arms dealer who sold weapons for Molyneux so she could fund her terrorism?"

"How did you figure that out?" Jake asked.

"It was easy." Beatrice produced the bag she had brought into the room. Inside was a small wooden box.

"Is that a puzzle box?" Jake asked.

"Not just any puzzle box. It's a Japanese puzzle box or himitsu-bako," Beatrice said. "This box is one of the original puzzle boxes from the Kanagawa prefectures, and made by local craftsmen in the late nineteenth century. That puts it in the Meiji era in Japan. Benjamin wants it, and I decided to get it for him."

"Go on," Stella said.

"819A said this box belonged to his dead uncle. How, I do not know." Beatrice studied the box. "We talked a bit more after the dance, and he was very sad that his uncle was dead."

"Yeah, but that wasn't us."

No, it wasn't an FBI operation. Jake had heard about it. It had been the work of several private groups, including the security forces of a Middle Eastern kingdom whose family members had been threatened by Buchanan, working with a private organization who had been targeted by Molyneux several years prior.

"So you just talked. That's why it took you a while to get up here," Jake said.

Beatrice smiled at him. "Were you worried?"

Stella laughed. "I don't think Jake wants you to do this type of stuff."

"I was going to be at the conference anyway," Beatrice said. "My brother wants this box badly."

Stella nodded. "When I found that our paths were crossing, I made sure that the bureau paid for everything if she could help us get some information out of 819A."

"Thank you for this nice suite," Beatrice said. "And my plane tickets."

"Sorry I couldn't get you first-class. No seats." Stella returned to her laptop. "So it says here that someone is trying to reestablish Buchanan's stronghold in Libya. Could it be 819A?"

"That makes sense." Beatrice stepped closer to Stella, walking by Jake. "He's living with the memory of his favorite uncle."

Jake did everything he could not to reach out and hold Beatrice's hand in front of Stella. He focused on the box instead. "Did 819A give you the puzzle box?"

Beatrice chuckled. "No. I negotiated the price down."

"To what?"

"Nothing for you to worry about. Suffice to say that Benjamin would have to sell something to pay for it. He doesn't have room for everything either."

Jake had nothing more to ask about the box. He had met Benjamin in Charleston over six months ago. They had parted amicably after their rescue mission in Poland, but Jake wondered if he would ever see Benjamin again.

Or Beatrice.

Maybe he should calm down. When this conference was over, he might not see Beatrice again. He should be grateful for this opportunity to see her.

"Well, thank you, Beatrice. That was very helpful." Stella closed her laptop. "Have a safe flight home tomorrow morning."

"Okay. Thanks."

"Tomorrow morning?" Jake asked. "You're not staying for the last session?"

"There's no reason to. Besides, I need to fly back to Charleston to deliver this box. My brother can't wait to see it."

Jake wondered if he should change his flight schedule from the afternoon to morning so he could fly home at the same time as Beatrice. Should he? Shouldn't he?

"How about some dessert?" Stella asked. "We can order in."

"I'll have to walk it off, but why not?" Beatrice replied. "What would you like, Jake?"

"Me?" Jake asked. "I was going to go back to my room and pack."

He thought he might see if he could change his flight to the morning so he could carpool to the airport with Beatrice.

"Really, Jake?" Stella laughed.

"Stay. Please." Beatrice lifted the puzzle box up. "Extra scoops of ice cream if you can figure out how to unlock this box."

"Ah, a mental challenge. How can I resist?"

CHAPTER FORTY-EIGHT

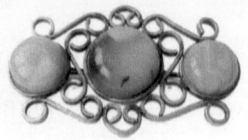

C harleston daily high temperatures in March fluctuated from the upper fifties to the low eighties. This afternoon, it was a pleasant sixty-two degrees with sunshine all around. Beatrice wandered into the garden, where Benjamin had ordered tulips, daffodils, and gardenias planted in the flower beds leading toward the butterfly garden on the other side of the herb garden.

Beatrice was sure that if Benjamin hadn't been a treasure hunter, he'd be a gentleman gardener. However, these days he was busy catching up with Dad, filling in the missing years, and then doing father-son things such as fishing...for information.

She knew that Benjamin was still searching for

his biological parents, but he also tried to forgive his adopted parents for what they had done to him and Beatrice all these years. He thought that perhaps if he spent more time with Dad, the truth about his birth might come to light.

Until then, father and son conversed on more mundane everything Glynn things, such as going on a treasure hunt or on an adventure together somewhere. They talked about searching for the lost Confederate gold, which Beatrice wasn't sure existed. It was certainly a folklore, but was it even true?

Still, it provided Benjamin and Dad something in common to talk about for the months remaining before the CIA had something else for Dad to do, and he would disappear again.

As for Beatrice, she was happy they had found Dad again, although that could never make up for the loss of her biological mother, who had been with them only for the first five years of Beatrice's life.

Beatrice wandered among the flowers and shady trees, and regretted leaving her phone in the house. All she had with her was a hardcover novel she was hoping to start reading. Stella had given it to her just before she flew out of Zurich back in November.

She remembered that Friday morning, eating breakfast with Jake one last time at the hotel. Since they were both undercover, they had been able to keep their disguises intact.

Jake had tried to put on a happy face, but she could tell he would have liked to fly with her back to the States. Unfortunately, Jake and Stella received word that the mole in the FBI was on the move. And off they went on their new assignment.

The sun was getting warmer, and Beatrice decided to head back to the house. There wasn't any bench to sit on among the flowers, and she did not want to sit on the grass where the ants and bugs were.

The porch was empty as was most of the ten-thousand-square-foot mansion. The personal chef came at certain times of the day. The maids cleaned the house at certain days of the week. The rest of the time, there were only five people in the house.

With their new mission, Benjamin and Dad kept Kenichi busy. Kenichi had seen his own potential of working with the hackers at Binary Systems, Inc., with whom he had collaborated to track down Molyneux. Now Beatrice and her brother were concerned he'd leave them for greener pastures.

To this day, Kenichi was still waiting for a call from Leland.

"Why go there when you get paid twice here?" Benjamin had blurted one fine day, pretty much confirming that Kenichi was working for Benjamin as well as Beatrice at the same time.

Double pay.

"I wish I could get double pay for the same amount of work," Beatrice whispered into the wind as she climbed the porch.

When she looked up, there he was.

Sitting in a rocker.

His hair was trimmed short. He was clean shaven. And he wore a plaid shirt and a pair of khaki shorts with hiking boots.

"Hey." Jake got up from the rocker and walked toward Beatrice. "Some hideaway you have here. No wonder your brother wouldn't leave."

Beatrice stood there at the edge of the porch.

She didn't know what to think.

Jake.

"How did they let you in?" Beatrice asked.

"Your brother invited me."

"Why?"

"I asked him if he would let me date his little sister." Jake lifted Beatrice's free hand—the other was still clutching the hardcover book—and gently kissed the back of her hand.

"I don't need his permission," Beatrice said

sweetly. Inside, she was pleased that Jake had respected her brother enough to check in with him.

"How did you contact him?"

"Your dad gave me his number."

"My dad?" Beatrice almost said she also didn't need Dad's permission to date. "I thought he was in WITSEC."

"Yes, but he's advising the FBI Art Crime Team on stolen World War II art pieces, so I got a message to him."

"What did he say?"

"That he's been out of your life for so long that he didn't feel he had the right to approve or disapprove."

"I don't need his approval either."

"He connected me to your brother." He rubbed the back of Beatrice's hand with his thumb.

"What did my brother say?" Beatrice knew her brother wanted the best for her.

"He said, 'Haven't you been together already?' I told him that was for work."

"We kissed on company time?" Beatrice rolled her eyes.

"Today I'm not on company time. Speaking of work, I bring you news from Stella. Your conversation with 819A yielded a treasure trove of data that goes a long way to protect national security. Your country thanks you."

"I'm glad to serve." It paid well, but that was part of the deal. And besides, she also achieved her goal of getting the Japanese puzzle box for Benjamin to add to his vast collection of puzzles.

"We handed the Libya information to the CIA, and they took care of it." That was all Jake said but Beatrice didn't ask for more information.

"You could have emailed or texted me regarding all that."

"I wouldn't be able to do this if I weren't here in person." Jake gently pulled Beatrice toward him.

She leaned against his chest. Feeling his warmth. Listening to his heartbeat.

They were silent for a while.

Then they were talking about work again.

"What are you doing these days?" Jake asked.

Beatrice wondered why he came all the way here to ask her about her work.

"I'm thinking of putting my doctorate to good use. Teach at some local colleges, or lecture at museums about World War II artifacts and such."

"Not much traveling there?" Jake's eyes were on hers.

"Only every now and then. And certainly no

undercover work. You? When do you go incommunicado again?"

Jake rubbed her shoulders. "About that, I moved into a supervisory role."

"Meaning a desk job?" Beatrice was surprised.

Jake nodded. "Thing is, I need to be myself after a while. I can't be undercover all the time. At my age..."

"You're what? Thirty-eight? You're talking like you're eighty-three."

"How did you know how old I am?"

Beatrice didn't say.

"That goes into the box of mystery questions that included how you knew I was drowning outside Cannes."

Beatrice didn't want to get into an argument with Jake, but she thought he should know the truth.

"My brother and I, with Kenichi, were tracking everyone who had anything to do with Molyneux. With your mole in the FBI selling data in the black web, your personal information was up for grabs."

"Personal? How personal?"

"Age, height, that sort of thing."

"How I squeeze my toothpaste?" Jake raised his eyebrows.

Beatrice laughed. "No, mainly your age and lots of photos of you."

"So you began tracking me."

"My whole team was. For only about a year. Not much to find, really. You weren't doing much."

Jake laughed. "Normally I'd argue with you, but it was true. I was transitioning out of being undercover."

"It helps that we were also watching Molyneux. I didn't out you."

"I know you didn't. The mole did—directly to Molyneux. That's how I ended up at sea outside Cannes."

"As for that, after we saw the news reports that Helen Hu and friends had helped to find the Petros eggs and a few broken panels from the Amber Room, we started tracking her. She was in Cannes. So we were in Cannes."

"And you were also after Philomena." Jake nodded. "All things considered, I'm glad we came out of the whole situation alive."

"Thank God." Beatrice grinned. "And now we're both going to be bored to tears being stuck at our new desk jobs."

"Are we?"

"Aren't we made for adventure?"

"I had fun while it lasted," Jake said. "Now I'm

all too happy to let young whippersnapper agents go instead of me. They have more energy, require less sleep, and they'd do daredevil things I don't want to do any more."

"What do you want to do?"

"I figured it's time for me to settle down and have my own family." Jake thumbed her jawline ever so gently.

A family? Did he say family?

"You know?" Jake whispered in her ear.

"Know what?"

"Know how I feel about you. That kiss on the bus. On the plane."

Beatrice remembered every moment, every touch.

"I have a surprise for you." Jake produced a small box from his pocket. "I know you like music boxes, but I don't know if you'll like this one."

Beatrice studied it. It was old. Maybe nineteenth century. "Where did you find this box?"

"I bought it at an antique shop."

"So tiny. What tune does it play?"

"Open it and see." Jake was on one knee before Beatrice opened the box.

"Twinkle, Twinkle, Little Star" filled their space.

Beatrice laughed so hard that she had tears in her eyes.

Not a classic tune that Beatrice had expected. Obviously, the music box was not an original, but more important to her was the fact that Jake had bought her one.

The tune went on for a while. Beatrice almost sang along.

When she looked inside the box again, she gasped at the diamond ring Jake had placed next to the pinned cylinder. "What..."

"Beatrice Glynn, love is your middle name. I've thought and prayed about this long and hard—more so after Zurich, where we met again after our death-defying adventure together." He blinked.

Were those tears in his eyes?

"Is it possible for me to fall in love with someone so fast, so hard, and never want to be with anyone else for the rest of my life? I say yes."

Beatrice nodded in agreement.

"The last four months without you have been the most tormenting time of my life, and I kept thinking I may never see you again, or that you would've have found someone new."

Beatrice shook her head. "No one else."

"That's good to know." Jake paused. "Clearly God

has brought us together again. I don't want to leave this place and never see you again. If I have to quit my job, I'll do it in a heartbeat just to be with you."

Beatrice was stunned. He had spoken what had been in her heart. She too would quit her job to be with him. In fact, she already had. She could teach anywhere in her new job.

"I know there are many details to sort out, but there is one most important thing. Do you love me?"

Tears pooled in Beatrice's eyes. Slowly, she nodded.

"Since when?"

"Since..." Dare she say it? Truth would always prevail, so she might as well tell him now. "I don't know when it all began... Perhaps Cannes. Perhaps earlier."

"I figured." Jake was still on his knees.

"You asked."

"While it seemed like a surprise to you that I'd pop the question today, I also know that you've known me longer than I've known you."

Beatrice's hand shook a little as she held the music box.

Jake wrapped his hands around hers. "You've done a lot for me."

"Anyone would have done those things," Beatrice admitted, knowing what he referred to.

"But none of them would have done it because they loved me that much."

"Did you forget something?"

"What?"

"You saved my life in the redwood forest—and Earl's life too. You confronted Molyneux to distract her from me."

"All in a day's work."

Beatrice smiled. "We do make a good team."

"Yes, we do." Jake held the diamond ring. "Beatrice Glynn, will you marry me?"

She closed her eyes, said a quick and nervous prayer, but she already knew what her answer would be.

"Yes."

And she extended her ring finger toward Jake, who happily placed the diamond ring there.

Beatrice pulled Jake to his feet, and they spent the next hour walking in the gardens as he kissed away her tears of joy.

CHAPTER FORTY-NINE

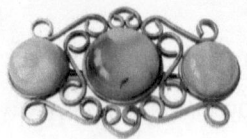

S ix months after Jake proposed to Beatrice on the porch of her family home, Dad finished his work for the CIA, but it came with a great cost. He re-entered the federal Witness Security Program for a second time, and his children would never see him again in his lifetime. Beatrice often wondered if he thought of them at all. No doubt he'd carry on his new life the way he had always done: away from his children.

Perhaps he was watching the wedding ceremony. Perhaps not.

Probably the former, if Beatrice had to guess. She knew now that most of the fortune that Benjamin and she inherited had not come from the Glynns, the venture capitalists in their own rights.

Instead, it had come from Chisolm Wright under the pseudonym of Thomas Peterson.

However, the government had not confiscated any of it because the money was legitimate. Apparently, Dad was quite the businessman and he had invested in whatever the Glynns had recommended. Whatever else Dad had done that was outside the law, that was where the penalty lay.

And that was where he was paying his penance.

Being banished to WITSEC would keep Dad alive.

That was all Beatrice could ask for. She had been praying for the last six months that God would get a hold of Dad. Perhaps he would attend church or meet Christians who could tell him about how Jesus could cleanse him of his many sins and offer him forgiveness and the gift of eternal life.

Perhaps praying would be the best thing she could do for Dad.

And so Benjamin would have the honor of giving Beatrice away today. Her bridesmaid was a reluctant Raynelle, who rarely wore dresses and gowns unless she was conducting an undercover operation.

Earl would be Jake's best man. His four brothers, his groomsmen. They were excited to meet

Beatrice and found her background fascinating. After she had given them the synopsis about her job as a treasure hunter, they all wanted to be one.

Ironically, she was leaving the high-flying adventure behind for a teaching job at a college in town. Jake would commute from Charleston to wherever his field assignment took him, until they moved him to a local FBI field office.

No, she did not believe she would miss her old job.

It was Benjamin's turn now. He seemed to have popped out of his cocoon after having to fly to Poland with Jake to rescue her. In fact, Beatrice heard through the grapevine that it had been Jake who invited Benjamin to go with him.

It would be nice to attend a real in-person church again after so many years of being on the road and catching podcasts on demand. The small church here had a women's group that Beatrice could socialize with whenever Jake was out of town.

He was going to find a way to not travel so much anymore, but Beatrice told him that she needed time to adjust to her new adjunct professor job, so she'd be busy with work and prepping the curriculum during the school year.

They agreed to regroup next summer to figure out where they would go from there.

Jake was determined that when they had kids, he did not want to be an absentee father.

But first we have to get married.

To protect everyone in attendance, Beatrice and Jake agreed to a small wedding at Glynn Chapel on the grounds of Glynn Estate. A small chapel, indeed, holding no more than a hundred people—fifty on the wooden pews on each side of the aisle.

A Glynn family friend, Pastor Wilcox must be pushing ninety or a hundred years old. He was wobbly on his legs, but was determined to stand through the entire wedding ceremony. All fifty minutes of it.

His wife had passed away many years ago, but Pastor Wilcox continued to preach "all the way to heaven." His personal goal was to go from the pulpit to heaven.

Beatrice prayed that he would live through their wedding day because for him to die while officiating the wedding would be awkward.

And tragic.

Speaking of *tragic*, Beatrice wondered what Philomena was really like as a mother. Her memories of her childhood until she was five were scanty as best. She wished she could sit down with Dad and ask him about Philomena. However, he had still been grieving before the U.S. Marshals whisked him away to parts unknown.

She did not want to broadcast this wedding online for anyone to see. So there would be no live-streaming, and thus no chance for Dad to watch his only daughter get married.

So sad.

Beatrice opened her eyes and found herself standing outside the bridal room, greeted by her brother, who had cleaned up and looked like a prince in that tuxedo.

"Ready?" Benjamin asked.

"Will we ever be?"

"I don't know. Never been married. Not sure if I'm going to marry any time soon."

"We don't know what will happen tomorrow. We're only given today." Beatrice recalled Matthew 6:34.

Take therefore no thought for the morrow: for the morrow shall take thought for the things of itself. Sufficient unto the day is the evil thereof.

"Let's focus on today then," Benjamin said.

"Focus on God for today? After all, the word

today is filled with evil—Oh!" She squeezed her brother's arm gently. "Forgive me, I've corrected you twice, and all you did was try to encourage me."

"Don't worry, little sister," Benjamin patted her gloved hand. "We know each other well. I'd rather you be transparent with me. And I promise to be honest with you the rest of my life."

"Thank you."

The wedding march started playing. Beatrice wanted to both smile and cry at the same time.

"I wish our parents were here," she whispered.

"God is with us. That's enough for us."

"Yes. God is enough." She sniffled.

The old chapel door opened. It was not a long walk up the aisle toward Jake, who grinned like a school boy. He looked dashing in his black tuxedo with a bow tie.

Standing next to him, Earl made faces, trying to make Beatrice laugh.

She chuckled. It was good to have friends like that, who knew that such a solemn moment sometimes required brief levity.

Benjamin handed Beatrice over to Jake, who smiled from ear to ear like he was going on a much-awaited field trip.

Pastor Wilcox held up—by sitting down on a

barstool—and conducted the ceremony flawlessly. Bride and groom exchanged traditional wedding vows to cherish each other until death.

Death.

The fact that it had to be brought up in a wedding reminded Beatrice of the brevity of life. Someday, she and Jake would grow old and pass away, leaving the next generation to fend for themselves and carry on. The cycle of life would continue until Jesus came back again.

But today was a happy day. A joyful day.

A peaceful day as a man and woman married in the presence of the Lord.

"I now pronounce you husband and wife. You may kiss the bride." The pastor closed his Bible.

Jake reached for Beatrice, as though they had all the time in the world, and that the fifty guests had no problem waiting. Slowly, he pushed aside her veil, which covered part of her face. He ran the back of his fingers across her chin.

Beatrice smiled. She did not want to get caught on camera saying, "Hurry up, will you?"

Jake found his way to her lips, a gentle touch that meant much to Beatrice. He had always been gentle with her. Always.

God knew the kind of man she needed in her life.

With her job as a treasure hunter, she'd had to go to some rough places to find clues and dig up artifacts. When she came home, she wanted to rest and relax and have everything quiet and just so.

Now that she would be at home for a long time, she wanted to continue living quietly with as little stress as possible.

God had sent a man who was calm in crisis, collected in conversation, and overall a charming hero for her daily life.

"Ladies and gentlemen, I introduce to you Mr. and Mrs. Jake and Beatrice Kessler."

Yes, Beatrice had decided to take her husband's last name. After all, she had been a Wright, Peterson, and Glynn. *What's a fourth last name?*

Everyone cheered and clapped as Beatrice and Jake waltzed down the aisle. They waved to Jake's parents sitting in front, and then to Jake's FBI friends. They waved to all the employees at Glynn Research, Inc. And they waved to—

There, sitting in the back row, were two people in wigs. Of course they were wigs. Beatrice could spot that nose and those eyes anywhere. He should have used a prosthetic nose.

Dad.

Beatrice smiled broadly. In her mind, she

JAN THOMPSON

suspected that he had sneaked out of WITSEC to be here today.

But who was that gorgeous fifty-something woman sitting next to him? She seemed to have a beach tan. Her arms were covered with freckles. And she had a hunk of a diamond on her ring finger.

Seriously, Dad?

Beatrice squeezed Jake's arm. He turned and nodded to Dad.

"Stay," Beatrice mouthed. She wanted to cry. "Please stay."

Slowly, Dad nodded.

And he did.

The reception was in Glynn Mansion ballroom a short walk away across the lawn. Half the FBI agents didn't stay, saying they had to get back to work. Jake's brothers were the life of the party. His sister merely sat to one side and kept busy on her phone.

As Jake chattered with well-wishers, Beatrice talked with Dad. He introduced the lovely lady as Amelia. "We eloped two days ago and this is our honeymoon."

"What?" Beatrice was stunned.

"At my age, there's no time to plan too much,"

Dad explained. "Better use the money for long honeymoons."

"Priorities."

"Exactly."

"Well, congratulations!" Beatrice hugged her new stepmother.

"Before we go, I want to leave you with this." Dad handed an envelope to Beatrice.

She felt a bump in the envelope. She peeked inside. There was a small USB drive.

"I wanted to write you a letter but I couldn't find the words," Dad said. "So Amelia recorded me while I talked about my life with your biological mother. I want you to know that you're very loved."

"I know."

"Someday when we meet again, you can tell me all about this Jesus who gives you strength and steadfastness."

Beatrice was taken aback by Dad's request. "What if we don't meet again?"

"Then it is what it is."

"No, Dad. It will be too late. May I tell you now what Jesus has done for me? How He took all my sins upon Himself, paid the death penalty that comes with sin, and set my soul free to experience eternal life with God in heaven?"

"What about the cake?" Dad asked. "You have to cut the cake."

"The cake can wait. Eternity is a very long time, Dad. Let's get on with it."

"All right." Dad followed Beatrice to a round table where she explained it all.

At the end of it, Dad said he would think about it some more.

Beatrice suggested he find a good local church where he lived—wherever it was—and start attending, in addition to reading the Bible, which he could get online or in an ebook format.

Dad hugged her, and then he and Amelia vanished.

"Was that real? Did that just happen?" Beatrice asked Jake. "I turned around and they were gone?"

"They went out that door. A chauffeur drove them away." Jake pointed.

As Beatrice stared at the open door, she saw Benjamin's back down the hallway beyond the door. He was in a hurry to get somewhere.

"Ray." Beatrice looked around.

"I'm here." Raynelle appeared out of nowhere in her bridesmaid gown. She was holding a glass of water. "I see he left sooner than expected."

"Be careful, okay?" Beatrice took the glass of

water from Raynelle's hand. "Go. You know what to do."

"Yes, ma'am." And off Raynelle went after Benjamin.

Jake leaned toward his wife. "What was that about?"

"Nothing." Beatrice handed the glass of water to a server passing by. "Glad you have good eyes and saw my father leave, or I'll still be searching for him."

"Are you sure your dad and Benjamin are not related? They both left abruptly."

"You meant rudeness is genetic?" Beatrice laughed. She pressed on the envelope that Dad had left her.

Jake lifted Beatrice's hand and kissed it. "What's in that envelope?"

"Family history."

"Would you like me to keep it since you don't have any pockets?" Jake asked.

"How observant you are."

"All the better to serve you." He put the white envelope inside his jacket pocket.

The music started to play.

"May I have this dance?" Jake asked. "I practiced."

"So have I." Beatrice chuckled at his silliness. They had practiced together for a few weeks.

"They're recording this for posterity." Jake led her to the dance floor for the slow waltz. "We'll do it for thirty seconds. That way we can show our grandkids that we know how to dance."

"Sounds like a plan." She laughed as they held each other, happy and content that they were where they needed to be at this time in their life together.

A gift from God.

Best treasure ever.

Dear Reader:

Thank you for reading *Once a Hero*. At Beatrice's wedding, we see her older brother, Benjamin, leave the reception early. Where does he go? We'll find out in *Once a Spy*, the next romantic suspense novel in the Protector Sweethearts series. Beatrice sends former CIA agent Raynelle Dryden to keep an eye on Benjamin. Amused, the billionaire lets Raynelle tag along as he hunts for the map of seventeenth-century pirate Blackbeard's last journey. Will Benjamin and Raynelle find more than sunken treasures in this enemies-to-lovers romantic suspense?

Once a Spy (Protector Sweethearts Book 3)
JanThompson.com/spy

Helen Hu is in ONCE A THIEF

In *Once a Hero*, we meet two private investigators, friends of Jake. Helen Hu is the owner of Hu Knows, Inc., where Earl works. Helen's story is in *Once a Thief*, in which she has to team up with a former art thief, Reuben Costa, to find her mother, who has disappeared after trying to return some bejeweled eggs she stole, back in her rebellious days. Will Reuben keep his end of the deal with Helen in this opposites-attract romantic suspense?

Once a Thief (Protector Sweethearts Book 1)
JanThompson.com/thief

Earl Young is in NEVER A TRAITOR

Jake's invaluable partner in *Once a Hero* is one of Helen's employees, Private Investigator Earl Young. After he recovers from his injuries, he is sent to protect a corporate whistleblower attending a conference in the Bahamas. He can't say no to a free vacation and free food. But first, he has to get Sienna Halstead out of the metropolis of Atlanta safely. Is Earl up to the task in this workplace romantic suspense?

Never a Traitor (Defender Sweethearts Book 1)
JanThompson.com/traitor

Stella Evans is in ZERO SUM

FBI Special Agent Stella Evans provides the inside track for Jake in *Once a Hero*. In the last chapters of this novel, Jake returns to the bureau and gets his badge back. Even though Molyneux is in jail awaiting trial, her network still needs to be dismantled. In Stella's story, *Zero Sum*, she finds out who created Molyneux's computer systems, and tracks down the software specialists. Unfortunately, they are all dead, except for one computer dude with a kill switch in his head. Will Stella be able to save Cayson Yang from certain death in this friends-to-more romantic technothriller?

Zero Sum (Binary Hackers Book 1)
JanThompson.com/zerosum

Sign up for my mailing list

If you like Christian romantic suspense, suspense thrillers, coastal and beach romance, and romantic women's fiction, feel free to sign up for my mailing list. I'm writing more books for you to enjoy.

JanThompson.com/newsletter

Would you please post a review?

Back to *Once a Hero*, if you enjoyed the novel, would you please write a review? Reviews are very helpful to other readers, especially those who are new to my books. You can find the book retailer link for *Once a Hero* here. Thank you.

Once a Hero (Protector Sweethearts Book 2)
JanThompson.com/hero

Sneak peek...

Continue reading for more information about the next book, *Once a Spy*...

THE NEXT NOVEL IS ONCE A SPY
PROTECTOR SWEETHEARTS BOOK 3

An adventurous billionaire.
A former CIA agent.
Treasures lost to time.

Hired to protect an adventurous billionaire, former CIA agent Raynelle Dryden gets too personal with her client in a treasure hunt, and both inadvertently introduce the other to their old enemies in this Christian romantic suspense.

A dangerous quest...

Billionaire treasure hunter Benjamin Glynn is on a quest to find pirate Blackbeard's lost treasures. So are his competitors, who stop at nothing to win the race. Benjamin finds himself unable to proceed as obstacle after obstacle comes his way.

A displeased protector...

Afraid that Benjamin is too reckless, his sister hires former CIA agent Raynelle Dryden to tag along in his escapades. Raynelle needs the money to fund a secret project she hasn't told anyone about, but being involved in Benjamin's adventure exposes him to her own shadow enemies.

And dark enemies...

As they get closer to unearthing the truth about where Blackbeard hid his treasures that no one has yet discovered, Raynelle and Benjamin find themselves walking into the crosshairs of their old enemies. Each has their own agenda and goal, even if it means destroying Benjamin and Raynelle and everyone around them in the process. Who will blink first?

Once a Spy is book 3 in *USA Today* bestselling author Jan Thompson's **Protector Sweethearts** Christian romantic suspense series, in which the heroes and heroines pair up on adventures to recover lost treasures and rescue lost people. You might also enjoy the other books in the same collection.

Once a Spy (Protector Sweethearts Book 3)
JanThompson.com/spy

Protector Sweethearts
JanThompson.com/protector

Keep up with Jan's publication schedule:
JanThompson.com/newsletter

ONCE A SPY SNEAK PEEK (PROLOGUE)
PROTECTOR SWEETHEARTS BOOK 3

Rising a thousand feet into the Tuscan sky, the clifftop town of Pitigliano looked ancient and weary under a sepia moonlight shroud. Former CIA agent Raynelle Dryden floored the Audi and tore up the mountain road, praying that she would reach Mr. 819A before her former colleague did.

Perhaps it had been a mistake to invite Leonard Calhoun to the hunt, but he was familiar with the province of Grosseto in the Italian countryside, and she hadn't been there before. Now Leonard was speeding ahead of her on the winding road that wrapped around the old town, as though Mr. 819A had been his own target all along.

No *polizia* showed up when she entered the edges of Pitigliano, chasing the wind through the narrow wall-lined roads, empty now in the middle of the night, save for dim street lights offering no help.

No way was she going to let Leonard get to their quarry first. There was no telling what Leonard would do to Mr. 819A.

Raynelle no longer trusted Leonard, not since their botched CIA operation in Tel Aviv that left at least three of their team members dead. Over the last few years, two more had died mysteriously in a brutal way. They had been tortured using methods that Leonard had formulated.

So no, Raynelle must get to Mr. 819A first, to find out why he had cheated her employer, Beatrice Glynn, out of two million dollars for an empty Himitsu-Bako puzzle box.

Where's the map inside the box, Mr. 819A?

Raynelle turned a corner and saw Leonard's Ducati up ahead. In front of him, a Morris Minor crashed into a parked scooter under a streetlamp, and came to a complete stop. The driver jumped out.

A scraggly fellow with dirty blond hair—that looked an absolute mess in the moonlight—the antiquities dealer, known as Mr. 819A, took off on foot ahead.

Raynelle was outside her Audi now, running on the cobblestone road toward Leonard, who had leapt off his Ducati. He tossed his helmet to Raynelle and sprinted after Mr. 819A.

The Ducati engine was still running. She strapped on the helmet and climbed onto the motorcycle just as Leonard and Mr. 819A disappeared down a narrow alley.

"Better not lose him this time," Raynelle mumbled as the Ducati followed the two men.

She had chased Mr. 819A all the way from Zurich to London to Rome, but Mr. 819A wouldn't yield the secret he alone kept. His next chess move made Raynelle wonder if he had been trying to lead them all into a trap in the shadows.

Shadows were Raynelle's speciality.

Yes, she was a hunter of a different sort from the employer who paid her to track down this conman and swindler, who now fled on foot, having fallen off his motorcycle half a block away.

He should be easy to catch, if only she could create her own roads on the fly.

She reached the alley, with her Ducati at full throttle, and spotted Mr. 819A turning a corner.

Where's Leonard?

Raynelle narrowly missed running over a cat crossing her path on the cobblestone road. When the road widened, she bounced the rental motorcycle onto the sidewalk, and someone spoke into her earpiece.

"I see him. One block down. Turn left," Leonard said.

"Got it." Raynelle almost thanked God for Leonard, until she remembered that Leonard couldn't answer all her questions surrounding the death of their former team member, Javonte Gerhard, a loving husband and a father of two.

In other words, she could not trust him.

However, he had helped her track down Mr. 819A, and sometimes she had to work with people she didn't trust.

Such was the world of spies and subterfuge.

In any case, Leonard had to make a living after having left the CIA in disgrace. An equal opportunity contractor, he took jobs from both sides of the fence—the good and the bad. Raynelle did not ask how he slept at night because the former spy didn't sleep.

Raynelle parked the Ducati, didn't bother to take off her helmet, and ran down the small alley that Leonard had told her. She had been here before in the daytime, but night light brought all sorts of shadows she had to adjust to quickly.

The alley was lined with doors—old wooden doors—all closed. She glanced up at some windows when she heard someone call her name.

"Ray!" Leonard hissed and grabbed her leather jacket, pulling her so hard that her shoulder smacked into his chest.

Leonard smelled of cigarettes. Obviously, he had failed to quit.

He smiled under the streetlamp, his fists still coiled around the edge of her jacket, as if it was a form of control.

Raynelle pushed back. "Where did he go?"

He pointed to a dark door next to him, up some stone steps.

Raynelle tested the old wooden door. It was locked. From the inside? She hated to break in, unless they were absolutely sure that Mr. 819A was inside.

Could she trust Leonard for that too?

"I didn't think you'd take such an easy job, chasing after garden-variety criminals," Leonard whispered. "Come work for me, and you'll do grander things."

Raynelle looked for a key under a flower container—with a half-dead plant in it—next to the door, making herself look silly.

Leonard chuckled. "You're seriously that helpless? Have I taught you nothing?"

Raynelle didn't forget that Leonard had trained her, back when she was new to the agency, long before he asked for her by name to be in an eight-person team to help MOSSAD take down the terrorist Molyneux in Tel Aviv. The same operation that had maimed some of security specialist Esperanza Diaz-Mendenhall's men.

Speaking of whom, Esperanza should still be hiding in the dark, watching her and Leonard, and preparing to take over.

Leonard stepped forward. "Shall we call for reinforcements, or can we take him, just the two of us?"

Raynelle didn't tell him more than he needed to know. As far as Leonard was concerned, Raynelle had come to Italy all alone and needy, looking for a man who had robbed two million dollars from her employer.

And here they were at the Little Jerusalem on top of a mountain ridge, hunting for another lone man, who was not so little himself. In fact, it was probably a stroke of genius for Mr. 819A to hide here in Pitigliano, where nobody would ever guess that the frail, pasty-faced British subject was the millionaire cousin of a more-than-nasty arms dealer based out of Libya, who had been killed in a raid that involved Esperanza's team.

For those two reasons, Esperanza had been interested in the operation the minute Raynelle had mentioned who she was going after.

She remembered Esperanza asking why she would even bother to call Leonard for assistance.

"Because I'm testing something," Raynelle had told her friend.

"Let it not be death."

"I hope not."

Raynelle drew a deep breath, and prayed for God's wisdom as she waited for Leonard to pick the lock. "Are you rusty or are you rusty?"

Leonard chuckled. "I used to be able to do this in seconds."

"Not on a door that looks like it's from the sixteenth century." Raynelle pointed this way and that. Not that she knew precisely what to do in the darkness.

"I yield to your expertise." Leonard's voice was low. "You're glad I'm here, but I know you're hiding something."

"Like what, exactly?" Raynelle glanced around to make sure nobody was paying attention to them.

The air around them was still, but the September night was cool in the mid-sixties or thereabouts. It would've been a pleasant night had she not been chasing Mr. 819A and working up a sweat.

Raynelle's gaze followed the stone walls upward, as she wondered if it might just be easier to scale the wall into the windows, although they might find people sleeping inside.

Leonard didn't answer her this time.

Raynelle walked around him. In the pale moonlight, she figured that the building had three floors from this side. Was it someone's house or an apartment? The latter would be hard to search for a single lone man—

Who might be long gone by now.

She walked to the edge of the building, and spotted another door. This door had only a latch. She looked around her to see if there might be a convenient stone somewhere, but no such fortune.

She turned on her phone flashlight for a quick

minute to check the condition of the latch. Rusty, as expected.

She withdrew her Glock from its holster inside her jacket, but Leonard stopped her next step.

"Save your bullets." He twisted on a silencer onto his Sig Sauer. "I need to be useful here."

He blew the rusty screws off the iron latch, and they were inside in no time.

However, they had lost minutes loitering outside. Raynelle didn't say anything. She didn't want Leonard to see her antsy, because he could break down her emotions if she displayed any worry. He could see through her worry and exploit her weakness.

This was a dangerous man.

All the more reason to suspect that he had something to do with the death of Raynelle's friend and their team member. Poor Javonte's widow, Carmine, had to raise two kids on her own, while hiding them from their father's enemies.

Raynelle wondered if there were more turncoat agents like Leonard.

Perhaps more than she wanted to know.

Then again, was Leonard really a turncoat?

Inside the door, the hallway was dark, and Raynelle realized she still had her motorcycle helmet on her head. She held back a chuckle. She lifted her visor so she could see dark outlines and the path to the stairs.

All was quiet, although the hallway smelled musty, as though it hadn't been aired out in a while.

Suddenly, a fear gripped Raynelle, a moment of clarity in her mind perhaps, that Leonard might have his own agenda this very minute, and she could be stepping closer to her own demise by following Leonard down the hallway.

Then again, better to have him walk ahead of her than to give him an opportunity to stab her in the back.

Her other earpiece came to life.

"You have the right building." Esperanza's voice. "We're waiting outside. Stay calm."

An angel from the Lord?

Raynelle couldn't reply, and Esperanza would know that.

Stay calm.

And that had been why she had to leave the CIA. That one emotional breakdown she had when Javonte and Millard were murdered had been too much for her to handle.

Her knee-jerk reaction was to move two of her team members, Rulon Smith and Dakara Dermott, to safety since they couldn't protect themselves anymore after Tel Aviv. They required constant care, one paralyzed from the blast, and the other blinded and maimed.

Once Raynelle had been sure they were safe in Wyoming, she had gone looking for more team members. Zarina Myers was nowhere to be found.

And then there was Leonard, the agent who could never die. He continued to work in the CIA. Or was he still working in the CIA? He hinted that he was in deep undercover. Where?

He extended his arm in front of Raynelle. "I hear something."

Someone climbing stairs?

Raynelle nodded. She knew she had to trust Leonard.

She wanted to trust him so badly.

It wasn't the one accidental kiss from long ago, but it was that Leonard had two sides. Ironically, his side that had feelings for her was probably the reason Leonard hadn't hurt her thus far.

The house echoed. The footfalls grew distant, ever upward.

"Stairs," Raynelle whispered as she pointed.

Leonard nodded.

They went up, weapons extended. Raynelle glanced back every now and then.

The stairs creaked in parts, slowing them down.

When Raynelle heard someone running on

wooden floor one level up, she sprinted and so did Leonard. They went up the third flight of stairs, and followed the noise.

In an empty room, with only a small wall lamp casting light, Mr. 819A was opening the shutters. Breathing heavily, he climbed out.

"Stop!" Raynelle yelled, freezing in place.

Mr. 819A turned. He was in his late-twenties, just as Beatrice Glynn-Kessler had described. However, he had bleached his hair another color. She couldn't precisely nail the dye color in the night light.

Outside the window, a moon glowed.

"Mr. 819A," Raynelle said, pointing her gun down.

"I go by Arkyn now." He adjusted his chest harness around his waist. The harness was connected to a long rope. The other end of the rope went around a pillar about five feet away. "You don't want to mess with me, once you know who my uncle is."

He seemed to be talking to Raynelle, but Arkyn's eyes were on Leonard.

"His uncle is Spencer Buchanan, arms manufacturer," Leonard explained to Raynelle.

Raynelle inched forward. "Arkyn, you may not know me, but I work for Sandra. You remember

Sandra, don't you? You sold her a puzzle box ten months ago in Zurich."

"Sandra?" The man formerly known as Mr. 819A asked. "Sandra with the flowing hair?"

"And who danced like a princess." Raynelle had reviewed the security cameras in the ballroom.

However, Beatrice Glynn had cut her hair since the event, and stopped using the nickname Sandra.

"What do you want? Can't you see I'm busy here?" His British accent thickened.

"What are you busy doing?" Leonard asked.

"Asks the man with a Sig pointing at me."

Slowly, Leonard put his weapon back in its holster.

"That's better," Arkyn said. "Normally, I'd ask you to step into my office, but right now, I'm in a hurry."

"Where are you going?" Raynelle kept her voice calm and friendly. "The front door is three floors down."

"Someone was chasing me." He squinted. "Might that be you?"

"No, we're just passing through." Leonard was playing, and Raynelle could tell.

"Arkyn, I've got to be honest with you since it's past midnight now, and you probably want to go

back to your hotel and get some sleep, right?"
Raynelle prayed that Arkyn hadn't been thinking of
jumping out the window, down the vertical cliff
outside, and into the ravine a thousand feet below.

When Arkyn didn't reply, Raynelle walked
slowly toward him. "As I mentioned, Sandra
sent me."

"What does she want?"

"She wants to know why the Himitsu-Bako box
is empty."

"I don't know. Not my problem, is it?"

Arkyn was still sitting on the window sill, and
that made Raynelle worried. Perhaps this wasn't
the time to ask for the missing map inside the
puzzle box.

When Raynelle didn't reply, Arkyn kept talking. "It was given to me as is. I sold it to Sandra
as is."

"I know you did, and it's not your fault."
Raynelle was within feet of him. "She wants to
know if there's another box like this."

"She wants another one?"

Raynelle nodded, not looking back at Leonard
who was probably wondering why she had told him
another story. Then again, Leonard would understand the need for deception.

Only Raynelle didn't like it at all, and wished

she didn't have to resort to lying to get her way. Right now, her main concern was to get this man off the windowsill before he fell out.

Was there a ledge outside, or was his other foot simply dangling in mid-air?

"Can you get another box?" Raynelle was close enough that she would be able to reach out and grab him and pull him from the window.

Arkyn flinched, startling her.

She glanced behind him to find Leonard's arm extended, his weapon pointing at them.

"Leonard, what are you doing?" Raynelle gasped.

Was Leonard trying to play the bad guy to get Arkyn to talk? Or was he aiming to kill? If so, who was his target? Was he targeting her or Arkyn?

"Tell her what she wants to know or I will damage your haircut," Leonard said.

Arkyn grinned and fell backward.

Raynelle's heart raced. She leapt toward the window, grabbing one of Arkyn's legs. Leonard grabbed the other.

Arkyn was screaming his head off. "Aaaaahhhh."

Like he was falling.

Raynelle didn't know whether to laugh or cry.

"Why don't we just let him go?" Leonard asked.

"Two million dollars say no way." Raynelle pulled the man in through the window with Leonard's help.

Arkyn's eyes widened as he stared at Leonard. "I know you..."

"Must be mistaken." Leonard stepped back.

"Why didn't you say so earlier?" Raynelle asked.

"I didn't have my glasses on," Arkyn said. "I lost them on the way here."

That was a fair explanation, Raynelle though. She glanced at Leonard. His face was calm, and he looked like he didn't know what Arkyn was talking about.

Raynelle stepped between Arkyn and Leonard. Perhaps Leonard had meant to shoot Arkyn after all. He could give any excuses later on, but Arkyn would've been dead.

The fact that Arkyn though he knew Leonard could mean many things.

However, Arkyn had lived a sheltered live in Libya as a British expatriate until his uncle's demise. How many places could he have met Leonard?

Leonard drew his gun back. "Step away, Ray."

"Leonard, please." Raynelle barely got her words out.

"We both have a job to do." Leonard pointed his Sig Sauer again.

Raynelle hugged Arkyn tightly and pushed him backward. They both dropped out the window.

Arkyn screamed again.

Raynelle hoped the rope could hold the weight of both of them as she counted the floors. Five floors of windows on this side of the building. She glanced below. Vertical cliffs. Sheer tufa rocks made of calcium carbonate—but would still break their bones if they smashed against them.

Great.

The rope was long, but it wasn't long enough. It jerked to a complete stop, causing Raynelle to smash up against Arkyn, pinning him to the wall. Unfortunately, her helmet smashed into Arkyn's forehead.

He passed out.

They dangled in midair where the building ended and the rock cliffs began. Raynelle was on the outside, holding on to Arkyn, the only one with a harness.

"Espy, now would be a great time to rescue us," Raynelle spoke into her headset.

"Roger that," Esperanza replied. "We just arrived. See the white van on the road below?"

"No. It's dark."

Something flashed on the road.

"Okay, I see it now. Do you see me?"

A spotlight shone on Raynelle.

"You're five floors down from the roof and five floors up from the road."

"Is that right?" Raynelle prayed that her arms were strong enough to hold on to Arkyn until help arrived.

The man was still knocked out. The force of Raynelle's helmet had been brutal. She hoped he didn't suffer a concussion or memory loss. As long as he still remembered the map...

"Hold still. We're coming up to get you," Esperanza said. "Is that Mr. 819A?"

"He goes by Arkyn now." Raynelle looked up. Nobody peeked out the top floor window. "Leonard is on the third floor—or was it the fifth?"

"He's not anymore. My people are up there but he vanished."

"How does he vanish? There's only one flight of stairs up and down."

"We'll keep searching the building."

"Thanks," Raynelle said. "By the way, I have no harness."

That made Esperanza sound frantic in Raynelle's earpiece.

It meant that help was coming faster than expected.

Until then, Raynelle hugged the unconscious Arkyn.

"Ray?" Esperanza spoke into her earpiece.

"I'm still here." Raynelle chuckled, trying to take shallow breaths to stave off the smell of Arkyn's sweat.

"We're going to lower a new harness from the window above you."

Raynelle looked up to where the spotlight shone, and spotted masked men leaning out of the window.

She closed her eyes and waited.

Fifteen minutes later, she was off the wall and craggy cliffs, and sitting on the asphalt talking to Esperanza, who'd just handed her a bottled water. Somewhere between up and down, Arkyn had stirred, and they had handcuffed him and whisked him away in one of the vans.

"All right, Espy. I'll see you in Malta." Raynelle stood up and stretched. "Right now, I have to get back to Charleston. I hope to hear from you about the map before the rehearsal dinner. It will be your gift to her."

"The wedding is in two weeks. I don't know if we can get the information that soon."

"Do your best."

"All we can do." Esperanza waved to one of her people. "Will you get Miss Dryden to the airport? She has to return home for wedding preparations—not hers, unfortunately."

"Thank you." Raynelle hugged her.

Esperanza was about to leave her when she stopped. "Hey, you still sure you don't want to come work with us? We could use someone with your skillset."

"I'm happy freelancing, as I mentioned before. Haven't changed my mind about that." Although her next gig was to babysit a billionaire, Beatrice's irritating older brother.

How hard could it be to monitor a recluse? His whereabouts were so confined to a particular radius that it could turn out to be her most boring assignment ever.

Well, as long as Beatrice paid her, Raynelle couldn't complain. She needed the money to fund medical costs, living expenses, and personal security for people she owed her life to. More than former colleagues, her two dear friends had shielded her with their bodies when Molyneux's bomb blew off, injuring themselves into disability for the rest of their lives.

Supporting them was the least Raynelle could do. The least.

She turned away from the vehicle lights to blink into the night shadows, trying not to wipe a tear.

ACKNOWLEDGEMENTS

Many thanks to my Georgia Press publishing team for keeping up with my writing schedule.

Special thanks to editor Lesley Ann McDaniel for copyediting this novel.

With God-given eyes for copyediting details, Lenda Selph is my patient proofreader extraordinaire. I appreciate her and thank God for her invaluable hard work.

I am grateful to God for my husband and son for their support and encouragement.

And I'll always remember my beloved mother and my late father for having instilled in me the love of reading and writing from a very early age. I miss my father here on earth, but I will see him in Heaven some bright day.

Most of all, I am eternally thankful to my Lord and Savior, Jesus Christ, who died on the cross to save me from my sins and rose again from the grave to give me eternal life. Without Him, I can write and do nothing.

HYMN: ALAS AND DID MY SAVIOR BLEED

Alas, and did my Savior bleed?
    And did my Sovereign die?
    Would He devote that sacred head
    For such a worm as I?

Chorus:
    At the cross, at the cross where
    I first saw the light,
    And the burden of my heart rolled away,
    It was there by faith I received my sight,
    And now I am happy all the day!

Was it for sins that I had done
    He groaned upon the tree?
    Amazing pity! grace unknown!

And love beyond degree!

Well might the sun in darkness hide,
    And shut His glories in,
    When Christ, the mighty Maker, died
    For man, His creature's sin.

Thus might I hide my blushing face
    While His dear cross appears.
    Dissolve my heart in thankfulness,
    And melt mine eyes to tears.

But drops of grief can ne'er repay
    The debt of love I owe;
    Here, Lord, I give myself away,
    'Tis all that I can do.

The lyrics for this "Alas and Did My Savior Bleed" hymn penned by Isaac Watts in 1707, with additional chorus by Ralph E. Hudson are in the public domain.

BOOKS BY JAN THOMPSON

CHRISTIAN ROMANTIC SUSPENSE & BEACH ROMANCE

BINARY HACKERS (Near-Future Inspirational Romantic Thrillers)

- Book 1: Zero Sum
- Book 2: Zero Day
- Book 3: Zero Base

PROTECTOR SWEETHEARTS (Christian Romantic Suspense)

- Book 1: Once a Thief
- Book 2: Once a Hero
- Book 3: Once a Spy

- Book 4: Twice a Fighter
- Book 5: Twice a Convict
- Book 6: Twice a Soldier

DEFENDER SWEETHEARTS (Christian Romantic Suspense)

- Book 1: Never a Traitor
- Book 2: Never a Hostage
- Book 3: Never a Fugitive
- Book 4: Always a Maverick
- Book 5: Always a Champion
- Book 6: Always a Guardian

SAVANNAH SWEETHEARTS (Christian Coastal City & Beach Town Romance)

- Prequel: Ask You Later
- Book 1: Know You More
- Book 2: Tell You Soon (Romance with Suspense)
- Book 3: Draw You Near
- Book 4: Cherish You So
- Book 5: Walk You There
- Book 6: Love You Always (Romance with Suspense)

- Book 7: Kiss You Now
- Book 8: Find You Again
- Book 9: Wish You Joy (Christmas Year Round)
- Book 10: Call You Home

VACATION SWEETHEARTS (Christian Travel Romance)

- Book 1: Smile for Me
- Book 2: Reach for Me (Romance with Suspense)
- Book 3: Wait for Me (Romance with Suspense)
- Book 4: Look for Me (Romance with Suspense)
- Book 5: Pray for Me
- Book 6: Care for Me
- Book 7: Cheer for Me

SEASIDE CHAPEL (Christian Small Town Beach Romance)

- Book 1: His Longing Heart (second edition of Share with Me)
- Book 2: His Wake-Up Call (second

edition of Step with Me)

- Book 3: His Morning Kiss (previously published as Sing with Me)
- Book 4: His Quiet Serenade
- Books 5-12: Coming Soon

Subscribe to Jan Thompson's mailing list:
JanThompson.com/newsletter

PROTECTOR SWEETHEARTS

Private investigator Helen Hu and her associates specialize in searching for missing persons and hunting for lost treasures. Join them in their adventure suspense around the world in *USA Today* bestselling author Jan Thompson's Protector Sweethearts, a series of Christian Romantic Suspense with a side of mystery. Protector Sweethearts is a spin-off of Savannah Sweethearts and Vacation Sweethearts.

JanThompson.com/protector

- Book 1: Once a Thief

- Book 2: Once a Hero
- Book 3: Once a Spy
- Book 4: Twice a Fighter
- Book 5: Twice a Convict
- Book 6: Twice a Soldier

DEFENDER SWEETHEARTS

Defender Sweethearts is a sister series to the Protector Sweethearts Christian romantic suspense collection. While the heroes in Protector Sweethearts search for lost treasures and lost people, the Defender Sweethearts novels focus on protecting the helpless and hopeless. The main characters in Defender Sweethearts come from the supporting cast in Protector Sweethearts.

JanThompson.com/defender

- Book 1: Never a Traitor

- Book 2: Never a Hostage
- Book 3: Never a Fugitive
- Book 4: Always a Maverick
- Book 5: Always a Champion
- Book 6: Always a Guardian

BINARY HACKERS

Like more suspense with your Christian romance? Like to read suspense thrillers? If you're looking for clean near-future romantic suspense without compromising the Christian faith, these books are for you.

From *USA Today* bestselling author Jan Thompson come these inspirational near-future cyberthrillers combining technothriller and romance, starting with Binary Hackers that feature computer specialists living at the edge of cyberspace, where they have to juggle being law-abiding truth-telling Christians while carrying out their assignments by any and all means possible.

The Binary Hackers series is set in the same story world as Jan's other books, and characters from the other series may make cameo appearances in this series and vice versa.

JanThompson.com/binary

- Book 1: Zero Sum
- Book 2: Zero Day
- Book 3: Zero Base

SAVANNAH SWEETHEARTS

Welcome to the new south! From *USA Today* bestselling author Jan Thompson come these clean and wholesome, sweet and inspirational Christian romances set on the romantic beaches of Tybee Island and in the coastal town of Savannah, Georgia.

Meet a group of multiracial and multiethnic churchgoing Christians who love the Lord, work hard in their careers, and seek God's will for their love lives. Against a backdrop of ocean, sand, and sun, these inspirational romances showcase aspects of the human need for God and for one another. Have some tea, settle in a comfortable reading chair, and enjoy these sweet celebrations of faith, hope, and love in Jesus Christ.

JanThompson.com/savannah

- Prequel: Ask You Later
- Book 1: Know You More
- Book 2: Tell You Soon (Romance with Suspense)
- Book 3: Draw You Near
- Book 4: Cherish You So
- Book 5: Walk You There
- Book 6: Love You Always (Romance with Suspense)
- Book 7: Kiss You Now
- Book 8: Find You Again
- Book 9: Wish You Joy (Christmas Year Round)
- Book 10: Call You Home

VACATION SWEETHEARTS

Travel with our friends from Savannah, Georgia, to the coast and to the mountains. Cheer them on as they celebrate the immeasurable grace and unde-served mercy of God through Jesus Christ.

The Vacation Sweethearts novels are a spin-off of Jan's Savannah Sweethearts series, and fans will recognize familiar faces from Riverside Chapel, a church in the coastal city of Savannah, Georgia. In fact, we might even visit the beach town of Tybee Island from time to time to visit old friends and beloved families...

JanThompson.com/vacation

- Book 0 (Prequel): Time for Me
- Book 1: Smile for Me (International Romance)
- Book 2: Reach for Me (Romance with Suspense)
- Book 3: Wait for Me (Romance with Suspense)
- Book 4: Look for Me (Romance with Suspense)
- Book 5: Pray for Me (International Romance)
- Book 6: Care for Me
- Book 7: Cheer for Me (International Romance)

SEASIDE CHAPEL

Welcome to *USA Today* bestselling author Jan Thompson's Seaside Chapel Christian beach romance series. These novels are set on real-life St. Simon's Island, Georgia—a beach town where history is all around and the future is a moment away—and the neighboring fictitious Seaside Island, where the rich and famous live.

Savor the small-town atmosphere and the warm southern beaches of St. Simon's Island and the idyllic Golden Isles along the Atlantic Ocean. Enjoy the music of the orchestra and hymns of the church, and hang out with our Christian friends who attend Seaside Chapel, a little church by the sea known for its beach weddings and fair share of love and life.

As these Christians grow in their knowledge and understanding of God, they are tested in their spiritual maturity, their love lives, and their relationships with others. Share their heartaches and healing, and cheer them on as they celebrate faith, family, and friends.

JanThompson.com/seaside

- Book 1: His Longing Heart (second edition of Share with Me)
- Book 2: His Wake-Up Call (second edition of Step with Me)
- Book 3: His Morning Kiss (previously published as Sing with Me)
- Book 4: His Quiet Serenade
- Books 5-12: Coming Soon

ABOUT JAN THOMPSON

USA Today bestselling author Jan Thompson writes clean and wholesome contemporary Christian romance with elements of women's fiction, Christian romantic suspense with an air of mystery, and inspirational international thrillers with threads of sweet Christian romance.

Raised on a tropical island in the eastern hemisphere, Jan now lives and writes in the western hemisphere. Her international background gives her a unique multicultural and multiracial perspective to her novels and books.

After earning a Bachelor of Science degree in Computer Science, Jan worked as a database programmer and website developer for many years collectively before transitioning from writing software to her lifelong dream job of writing fiction.

Jan's books are for readers who love inspiring stories of faith, hope, and love in Jesus Christ.

JanThompson.com

For God so loved the world
that He gave His only begotten Son,
that whoever believes in Him
should not perish but have everlasting life.
—John 3:16